STARS IN THE STORM

ALSO BY KELSEY GIETL

HOPE OR HIGH WATER — OVER THE ATLANTIC
Across Oceans
Twisted River

HOPE OR HIGH WATER — WAR ACROSS WATERS
Broken Lines
Unsettled Shores

LARKSONG LEGACY
For a Noble Purpose
Dusk Shall Weep
Sparks Fly Upward
Stars in the Storm

For updates and behind the scenes info, subscribe to the author's newsletter at: https://kelseygietl.com/newsletter

LARKSONG LEGACY • 4

STARS *in the* STORM

KELSEY GIETL

Purple Mask Publishing
Saint Charles, Missouri

+JMJ+AMDG+

Stars in the Storm
Copyright © 2025 by Kelsey Gietl.
All rights reserved.

This is a work of historical fiction. References to real events and locales are only intended to provide a sense of authenticity. All other characters, places, incidents, and dialogue are a product of the author's imagination. Any resemblance to actual events, locales, or persons, living or dead, is entirely coincidental.

ISBN-13: 979-8-9856744-6-0
ebook ISBN: 979-8-9856744-5-3
Library of Congress Control Number: 2024924821
First Edition

Scripture quotations are taken from The New American Bible, St. Joseph Edition.

Cover design by Kelsey Gietl (kelseygietl.com)
Cover photos: Lark Tattoo by Amelia Gietl. Head, arms, and belt bag of woman used under license by Adobe Stock. "Person Holding Compass" by Jamie Street and "Brown Belt" by NordWood Themes used under free license by Unsplash. Additional images from The Metropolitan Museum of Art, New York, Open Access Collection.
Back cover photo: "Brown Cardboard Box on White Table" by Dan-Cristian Pădureț.

For Adam
We don't get to pick our brothers, but I'm glad you're mine.

"Unfurl the sails and let God steer us where He will."
St. Bede the Venerable

Prayer of St. Brendan the Navigator

Help me to journey beyond the familiar
and into the unknown.
Give me the faith to leave old ways
and break fresh ground with You.
Christ of the mysteries, I trust You
to be stronger than each storm within me.
I will trust in the darkness and know
that my times, even now, are in Your hand.
Tune my spirit to the music of heaven,
and somehow, make my obedience count for You.
Amen.

KEY CHARACTERS

Alice Ann Owens Lark — 24-year-old with a Gift for memory who left her husband and daughter to fulfill her sailor's dreams, sister to Coraline Lark and Mercy Owens

Cade Lark — 27-year-old former plantation son with a Gift for predicting the weather. Has been raising his daughter alone since his wife left almost four years ago.

    Julep Lark — Cade and Alice Ann's 5-year-old daughter

Daniel Lark — Cade's 39-year-old brother

Tobias Lark — Cade's 37-year-old brother

    Sarah Walcott Lark — Tobias's 35-year-old wife

    Philip Lark — Tobias and Sarah's 5-year-old son

Garrett Lark — Cade's 35-year-old brother

    Martha Louis Lark— Garrett's 37-year-old wife

    Josephine Lark — Garrett and Martha's newborn daughter

Jamison Lark — Cade's 33-year-old brother

    Coraline Owens Shay Lark — Jamison's 30-year-old wife

    James Lark — Jamison and Coraline's 3-year-old son

Josiah — The Larks' former butler who is like a second father. He now lives with his daughter, Clary, at Stella Maris Mission.

Anwillik (*ann-will-ick*)— The 29-year-old Chinook leader in Larksong

    Tleyuk (*tay-yook*)— Anwillik's 10-year-old son

Alonzo and Geraldine Lark — The Lark brothers' parents (deceased)

Ned and Octavia Owens — Alice Ann's parents in South Carolina

Mercy Owens — Alice Ann's 34-year-old sister in South Carolina

SAILING SHIPS

Gratia — Cade's fishing schooner

    Winasie, Thatcher, and Jones – *Gratia*'s crew

Oblique — sailing ship of the first Gifted ancestors, sank in 1700

Arletta — the ship Cade, Garrett, and Josiah were enslaved on

At the beginning of the eighteenth century,
in the first month of the year of our Lord,
the sailing ship Oblique
made her final stand against the sea.

After the earth moved and the waves crashed,
only seven of her crew remained.
Forever changed by God's great thunder,
their legacies carried on.

One-hundred-and-fifty-nine years later,
this is but one of their stories...

1

AUGUST 1859
GHOST FOREST, WASHINGTON TERRITORY

A lice Ann Owens Lark remembered everything. Why she left her husband, Cade, and baby daughter, Julep. Why she stayed away. Why she would never be welcomed back should she choose to return, which she never would.

Alice Ann remembered everything; as much as she tried not to, she had no choice. Like her sister Coraline's Gift for translation, Alice Ann's perfect memory had appeared without warning, and it seemed there was no way to rid herself of it. From today's first blink until she breathed her last, these horrid memories would always be with her.

Throughout their short marriage, Cade had often asked, "Are you happy, Alice?"

In the beginning, she would laugh and lightly smack his arm. "Of course, you idiot." But as time wore on, as her dissatisfaction with her mediocre husband grew, her responses held more hostility than joking affection.

"How can you be happy in such a dismal place?" she had seethed. "There is nothing for us here. You have no ambition, no sense of adventure. If only you would let us sail away, then perhaps I could be happy."

"Larksong is my home, Alice Ann," he would reply. "Our family is here."

"I'm your family, too! I'm your wife. Don't I matter?"

"Of course, but everyone else matters, too."

That was always where their quarrel ended. He would leave the house for his brothers' or the fields or would play with Julep to avoid further confrontation. Often, she considered telling him the truth behind her request, that it wasn't only her sailor's dreams that drove her, but there seemed little point in mentioning it. Whether she was Gifted or not, he would never leave Larksong, no matter how many arguments she threw his way.

Eventually, to her relief, he stopped asking. That was how she knew her time in Larksong was truly at an end. After penning Cade a letter she knew he would never forgive, she left it and their two-year-old daughter with Coraline. There on the Pacific shore, Julep snuggled into her blind aunt's lap, finally asleep after her tiny fingers had shoveled sand into her mouth for the fifth time that hour. Small clumps of saliva-laced granules stuck to her dress and her sticky hands, a baby trait Alice Ann would never find endearing.

"This is selfish," Coraline had scolded, while cradling the child close.

"No, Cora," Alice Ann told her. "This is the *least* selfish thing I've ever done. All my life, I've only looked out for myself, and you looked out for me. I was a bad sister, bad daughter, bad wife, bad mother. I'm the only one in our family who deserved to go blind, but I didn't. You're going to let me do this one good deed and take a little of the burden off your shoulders, since I know I placed so much of it there. Tomorrow, hopefully, I'll be the best of everything everyone wanted."

"This isn't what we want," her sister had begged; however, Alice Ann still walked away.

A year later, she had no sea-faring prospects and was living on her last dime. But she wouldn't go back. Couldn't. Didn't deserve to, didn't want to. Life was as she had told Cora—Alice Ann *was* a bad sister, bad daughter, bad wife, bad mother. The unwelcome memories—what she now referred to as memory moments—hadn't stopped, but she would rather be alone and tortured in her mind than beg for forgiveness. Cade still had Julep and his family. That was who he truly wanted anyway. That was why he'd refused to sail away with her time and time again.

Are you happy now? she often asked herself. *Now that you've gone?*

She should have been happy *then*. She was certainly not happy now, and never would be.

All around her, the Ghost Forest's barren trees rose from the stagnant waters before Washington's mountainous splendor, their juxtaposition the perfect metaphor to all she was. Alone and broken, yet surrounded by beauty. Longing for home, yet resigned to shame and regret as her only companions, the only ones she deserved after all she had done...or considered doing. The intense nature of her frequent reminiscences was punishment enough, without peering into the eyes of all those she had wronged.

No one would come here. No one would think to. Not even Garrett could find her if he tried. As far as she knew, he had never been able to find another Gifted.

A ramshackle hut became her home, the last page of her desolate story. A place where she could open her mind to the Gift of her memories. Where she could scream and no one would hear.

2

AUGUST 26, 1859
GHOST FOREST, WASHINGTON TERRITORY

Grey bones of preserved spruce and cedar beckoned the oars of Cade Lark's captain's gig through the marshland. Barren trees, ravaged stumps, and tidal pools marred the Ghost Forest's otherwise mesmerizing shades of olive green and golden brown, providing a sense of eerie calm. In the gig beside him rowed his brothers—Daniel, Tobias, Garrett, and Jamison—all silent in the space between the life they knew and the one that awaited them. Despite the quiet, the air hummed with energy ready to snap into a typical Washington rain shower at a moment's notice. His Gift told him that today's clouds were but an illusion; no rain was to come. But they would face storms enough once they arrived at the place his wife now called home.

Cade hadn't seen Alice Ann in almost four years. What was he going to say to the woman who had left him completely devastated? Who had forced him to raise a child by himself. Yes, he had help from his ever-expanding family, but it wasn't an adequate substitute. His precious Julep was old enough now to ask where her mother was, forever wondering why her cousins had two parents and she did not. That explanation fell to him, not his brothers or their wives.

And he had to lie to his daughter every day.

Did her mother love her? Of course, she did.

Did she miss her? Once again, yes.

Was she coming back? ... Not such an easy lie to give. Did Cade want Alice Ann to return home? Yes. And no. And definitely. And never.

The clench of anxiety began to squeeze his chest and caused his legs to feel less solid than the waterlogged land around him. Thanks to Jamison, he could now define the fits he had experienced since childhood, instances when he desired to escape, to run away and scream and hide under his blankets. Where his lungs physically hurt and his chest pounded like death waited at his heels. It reassured him that his brothers now understood his affliction, even if no ordinary person could.

Lord, please lead me.

He couldn't succumb to his terrors here. He had a job to do. Get the compass his estranged wife had stolen and hope it would reveal some clue to the origin of their unusual Gifts. His mother had died for the information on that compass and had trusted him to keep it safe. That navigational device was his sole reason for being here, not to confront his wife in anger or reconciliation. Not to invite her back to Larksong or try to be a family. If she wanted that, she would return on her own. Mere months ago, he had finally decided to lay the past to rest, to accept his life as a chaste man and devoted father. Although he could not remarry, he could still serve God in a family capacity. With that, he was satisfied.

"Beach the boat over there," Garrett said. He pointed to a wooden shack set about ten yards off the riverbank and built against one of the thicker ghost trees. Three garden boxes lined the shack's front wall, each made from branches and twigs lashed together with some sort of braided twine. There were no windows on this side and mud chinking patched several places between the wall logs. Water pooled only thirty feet from the shack's front entrance.

What happened when the river flooded? Did her home flood, too? It wasn't built up very high. Alice Ann had always been resourceful though; perhaps, he shouldn't doubt her. Her resourcefulness, however, was what now surprised him at the way she was living. He'd figured she would have gone out and conquered the oceans by now, perhaps been a sea captain in her own right with a hundred-man crew. How had she ended up here? Why hadn't she come home?

"Are you certain this is the place?" he asked Garrett. His brother's Gift was locating people, a type of navigational ability and the reason they knew where Alice Ann was at all. Without him, Cade would have never found this place on his own. He wouldn't have even thought to look.

Garrett glared at him, one hand clenched around the strap of the Colt rifle slung across his back. "After all we dealt with this past year, you're doubting me now?"

His brother had been the one to help locate a myriad of Gifted over the past year, inadvertently also informing a mad circus master, Ashley Sterling, of their whereabouts which had led to Cade and Garrett's kidnapping and forced servitude. They had been enslaved as coal stokers on the steamship *Arletta*, nearly died several times, and finally returned to rescue Cade's daughter, Julep, and Garrett's wife, Martha. Together with their other brothers, they had overcome Sterling and brought the imprisoned circus workers home to Larksong. Even though Garrett had caused his share of problems, Cade was exceptionally grateful.

"No," he said slowly. "I don't doubt your ability, but look at this place. This doesn't seem like somewhere Alice would live."

"Likely or not, she's inside and probably listening to this conversation with one hand on a pistol and the other on a pitchfork."

"Why would she need a pitchfork?" Tobias asked. "There's no hay anywhere around, nothing even to farm."

"Tobias, do I tell you how to use your Gift?"

"First, I don't have a Gift anymore as you well know. Second, thanks for bringing it up *again*—you'll pay for that later. And third, yes, when I had one, you did tell me how to use it all the time."

Garrett smirked. "Oh, you're right. I did."

The men went silent as the shack's door creaked open an inch; however, darkness concealed whomever might be watching from beyond it.

"Is she alone?" Cade asked Garrett.

"How would I know? I can only find specific people, not see through walls."

"Although that would be a nice Gift to have," Daniel said, downcast as usual because he had lived thirty-nine years on this earth and still didn't possess any extraordinary talents.

"Go find out," Tobias hissed. He jabbed Cade in the ribs with his elbow causing him to lose his grip on the oar. It swung up and clattered against the oar lock with a thud that echoed across the marsh. So much for subtlety.

Swinging one boot over the side, Cade landed ankle-deep in the river and splashed his way onto shore. With every step forward, his boots squelched into the mud, each step releasing with a substantial upward tug. He heard his brothers splash into the water behind him, dragging the gig onto the shore. Five feet from the door, it swung open and there, as foretold, stood his wife.

After all these years, constantly hoping he'd see her again, chasing after women who looked like her, losing his mind in quiet corners and stifled sobs, here she was. She looked like Alice Ann, yet she didn't. She was thinner, but then again, after five months enslaved on *Arletta*, so had he been. He was only now returning to his normal physique. Alice's crimson hair, normally streaked with bright highlights, appeared dull beneath the overcast sky. He glanced past her to see a straw tick on the floor with a tan knitted blanket, another stick and twine crate stuffed with clothes, and the corner of a roughhewn table, the rest hidden from sight. Did she have a stove? No, probably only a fire pit out back.

Her fingers tugged at her bodice sleeves, pulling them lower on her wrists, while her brown eyes roved over him from toe to head. When she met his eyes, her lips parted slightly in astonishment and a tiny gasp escaped. What did she see that had her so astounded? His beard, his hair, perhaps the overall coarser nature of his physique? All these things had changed over the years, although she knew nothing of his most substantial alterations. The ones deep inside, many he couldn't even bring himself to speak of to anyone except God.

Uncomfortable, he dropped his gaze to find bare dirt-caked feet beneath her skirt's jagged hemline. A smile passed over his lips; he couldn't help it. His wild girl never had liked shoes or socks. In fact, she had somehow managed to walk much of the westward trail

7

without them. Iron feet, they all said she must have. But when he rubbed those toes after a long day's walk, despite the callouses, they still felt soft beneath his hands.

Someone cleared his throat and Cade jolted, tripping forward into the doorframe. He braced a shoulder against it as though he meant to land there, but his brothers' sniggers told him he had failed at nonchalance.

Alice's eyes flicked to the Lark brothers then back to him. "Hello, Cade." Her voice sounded the same, although it carried an undertone of uncertainty.

"Uh, hi."

An excruciatingly intense pause followed, punctuated by boot heels shuffling behind him, toe tapping—probably from Garrett—and a shush from Jamison.

"I...I don't know what to say," Cade stammered. "It's, uh, it's good...good to see you."

Alice's lips turned down. "It is not. I look terrible."

True, she did, but at the same time, she was beautiful. Always had been, at least to him. From the day he'd met her, he had been hung up with attraction. He supposed love did that to a man, made him a blind fool.

He tried for a smile and was certain he failed at that, too. "We've, uh, both looked better."

"Oh, for the sake of the Union, move this along." Garrett jostled against Cade, their shoulders pressed close together in the doorway. He held out his hand, palm up. "Where's the compass, Alice Ann? Hand it over."

Her eyebrows tented, and three sharp creases shadowed her forehead. "Compass?"

Tobias flanked Garrett's opposite side. He held his thumbs and index fingers up in a small circle above Garrett's shoulder. "When you left, Cade had a compass about this size in his possession. It's now missing and he claims you're the only other person who had a key to the trunk it was in. It's imperative we get it back."

"The key? I don't have that."

Tobias frowned. "You know I meant the compass."

"If you sold it," Garrett growled, "so help me, I'll—" He lunged forward and Jamison yanked him away by the arm. "Stand over there. You're not helping."

"Neither is she!" Garrett jabbed a finger back at Alice. "I know you know where it is."

Alice Ann, finally seeming to get a grip on herself, pressed her lips into a tight line. She turned into the shack without another glance at any of them.

"Do we follow her?" Daniel asked. He had the least experience with Alice Ann's antics, having met her but once over eight years ago. Until last year, when the brothers had reconciled, he had remained in Charleston at their family's townhome.

"I think we should," Cade said. He started forward, and Garrett's hand grabbed his elbow.

"How about we let Tobias or Jamison take care of it? Your head isn't in the right place for this."

"She's *my* wife, and my head is just fine, thanks." He ripped his arm away. "I'll take care of it." As he strode into the room, he heard his brother mutter, "You know, I think I liked him better when he had no spine."

The joke was on Garrett. Cade still had no spine; he was simply able to hide his distress better than before. Little did his brother know that right now, he was shaking inside like a set of altar bells during Eucharistic consecration.

The five men squeezed into the room, leaving the door open to lessen the heat within. As suspected, the inside held no stove or fireplace, which meant all the cooking must be completed behind the house. Another narrow door hung on the opposite wall, daylight rimming its borders. The table Cade had seen was the only other object in the room with a cedar tree stump for its single chair. Tears pinched his vision. His wife would rather live like this than be with him? What had happened to her during their time apart? Why wasn't she "off at sea" as she always said she wanted?

Alice stretched her arms out wide with a grin that landed somewhere between a bitter smile and a cheeky smirk. "As you can see, fellas, I have all the latest in luxury. Can I offer you a cup of

9

absolutely nothing?" She knelt before the crate of clothes and dug to the bottom.

"Where's the compass?" demanded Garrett.

"Alice—" Cade tried, but Jamison spoke over him.

"Garrett, show a little compassion. Maybe she wants to—"

"What, be welcomed back without a fuss?" Tobias quirked a brow. "Is that even a possibility?"

Alice shoved her meager clothing back in the crate and rose, her fingers wrapped around a metal object. "I've got your compass right here."

"Why are you living here, Alice?" Cade asked. He reached for her, but she pressed the compass into his open palm instead.

"Here, take it and go." Before he could say more, she retreated to the other side of the cabin, laid down on her straw tick, and dramatically threw the knitted blanket over her head.

"Well, that's one question answered," Garrett muttered.

Cade tried to stifle the sharp stab of rejection to his heart. He hadn't come all this way to have his wife shove him away without so much as a conversation, however brief it may end up being. But first things were first.

Emotions torn, he turned his attention back to the compass. It didn't look special, never had. It appeared to be an old compass complete with scratches and smudges, now tarnished after years in this moist dusty shanty. He examined the face. Nothing unusual there either. All the coordinates were in place, cardinal directions on four sides, magnetic arrow pointing north. He shifted the instrument 90 degrees, and the arrow turned with it. The back etching contained a geometric design, long jagged lines connected by waves with a circle at their center like the sun. Those had been there before, too. Many compasses had decorations. Nothing odd about that. Otherwise, no unique markings, no secret compartments so far as he could tell.

"I don't see anything unusual. What is this supposed to tell us?"

He handed it to Tobias who first examined it before passing it around to each of the brothers, landing with Jamison last, who shrugged. "Well, I'm plumb stumped. Without taking it apart to see if there's some secret inside, it appears to be just a compass."

"It doesn't make sense," Tobias said. "How is the compass the key? The key to what?"

Daniel peered over his shoulder. "Do you think the entire compass opens something? That the compass is a literal key, not a solution?"

"Maybe," said Jamison, "but how would one know what it unlocks? It obviously won't fit in a normal keyhole. Where would we even begin to search?"

"Could be on the inside. Let's break it open and see." Garrett swiped the compass from his brother's hand and turned to the lump that was Alice Ann. "You have a hammer or a big rock?"

The blanket ruffled as Alice shook her head. "But you have both back in Larksong. Maybe you should try there."

Cade ignored her. He grabbed the compass back and, clutching it, pocketed his fist. "If we must break it open, we do so back at home and in the right way. If we start smashing things, we could destroy a clue."

"What clue?" came Alice Ann's muffled response. "I've looked that thing up and down. It's just a compass."

"It's not just a compass, Alice!" He rounded on her, the instrument digging into his palm. With his shout, her figure stilled under the blanket. He forced a calming breath before continuing. "Our mother gave me this. It's the last thing she ever gave me and then she died for it. She lied to my father and said she stole it from him when I had it all the while. She told me it was the key to our Gifts, to who we are. She trusted me to keep it safe, and that's what I'm going to do."

Slowly, the blanket lowered, barely enough to see her eyes. "It wasn't your fault she died."

"I know it wasn't. But I felt guilty for a long time before I realized it."

Releasing the compass to the depths of his duster pocket, he lowered himself onto the tick, the straw crunching beneath him. He eased the blanket away from the rest of her face. "I've missed you, Alice."

"Seriously?" Garrett groaned. "We've got the compass. Let's just leave."

Cade ignored him, but Jamison didn't. "If you can't say anything polite, then get out." Cade heard a scuffle behind him followed by Jamison shoving Garrett out and closing the door. Alice's eyes flicked toward them, but Cade's remained on her.

"You owe me an explanation for leaving without a word."

Abruptly, she sat up, shoving both palms against his chest as she scurried to stand. Surrounded by the other brothers crowding the room, she backed against the wall, her arms folded tightly against her chest. "I gave you a word, many in fact. Didn't Cora give you my letter?

"She did."

"Did you read it?"

"Yes."

"Then you know exactly why I left."

"Sure, for the sea, for adventure. Because I was a weakling and we were ill-suited. I believe those were the words you used. But things have changed, Alice. You didn't go to sea at all, did you?"

She lifted her chin higher. "I made a life here instead."

"What life?" asked Tobias. "You live alone in a dead forest in a shack."

Jamison stepped closer, his gaze gentle. "What happened? Wasn't being a sailor your dream, more important than anything?"

"Like keeping your vows and your family together," muttered Tobias.

She huffed, the breath blowing stray hairs from her lips. "It turns out being a sailor and a woman is more difficult than I'd anticipated."

Jamison cocked a brow. "You told Cora you'd make yourself into a man."

"I decided it was better to earn my way as myself. I wanted everyone to know that Alice Ann Lark set out on an adventure and she succeeded by the skin of her teeth and the sweat of her brow. I can't help it if men are idiots who don't see true talent when it smacks them in the cheek."

"So, you hit someone did you?" Garrett called through the crack in the door. "I always did like your spunk. Nothing else, mind you, but that I could appreciate."

With a roll of his eyes to heaven, Jamison opened the door. Garrett grinned down at him. "Might as well let me back in, since there's no point in keeping me out."

The point Cade was stuck on was that she referred to herself as Alice Ann *Lark*. She was still using his last name. That must have meaning, right? Then again, perhaps not. Perhaps he was as deluded as he had been so many times before. But wasn't it worth the asking?

If adventure was what she wanted, adventure he could give her. Maybe then she would see that they could be well-suited. Maybe then they might have a chance.

Rising to his knees, he reached out to embrace her. She gasped and tried to step out of reach, but found only the wall against her back. Eyes wide, she tried to sidestep him, but he secured a hand on either side of her waist. Such behavior wasn't like him, or hadn't been like him four years ago. He had caught her off guard and hoped it would play in his favor.

"Alice, come with us. We'll decipher the compass and find the source of our Gifts. Once we do, if I haven't won you over, you can leave, no questions asked. I promise."

Garrett grunted and muttered something Cade chose to not interpret. "Come home and see your sister. Coraline misses you something awful and Julep—" He glanced away. How to describe their daughter? She spoke of her mother often, how she wished for her to come home and be a family. After being trapped in that circus for over a year, Julep needed a normal life. She was almost six years old, and while she loved her Auntie Martha, she knew that Martha wasn't her real mother. Martha needed to focus on Garrett and baby Josephine, not run ragged trying to make everyone else's ends meet.

Cade needed to offer his daughter more than a father without a clue what he was doing. And he needed a wife—*his* wife. He needed to believe that the collapse of all Alice Ann's dreams and what she perceived to be failures was really a blessing from God to reunite them. He could forgive her. He hadn't realized it before, but now that they were together, with him holding onto her flesh-and-blood, looking into the eyes he loved, he knew he could. It would be difficult, but he could.

"Please, Alice, Julep needs her mother. We want you to come

home. It doesn't matter why you left or why you've stayed away. I forgive you for it."

"Cade, I...I can't. It's too complicated."

"It isn't."

Garrett snorted again and rolled his eyes. Cade shot him a scowl as Alice's jaw tightened and her lips drew into a straight line. She gestured at her brother-in-law. "You see? No one wants me there."

"Ignore him. You know how he is. He holds a grudge, but he's really become much softer. He married Martha. They have a daughter now."

Alice stared at Garrett, eyebrows raised. He shrugged. "The Lord works in mysterious ways."

"So, what do you say?" Cade asked. "If my brother can become a boring farmer, maybe there's hope for me to become an audacious sailor. I even own a ship."

The right side of her lip lifted. "You have a ship?"

"That's right," Tobias drawled. "Nothing says love like an ocean vessel."

Cade glared at him. "You built your wife a prairie schooner."

"So?"

"So, I think he's saying that he won," Jamison chuckled. "Ship beats wagon any day."

"Exactly." Cade took Alice's hands in his and turned her back toward his brothers. Enough distractions. He gripped her fingers tighter. "I bought my schooner a couple years ago. It was in rough shape, but Tobias and Jamison helped me clean it up and make it seaworthy."

"When did you learn to sail?" she said softly.

"I worked on a ship for about five months."

"You did? What role did you have?"

"Stoker and then later, on the quarterdeck using my Gift to help the captain. Not that I had much choice after being shanghaied."

She gasped. "*Shanghaied*?"

"Garrett, too. And Josiah. Then we discovered Martha's brother on board, escaped, washed up in Charleston, and found Daniel. We all returned to San Francisco where we rescued Julep and Martha from a maniacal circus master along with a few hundred others, many of whom now live in Larksong."

She gawked, and he couldn't help but delight in the sheer shock on her expression. He had never dumbfounded her before and he rather enjoyed it.

He shrugged. "A lot has happened since you went away."

"Clearly. It sounds like you've grown a lot."

The knife of rejection began to retract from his chest. He was winning her over! He rushed ahead, determined to recount every last detail that might convince her to return home. Today would be the day God finally answered his prayers. Everything would be normal, like it should.

"You don't even know the half of it, Alice. I've taken over our fishing business. It suffered for a little while, but thanks to help from our Chinook friends, it's doing well after this summer. I've become more assertive and I even punched someone once. I've stoked fires and sailed through storms, almost died, and gone a little crazy. Oh, once in Georgia, I chased a lady down the street because I thought she was you. Obviously, she wasn't, but I thought so at the time. She had red hair just like yours. You and I can have a good life in Larksong. A grand life. I promise things will be better this time."

Suddenly, her half smile was all anger. She ripped her hands from his and pushed away, turned a circle to shout at each of them in turn. "I told you, I don't want to come back. This is my life, right here. I don't care that I live in a shack. I don't care that I left any of you. This is my life, and I chose it. Not you, do you hear me? I chose me." Her chest rose and fell with deep breaths, growing closer and closer together. She pressed a palm to her forehead. "I told you it was complicated. I told you. I told you."

She was panicking. Cade knew those reactions for he had felt them in his own being for most of his life. Living alone in the wilderness, what had such isolation done to his confident wife?

He reached for her, but when his fingers touched her arm, she spun and backhanded him across the cheek. A groan fell from his lips, and his brothers rushed forward. He saw Garrett make a fist and grabbed his arm. "Stop." He gasped. "You don't understand what's happening."

"She just hit you!"

"I know she did."

His wife's gasps grew louder as she stumbled for the door and ran outside. He rushed after her and caught her around the shoulders as she tried to flee through the marsh. She shoved him, palms pressed against his chest with all her might, tangled hair flying, her eyes darting everywhere but into his. "Let me go! I have to leave. I can't be here. You don't want me."

He grabbed her face between his palms and looked into her eyes. "Yes, Alice, I do."

Tears streaked her cheeks. "You have a wonderful life and I...I have nothing."

"You have me."

Her chest rose in a deep inhale. "No," she breathed. "I should have never been yours to begin with." Then her eyes rolled up and she pitched forward, tumbling unconscious into his arms.

3

Alice Ann swam through the depths of another memory, struggling to escape. If she could swim to the surface before it took hold, then maybe she wouldn't remember. She could have a normal mind like ordinary people who recalled events with that perfect haze across them. The one that obscured things just a little, like looking at the sepia tones of a tintype rather than the colorful hues of a painting. The photograph still showed what had been, but with a little something missing. You could fill in the blanks if you wanted, but for unfortunate events, why would you wish to do so? Instead, you could look on the photograph with a sad type of fondness without the sharp pains inside your soul.

Not for her. Pain was all these memory moments ever brought her. Like a novelist's pen or an artist's brush, sounds, scents, and emotions charted a path through her mind with perfect clarity. As though she was there again, reliving the event, word for word, touch by touch. For the new memory, in all its crisp detail and heightened emotion, would be with her forever, ready to retrieve at a moment's notice like a book from a shelf. Showing her how she had hurt others because she could, so she could always be a step ahead. Always so determined to put her desires before anyone else's. She had lost much of her childhood and her growing years to the needs of her father and her family. To them, Alice Ann's dreams were never as important as those of her sister, Coraline, simply because Cora was going blind and

17

Alice Ann was not.

"Go west with your sister," her parents had told her. "She deserves to see all the beauty of this world while she still can. She will need you to help her once the day comes that she cannot."

Alice Ann had opened her mouth to declare that she didn't want to help Cora, that this was all so unfair, but her father spoke first. Even in his blindness, he always sensed her coming arguments. "Think on this as your faithful calling. An adventure the Lord has given you to share with your sister."

Some adventure. More like a jail cell. To see the world pass by her through the bars like ships on the edge of the ocean.

"It's always about Cora. What about me? What about my dreams?"

"Sometimes our dreams must change," her mother had said. *She would know*, Alice thought. Her mother had sacrificed everything for their father's health. She had given up her home, her livelihood, her friends, and her money—all deferred to his interests. There had been nothing left for her, and that in turn leached onto Alice's eldest sister, Mercy. Mercy never married; she couldn't for she could never leave their mother to tend their father alone. Mercy also sacrificed her dreams for her family, to be a laundress in a fisherman's cabin while all her lost friends became debutantes and married wealthy men.

Mercy never complained, although Alice Ann knew that inside she must be dying with regret.

"You will do this for Coraline," their father continued. "Think if it were you who had gone blind."

"Isn't that why she married Oliver?" Alice asked. "He's a doctor. Let him take care of her."

"Alice," her mother said gently. "I know it is difficult for you to understand being young as you are—sixteen is such a tender age—but Coraline will do the same for you as long as she is able. You can trust her to guide you on the trail, all the way to Washington."

"And what then? After she's blind and *I* have to guide *her* every day for the rest of my life." Alice Ann stomped her foot, as though that would actually create any sway with her father. She knew it would only anger him, yet she did so anyway. Twice.

"You, daughter, listen well. This is the end of all arguments.

Coraline and Oliver are wed. They have signed on with the Larksong wagon train and generously agreed to take you with them. Sometimes we are given a path we do not wish to follow, but we have no choice."

"That is how this ends then? I have no choice?" The room fell silent, her father's glassy eyes staring into space, her mother's staring at the floor. Mercy quietly dried dishes at the wash basin, and Alice Ann released one final huff. "Well, isn't that simply splendid."

She stomped to the door and ripped it open.

"Alice Ann Owens!" her father's voice stopped her. "I've had enough of your defiance."

"Good news then, Papa. Soon I'll be headed to Washington and you'll never need to experience my defiance ever again. But just so you know, I would rather gouge my own eyes out than go to this godforsaken land where you're sending me."

Slamming the cottage door, she ran to the end of the dock and released their fishing dory from its anchor. It was nothing as grand as the schooner they used to have, but now, it was all they had. Taking both oars in hand, she rowed far out into the harbor, until she could no longer differentiate her family's home from all the others. There she dropped the oars in their locks, buried her face in her hands, and cried.

4

AUGUST 26, 1859
GHOST FOREST, WASHINGTON TERRITORY

Over an hour had passed before Alice Ann awoke. Cade had spent the past sixty-seven minutes pacing the room, then circling the shack, then pacing again, convinced his heart was going to beat so hard it would eventually stop beating. His other brothers had settled themselves around the room, simply waiting, sympathy in their eyes. To him, it felt like the night Alice had fallen off a cliff, hit her head, broke her leg, and almost died. Thankfully their friend Quea'Quim had been there to save her, only to later, in a sad twist, take a war arrow aimed for Jamison.

The night of Alice's accidental cliff dive, she had recovered easily. Her injuries had been straightforward for Jamison's medicinal Gift to fix. Whatever afflicted her now, however...this was something entirely different.

The moment her eyes opened, Cade ran to her side. He knelt on the straw tick where Jamison had frequently sat to check her pulse and assess her constitution.

Cade squeezed her hand, her skin cool against his. "How are you feeling? We were so worried." Daniel offered him a wet cloth from the water bucket they'd procured, which Cade gently patted along his wife's forehead.

Her lashes fluttered as though she might go under again, but then rose and met his gaze. The irises were dark, the pupils dilated. "How long was I asleep?" she asked.

"Over an hour. Jamison couldn't figure out what was wrong. He thought his Gift was broken. He thought you were dying!"

"Her pulse is normal now," Jamison assessed. He scooted back on the tick, allowing more space for his patient. "Alice Ann, can you tell me how you felt immediately before you fainted? When did you last eat or drink?"

Considering his own affliction, Cade doubted her problem was lack of sustenance or any other medical ailment. She had likely developed the same all-consuming fear he suffered from and in her panic, encountered a fainting spell. He had told Jamison as much while Alice Ann slept, but his brother hadn't been convinced.

"If it was merely panic, she would have woken up by now," Jamison had said while they'd watched her sleep. "Fainting spells last minutes or moments, not hours."

"Maybe it's different with women," Cade had countered.

"It isn't."

Now, Alice watched him with faraway consideration, likely remembering their frenzied conversation immediately before she'd lost consciousness. She had been trying to escape. Escape from him.

Her gaze slid to his cheek where she had struck him. Although it no longer stung, he imagined the skin must still be splotched crimson. Squeezing her eyes shut, she turned away. "I hate when these happen."

"You've had this happen before?"

She nodded and grimaced with the motion. Her lips raised in a bitter laugh. "It's part of my Gift. As fate would have it, I'm a freak of nature after all, the same as all of you."

A chorus of disbelieving, *"Excuse me?—What?—Are you serious?—Yes, I knew it!"* filled the room from each of the brothers, while Cade's jaw merely fell slack. His wife was *Gifted*? He thought he'd had enough of a shock when they'd discovered Coraline could translate anything, then when they learned Josiah healed quickly, and never did he think he could be knocked over more than when they'd brought an entire group of Gifted circus performers home to stay. But this topped them all.

He and Alice Ann had lived for two and a half years as man and wife and regrettably, as intimate friends for nearly a year before that. Shouldn't he have at least suspected her to be Gifted when the woman shared his bed? But he hadn't. He hadn't had an inkling about any of them. Had Julep developed her Gift, too, and he'd completely missed it? Was she skipping around town performing miracles while her father remained oblivious?

"What is your Gift?" Tobias asked her. He slumped on the tree trunk stool, elbows on his knees and astonishment on his face.

"I remember everything."

"You've always had a good memory."

"But now it's perfect. I remember every tiny detail, every conversation word for word, what I did and the order I did it, dates and times and places exactly as they happened. It began when I fell off that cliff and hit my head. From then on, every day was branded into my brain. I could recall things months later with precision, as though they had happened the minute before. Always being reminded of my mistakes, the horrid things I'd said and every time I'd said them...it only made me angrier and more horrid. But that wasn't the worst of it. The worst part happened when...when Julep was born."

Cade ran the damp rag against his own flushed neck. "But you seemed happy when she was born. Remember when we were all three there together? Before anyone else came to see her? We used to say that was the happiest we had ever been."

She swiped the rag from his hand and laid it over her eyes with a sigh. "I was happy. I think, perhaps, that was the only time I've been really and truly happy. Not only because of having this beautiful baby, but because I thought that now remembering things would be good. Because then I could teach them to her."

He began to affirm her statement, but she held up a hand. "You haven't heard the rest yet. Despite my happiness, within hours, I started experiencing these strange spells, like what you just witnessed. I call them memory moments. Remembrances from before the cliff accident, all the way back to my childhood, in the same heightened detail. Back then, I didn't lose consciousness, but my head would ache and sometimes I would be sick to my stomach. I knew what it was; I had seen you and Garrett experience the same symptoms with your Gifts."

"Then why didn't you tell me?"

"And be a burden? You worry over the smallest things, Cade. You're afraid of grass—"

"That grass was taller than me! I'm not afraid of regular grass."

"—and I knew I needed to find a way to deal with my own problems, like I always have. On. My. Own."

"So, you didn't trust me."

"I didn't trust anyone."

There it was. The root of the problem. His anxieties had caused her to not trust him with her welfare and protection, nor her secrets. They had lived as husband and wife, but she had always lived inside herself, relying on no one else.

He had failed her as a husband. It was his fault she'd left, exactly as her letter had said. He stared at her, lost for words. Thankfully, he had four brothers with more than enough opinions to fill the space.

"I can't believe this," Tobias muttered.

Jamison ran both palms over his scalp. "My speculation is her head injury at the cliff initially triggered her Gift and then childbirth sent it spiraling. Different parts of our brain are designed to do different tasks in specific instances. The brain evolves over time to handle its full capacity. That's why Alice Ann's symptoms are growing worse. Her brain can't handle such frequent ingestion of emotional information; a person could go insane."

"Or die?" asked Garrett. For the first time, he appeared genuinely alarmed. Of all the brothers, only he and Cade had experienced severe physical symptoms from their Gifts. Those symptoms had diminished over time, but even so, one had to wonder.

"There's a chance," Jamison admitted. "Without more information on our Gifts' origin, we don't know where they could lead. We've never known anyone of an older generation who was truthful about them before."

Lying had been their father's daily bread and butter. While fully capable of lashing his youngest son's back and striking the others with a fire poker, when it came to information that could save their lives, Alonzo Lark kept that close to the chest. Likewise, his closest friend had also been his greatest rival. Together, he and Ashley Sterling had persuaded, negotiated, lied, maimed, and murdered from one coast to the other until the days they'd died. Even their unGifted mother had left them little but secrets and riddles.

The brothers all quietly looked at each other. "What do we do?" Cade asked.

Alice Ann's fingers tightened around his. "You leave me here and go home."

He squeezed her hand even harder. "Not if you're dying, I'm not."

"Julep needs you, and I'd rather die alone."

"No one wants to die alone."

"I do."

"You can't die without a priest to perform last rites," Jamison cut in. "I won't allow it."

"You can pray over me."

"I'm not a priest."

"Close enough."

"Good gravy, stop!" Tobias shouted. "Daniel, what do you think?"

Their brother's chin jerked up from the far corner, where he had been sitting practically silent since they'd walked through the door. He had always been a somber soul, but today more so than usual. He glanced between the group and shrugged. "I've never been Gifted. I don't have a say."

"You're our brother, so, yes, you do. What's your opinion?"

"Well..." Daniel pushed to his feet and stretched his back, twisting each direction with a satisfying pop. He settled a hand on either hip. "I think we find the source and hopefully, it removes her Gift the same as it gave our ancestors theirs."

Alice Ann flung the rag off her eyes and wrenched her grip from Cade's. "Don't. You shouldn't waste your time finding the source just for me. I'm not worth the trouble."

"We're searching for it either way, so you might as well come with us. Besides, Garrett and I get sick from our Gifts sometimes, but we're still here."

Yes, exactly, he thought. *We're still here.* They weren't dying and neither was she. He must believe that, otherwise he would need to contemplate the mortality of every person in that room and back in Larksong. Such fears would drive him deeper into the pit he had worked so hard to climb out of. "Our symptoms have improved quite a lot over the years, Alice. Yours will, too."

"You don't know that."

"There's much I don't know. You liked to remind me frequently." She glared at him, and he returned her hostility with a wary smile. After a second, she rewarded him with a tightlipped smile in return.

"I can't come home with you, Cade. You think you want me there, but you don't."

"That's what I thought, too, the day they came for me," said Daniel. He crossed the room and laid a hand on either of their shoulders, but his eyes were all for Alice Ann. "But I, like you, was wrong."

Alice shrugged his hand away. "I don't know you, Daniel."

"And I don't know you. I'm the only one who can be objective. This here is the truth: I know what it is to feel you've failed everyone and don't deserve forgiveness. But it's better to be with people. It isn't too late to go home."

"I'm not begging their forgiveness."

"Then don't. Just take the first step. Reconsider Cade's offer and sail home with us. Start there and let the rest happen with time."

Cade extended his hand. "Please, Alice." He willed that hand to speak of promises for both of them. If she accepted it, then maybe she would come home to stay. Their life could be like it was for those few happy minutes after Julep was born, wanting nothing more than to be together.

Her eyes met his, the pupils having contracted back to their normal state. Whatever affliction she had was now past. He extended his hand farther. *Just take it*, he prayed.

"Very well," she said finally. "I'll come back to Larksong, but there's little I can promise after that." Then ignoring the brothers, Cade's hand, and her meager belongings, she collected her bonnet and walked out the door.

5

All five brothers and Alice Ann crammed into the gig, sitting shoulder-to-shoulder on the three wooden thwarts. They navigated away from the Ghost Forest and downriver, crossing through the estuary to where Cade's fishing schooner, *Gratia* was anchored. As they approached, he watched his wife's somber expression break in a way she had never looked at him. That light in her eyes over a ship—a lifeless soulless object—nearly cracked whatever remained of his flimsy heart.

"Would you look at her!" Alice exclaimed. "How majestic."

"Yes, she is at that," Cade replied sourly.

"Outmatched by a boat," Garrett whispered beside him. "Should we count this quest as a loss and take her back now?"

They could have come without the schooner—the distance wasn't more than fifty miles each way—but truth be told, Cade had wanted her to see it. Part of him wanted her to recognize that he wasn't the disappointment she believed him to be. But even living in that swamp as she had, rather than delight at seeing him rescue her, she only delighted in the means with which he did so.

Gratia was a handsome ship now that they had repaired her. It hadn't been so at first. She had barely been able to stay afloat until they could careen her to clean, caulk, and paint the hull. Most of her sails required mending and her rigging needed to be replaced. Most of that, they'd accomplished before he had been shanghaied by the *Arletta*. The rest, including cabin repairs, had been completed after his return. His hope was to take Julep on multi-day trips along the

Pacific coast, storing fish up in the hold, traveling from Seattle to Astoria and perhaps even farther. Thus far, however, he had only entertained short jaunts around Larksong Bay, catching enough fish to help sustain the town. Their journey to collect the compass was the schooner's true maiden sea voyage.

If only he had wrestled his fears years ago and listened when his wife asked to leave Larksong, they could have taken *Gratia's* first voyage together. Yet he also knew that if Alice had never left, he would have never found the motivation to purchase the schooner. Even now, he wished for no more physical distance from Larksong than that which he had just traveled. Leaving his family to cross an ocean, as Alice Ann had often suggested, struck him to the core.

She gripped Cade's sleeve, finally turning those brown eyes upon him. "What'd you name her?"

"*Gratia.*"

"Oh, of course. How appropriate." Releasing him, she clasped her hands against her chest. *As though in prayer*, Cade thought, but he very much doubted she would be. Or that she truly understood the significance of his ship's name meaning *grace*. Did she even speak to God anymore? Throughout their short marriage, they had prayed together at times—mostly before meals and before bed—but the offerings had been short, and he had always led the intentions. Sometimes in the evening, he would read scripture while she mended her fishing poles or ropes. Occasionally, they would even discuss the meaning behind the passages. Rather predictably, however, Alice Ann saw the lessons as a ship's hold half empty, while Cade would comment, "At least there's cargo in the hold at all."

Was it that sense of negativity which had driven her to the Ghost Forest? She could have obtained work in one of the towns, even if she hadn't found luck seafaring. Surely Astoria, Seattle, or even Vancouver would have had something to offer. Olympia or farther south to Portland, perhaps. She was smart, knew much from her book reading, was a crack shot, a talented fisherman, and knew how to convince people of things they shouldn't be convinced of. How had no one else recognized that? Simply because they weren't in love with her and he was?

His brothers shipped the starboard oars as the gig knocked against the schooner's hull beside the ship's side ladder. Jamison stood to grab one of the manropes and Cade extended a hand to Alice. "Ladies first." Without a word, she ignored the proffered hand and gripped the manropes herself, shimmying up the hull and over the gunwale with ease.

"At least we know her staunch independence hasn't changed," Jamison muttered. He glanced once at Cade with clear uncertainty and then followed Alice up the ladder.

Garrett leaned into Cade's shoulder and thumbed back across the water. "The shore's right there. Say the word and we plunk her right back on it."

"No, I gave her my word we'd help her."

"What did she give you?" Tobias asked. "She made no promises." He reached for the manropes, the gig bobbing beneath him. "We'll help her because she's our sister-in-law, but if she doesn't get respectable, I can't see how we can accept her back into the fold."

Perfect. Three of his brothers had doomed this mission before it began. Even Tobias, the most open-minded of them all.

"Don't allow our brothers to discourage you," Daniel told him. "They loathed me once, too, for a lot longer than they've hated your wife. And now, here I am, back among you."

"You're family. It's easier for them to forgive you."

"She's our family, too. True, she left, but she's here now, and you have a responsibility to her. You'd be careless to forget that."

"What if nothing changes? What if, when we're back home, it's all how it was before? What if we don't find the source of our Gifts? What if she keeps getting worse and worse? What then?"

"That's a lot of fear over things that may never happen. Use your logic, Cade, not your heart. For better or worse. You made the promise, remember?"

"I know." He glanced up at his eldest brother. They had never had much of a relationship in all their years together, and even now, Cade barely knew him. But he spoke wisdom, something Cade always valued from Tobias and Jamison and much later, from Garrett, too. In a way, it seemed they were all prodigals, every one of them trying to return to a home they didn't feel worthy of. Maybe there was a chance for more reconciliation than just him and Alice Ann. Maybe he and Daniel could find a new friendship as well.

"Hullo, Captain!" His first mate, Winasie's tanned face popped over the rail, the Chinook man's rounded cheeks puffed out in concern. "Need help hoisting her up?"

"Not necessary, Win. Daniel and I will handle it. Prepare to weigh anchor."

"Aye, Captain." With a nod, he disappeared again.

The native was one of three sailors Cade had hired to help sail, perform regular ship maintenance, and act as guards when he went ashore. Although he would have preferred for his brothers to also be his crew, he knew how unrealistic that request would have been. They had families and fields to tend to, a town full of people needing their counsel, and except for Garrett who joined the *Gratia* when he could, they held little desire to live on the sea. Instead, they had provided their top recommendations for potential hires.

Their first choice had been Melvin, Martha's brother who had served as *Arletta*'s boatswain for over a decade after being enslaved on her for three years longer. However, the instant Cade made him the offer, he vehemently declined.

"I didn't work half my life to get off a ship, just to get back on one," he had groused. Instead, he remained content—and very busy— tending his new acres of land. He had earned them for helping to save them all from Ashley Sterling's wicked ways, and despite often butting heads with Garrett, had shown his diligence in tending the soil since his arrival.

Winasie had been recommended by Jamison as one of the recent Christian converts from Stella Maris Mission. As far as sailors went, the native was past his prime, but he was eager to work and eager to learn. Most importantly, he had over fifty years of cultural and fishing knowledge among the natives and fluency in the Jargon, the trade language of the Pacific Coast. His expertise made for smoother conversations and less potential for hostility.

Gratia's other two crewmates, Thatcher and Jones, had traveled with them from Sterling's circus in San Francisco, which meant they understood the importance of discretion. Thatcher's agility as a prior equine acrobat served him well while up in *Gratia*'s rigging, and Jones's experience as a stage hand made him particularly adept at knots and repairs. Along with Winasie, they had proven to be trustworthy investments.

Cade followed Daniel up the ladder, pausing as the last aboard to help him hoist and secure the gig, while the other men readied for departure. Alice stood at a distance, hands fisted on her hips as she watched them work. He wondered how *Gratia* compared with the fisherman's boat her father had sailed in Charleston harbor. From his recollection, Ned Owens had captained a one-sail dory with barely room for two aboard. This may have been the first time she had ever boarded a ship of this size; he honestly had no idea.

He turned to Daniel. "Take the spyglass to the bow and see if anything may delay our departure."

"Aye, Captain. That still feels strange to say."

"Truth be told, it still feels strange to hear." With a slap to his brother's arm, Cade left him to join Alice Ann. "We'll be weighing anchor soon. Would you like to rest below decks or join me on the quarterdeck?"

"The quarterdeck, of course." She strode aft like she was made to be there, easily skirting crates and coiled rigging, her bare feet slapping the steps as she ascended to the quarterdeck. Her fingers lighted above the ship's helm, seeming to shiver in delight before ever so slowly lowering toward the wheel's handles.

Before she made contact, however, Cade slipped his hands onto the handles beneath hers. She glanced up at him in confusion. "It's my ship, Alice. I man the helm."

"But—"

"It's my ship. I man the helm," he repeated. "If all goes well, and you decide to stay, I would be glad to have you on my crew."

He noticed her flinch at the words, which were both unusually assertive for him and likely a shock to her ego. When they lived together as man and wife, she had consistently squelched his ability to lead through her own demands. He had failed as a husband in that regard, and it wasn't a mistake he would make twice.

"Do you still want to come back with us?" he asked. Surprisingly, she nodded and stepped away to lean both elbows on the rail. Chin in her palm, she peered across the surf, back to where the Ghost Forest beckoned. With a deep exhale, Cade gripped the helm and hollered for the crew to weigh anchor and prepare to sail.

"Daniel," he called. "Are we clear to sail?" His brother stood at the bow, a spyglass raised as he scanned for any impediments. One final pass was followed by a nod of confirmation. Truthfully, the action wasn't needed to set sail; however, Daniel hadn't shown himself to be the most adept sailor on their way in from Larksong and needed something simple to occupy his time.

"Hoist sail!" At Cade's command, Jones and Tobias set the mainsail, while Thatcher and Garrett did the same on the foresail, with Winasie and Jamison ready to hoist the jib. Soon a light midday breeze filled the sails, and they were headed out to sea.

Gripping the helm in one hand, Cade removed the antiquated compass from his pocket with the other. According to the arrow, they were headed slightly southeast, exactly the direction that would take them home. If only he knew what else this instrument could tell him. Was God's purpose in having him obtain it as a child only to reunite him with his wife now? His mother's death seemed a shameful expense for a floundering marriage.

Ah, but those were thoughts to consider at another time.

Once they were safely sailing, Alice Ann rejoined him at the helm. Her eyes flitted across the deck, taking it all in, before landing on him. "It seems you've made a good life here, Cade. Rather the accomplishment."

A compliment? He waited for the other shoe to drop, for the accolade to be followed by her usual criticism. That's how it had always been before. But when she continued to stare at him without comment, he considered it might have been genuine. "Thank you, but I would have preferred for us to have accomplished it together."

"I know." Then she spun from the rail and strode past him toward the cabin hatch. "I think I'll rest now. Show me the cabin." He sighed. So much for compliments. At least, he wouldn't need to worry about keeping track of her while also navigating a course.

"Garrett, take the helm?" he called, but his brother was already on his way. Elbowing Cade aside, he claimed the helm in both hands and gave a deep inhale. "Ah, she's my ship now. What shall my first edict as captain be?"

"To stop saying that every time I let you man the helm. She's still my ship."

He grinned. "Then you should stop letting me. You know I thirst for power. In the time you're gone, I could start a mutiny."

"My crew would never agree to that."

"Maybe not Winasa, but who's to say I couldn't convince Thatcher and Jones? I'm quite the charmer."

Cade narrowed his eyes. "I will hurt you."

"Empty threats, my brother. You know I'm your favorite."

"Not if you steal my ship."

Garrett's boisterous laughter followed him all the way down the ladder into the cabin below.

The cabin contained two portholes on either side, but being splattered with sea salt as they were, made for a cloudy lighting source. Even so, they illuminated four identical wooden berths with trunks nailed down between them. On either side of the ladder sat a side-flue cast-iron stove and a cramped table with two chairs, also fixed to the floor. At the cabin's far end, a second ladder led to the hold with compartments for both dry goods and fish transport. Each compartment could also be accessed via hatches from the deck above. Beyond that lay the crew's quarters with space for up to eight hammocks should he decide to expand their numbers.

As expected, Alice Ann had descended the ladder on her own and now stood blinking in the near darkness. At his descent, she had turned to face him, although stepped no closer. Her brows raised in silent question.

"It's only us here now," he said. "You can tell me the truth. Why didn't you go to sea? I can't believe not a single ship would take you."

Her gaze shifted away. "Believe it, for they wouldn't. What I told you before *is* true. No one wanted me. I went to Astoria first then tried the steamboats along the Columbia River. I heard every excuse. It's bad luck to have a woman on board. Women are too stupid to sail.

I'm too young, too pretty, only good for one thing to a sailor—and we both know what that is. So, I took to the Ghost Forest. No one ever goes there. I knew I could fish as often as I wanted whenever I wanted with only myself to care for. It was the closest to perfection I could ever hope to find."

That shack in the marsh, alone and impoverished, thinking she could be dying, was her idea of perfection?

"You shouldn't waste your time finding the source just for me," she had said. *"I'm not worth the trouble."* Crickets, she had certainly been her fair share of trouble over the years. No one else might understand his motivations, but to him, she was still worth fighting for.

"Oh, Alice, God has bigger plans for you than that."

"Yes, I'm sure He did," she said, her voice so soft he wondered if the words were meant for him at all.

She turned away and, removing her bonnet, laid it on one of the bottom berths. "I'm going to take a nap. You'll tell me when we arrive?"

"I will." He paused with his hand on the ladder, considering turning back, then instead trudged upward. At that same moment, the summer sun broke through the clouds, warm and full upon his face. He raised his chin to it, catching a glance of Thatcher and Garrett hoisting the forestay sail. Meanwhile, Daniel remained at the bow, spyglass still in hand. All seemed quiet for now, but one could never be too cautious, especially with the ship's greatest question mark currently in the cabin beneath their feet.

"Lord, did I make a mistake bringing her here?" he asked the empty air.

"Yes, probably."

He frowned at Garrett, who thankfully hadn't turned his crew against him. Striding over, he reclaimed the helm. "I wasn't talking to you. You're not God."

Garrett chuckled. "Thank goodness. The whole world would be far more disastrous than it already is." His expression sobered. "But I do think you're making a mistake bringing her home."

Cade gripped the wheel, focusing on his crew completing their tasks. "I can't have this conversation while I'm at the helm."

"Then have someone else man it. Your crew may be mutinous, so they're probably capable of floating this ship for ten minutes without you."

"Your jests aren't amusing, Garrett." Cade called out to Winasie. "Win, take the helm. I need to check something in the hold."

"Aye, Captain." As soon as Cade handed off the compass to the native and instructed him to keep them on course, he and Garrett descended the secondary hold ladder from the crew's quarters rather than through the cabin where Alice Ann rested.

He blinked in the dimly lit supply hold, taking in the rations of food and fishing supplies that would need to be restocked on their next trip to Astoria. Garrett immediately rooted through a crate as though he owned the place and crunched into an apple.

"We're not down here to eat," Cade admonished. "I have work to do, so tell me why you think I shouldn't have brought Alice home when you're the one who insisted on telling me where she was. You could have just left it alone."

Garrett gave a muffled chortle, half-coughed, then finally swallowed. "If you recall, I did finally leave it alone, but you're the one who demanded I tell you so we could retrieve the compass. Then, like a dolt, you invited her back with us. I never told you to do *that*."

"I couldn't help myself. Seeing her how she is after I'd been such a desperate wreck myself...I couldn't leave without trying one more time. Without knowing there isn't any hope for us."

"You really think there is?"

Cade stared at him, uncertain. "There was for you."

"Hmmm." Garrett took another bite of apple and chewed slowly before he finally replied. "I guess if God saved me, He can save any of us. I might not like your wife, but, as far as I know, her morality is still a sight better than mine ever was. Let's agree it's good the restoration of your marriage doesn't rest on me."

"I'm not certain it rests with me, either."

"Don't play jester. You've been doing everything for her."

"How did you gather that conclusion?"

"You continued the fishing business even though she wasn't there to help. You bought a fishing schooner when you didn't know how to sail. You've become more assertive, more outspoken. All things Alice Ann wanted you to be. Before that, you traveled west because Tobias wanted you to. Now, you stay in Larksong because our family's there. Have you ever made a goal simply because *you* wanted it?"

"Of course I have."

"Name one."

"I—" Cade dug deep and couldn't come up with anything. When was the last time he had done anything only for him and no one else? When he was a little boy maybe, but he hadn't known any better. Toddlers were always selfish. Growing up, he had never asked for anything special, and birthdays were rarely celebrated. His father loathed mediocre accomplishments and, in his mind, living another year was exactly that.

"If I tell you, will you promise not to mock me for it?"

Garrett's lip twitched. "That's an awfully tall order."

"Garrett!"

"Fine. You're such a squalling babe sometimes." At Cade's side eye, he relented. "Ok, I cede. I won't say anything."

"Thank you. Honestly, all I want is a loving family. Mama taught us to be gentlemen, that there was no greater role than head of the house. She tried to raise us to be good fathers even though our own father wasn't one. That's all I ever wanted, to make Mama proud."

"Do you really believe Mama's the best person to take your mark from?" Earlier that year, they had learned of a many-years-past affair between their mother and Josiah, their family's butler and the brothers' father-figure. Their forbidden romance had produced a half-sister, Clary, only recently discovered to be alive. Until then, they had believed all three of their sisters were stillborn.

Cade sighed. "What she did was wrong, but her heart was in the right place."

"That doesn't make it right."

"Never said it did."

Garrett's hand clenched around his apple. "That's still not a dream of your own. It's our mother's more than yours. And now you want to make Alice Ann proud, even with all she's done to you."

"She's my wife. Of course, I want her to be proud of me."

"Surprisingly, I understand how you feel. Martha makes me feel that way, too. She was the only one who ever made me want to be better. The difference though, Cade? She was actually better than me to begin with." He slapped him on the shoulder and headed for the ladder. "Don't lose heart. Heck, maybe she'll surprise us. You certainly have. Who'd have thought crybaby Cade would ever command a ship?"

"Yeah," Cade said as he followed his brother upward. "Who'd have thought?" Out of everything in his life, this ship was the only element he *could* command.

6

Evening had fallen by the time *Gratia* anchored in Larksong. The scent of woodsmoke and salmon greeted them long before they caught sight of the town, their Chinook residents preparing their usual suppertime provisions. Although Cade had only lived here for a few years, it felt more like home than their expansive Charleston plantation ever had. Here he could be himself, or as much as his scattered mind would let him.

Jamison, being Larksong's current mayor as well as head physician, led the way up the path from the shore, the other brothers behind and Cade and Alice Ann bringing up the rear. Per usual, *Gratia*'s crew had remained on board to complete their evening tasks and perform night watch.

Alice kept tossing glances over her shoulder as though she might bolt back down the hill at any moment, and the movements set Cade's nerves on edge. When he finally felt like he was about to scream, he gently took her arm and laced it through his, placing as little space between them as he could. At first, she resisted the gesture, but with a huff, finally relaxed against him and on they went.

Dirt paths ran between thirty-foot wide cedar plank lodges, each one's roof containing three round holes for releasing smoke from interior fire pits. A substantial garden had been cultivated at either end of town along with a smaller central herb garden, each tended to by the residents, pioneer and native alike. On Larksong's eastern and southern sides, wheat, corn, and squash fields were nearly ready for harvest. The western hill down to the Pacific shore remained cloaked in spruce and cedar trees, and the northern end had been set aside as an annex for new residents.

The original section of lodges, where the Larks lived, had been what remained of an old Chinook village, abandoned after its chief died. Believing that evil spirits had taken up residence, the natives had also believed that only the white men could frighten the spirits away. Six years ago, with the original Larksong failing, the brothers had agreed to join some of the Chinook converts here in Christian community, and they had lived amicably ever since.

As such, there were plenty of neighborly greetings as the group entered town, both in English and the Chinook Jargon. A few of the circus folks stared at Alice Ann, but as they themselves had arrived only months before, no one knew her significance. Once inside with the rest of the family, however, there would be no avoiding a confrontation. How was Cade going to explain his wife's presence or why he felt compelled to allow her back into his home?

A pain shot through his chest. He was going to have his wife in his home for the first time in nearly four years. Did that mean they would share a bed as well? They were married, but everything in him cautioned against it. He only had the one bed and he and Julep had shared it for years, since the day Alice Ann had left them. It wasn't fair to displace his daughter from her comfortable bedding—to the sofa or floor no less—on the same day he would practically uproot her life. More importantly, he didn't trust himself to make sound judgements concerning marital intimacy. How far was too far when you were married but also didn't know your wife? Certainly not on the first evening.

No, certainly not.

Right?

Oh, Lord, help him, he had no idea.

As they neared Tobias and Sarah's door, woodsmoke rose up through the roof, and the delicious aroma of roasted rabbit wafted out. He was simultaneously starving and unable to eat; however, supper would at least provide a few hours to decide how to approach his living arrangements. Although, it would also add another layer of discomfort as he was surrounded by family and peppered with questions. Worse, if he and Alice went to supper, then Julep would know her mother was home.

What, oh what, was he going to say to Julep? How could he hope to introduce her to her mother? She had been so young, barely two, when Alice Ann had left. He didn't know how much she could possibly remember or how comfortable she would be having a near stranger in their home. Julep always said she wanted her mother to come back, but only because the rest of them indulged her childish fantasies. Now that the dream had become real, would it meet the child's expectations?

He rubbed a palm against the dull ache beneath his sternum. One more day of fantasy wouldn't harm her. Twelve more hours allowed him time to think and pray.

"Wait," he called before Tobias could open the door. "Let's not hash this over tonight. A restful sleep would do us all good and have us thinking clearly. We have much to consider, and I want to make the right decisions."

"You know we're going straight home to tell our wives," said Garrett.

Of course, they were. What were wives for if not to tell things to? Especially difficult truths. Although, rarely had he experienced that kind of trust with his own wife.

"I know and I can't stop you, but we can wait until tomorrow to argue about it again. I'm afraid that once everyone else knows—"

"They'll toss me out," Alice interjected. She folded her arms in a huff. "No one wants me here, that much is plain. No one here ever liked me."

"I liked you," Cade muttered. His neck warmed considering exactly how much he had liked her at one time and how, even filthy as she was, he couldn't forget the woman underneath the grime.

Garrett's patronizing smirk jerked him back to the present. His brother pointed a finger at Alice Ann. "One minute, your highness." Gripping Cade's elbow, he drew him out of earshot. He jabbed his thumb over his shoulder in Alice Ann's direction and whispered, "Wipe that drunken smile off your face."

"What are you talking about?"

"It's so obvious, it's pathetic. As Tobias would say, you want to sing sweet Song of Solomon love to your wife tonight, don't you?"

Cade's face enflamed. He pinched his ears to make sure they hadn't combusted right off his face. Nope, still intact, unfortunately. Lighting on fire would have made for a good excuse to end this conversation.

"I don't know."

"Don't lie to me. I'm Mr. Eighty-Three-Women-Before-My Wife. I know what desire looks like, and you've got it painted in bright red all over that chubby little face of yours."

"My face isn't chubby."

"And your avoidance isn't going to work. Why else would you want to wait to tell the women? Because you know that once we do, they're going to say something logical and completely kill the romance. If you wait, you can joyfully claim ignorance."

"No, I really don't understand my feelings right now. I know I shouldn't even go near her—she hurt me so bad—but then I look at her and I just...well, you're a married man, you should know!"

"Nothing about that woman—" He waved his hand in Alice Ann's direction where she glared back at him from a dirt-smudged expression—"says attractive. She looks like a street beggar."

"Not to me she doesn't."

Garrett curled his fingers into a fist. "Do I need to deck you one? Brace yourself because here it comes."

Cade threw his arms up. "Stop! Nothing is happening tonight, I promise you. I'll give her the bed and I'll sleep on the sofa."

"You promise?"

"Promise."

Garrett's fist lowered. "Maybe I should come snuggle up with you just to make certain."

"Please don't."

His brother laughed, a great embarrassing guffaw that caused their other brothers to raise eyebrows in their direction. Garrett waved a hand at them. "No worries. Cade's just promised me that he'll behave himself."

"Was that ever a concern?" Tobias called back.

"If you'd spent months on the ocean with him, you'd understand." He tossed an arm across Cade's shoulders and leaned into his ear. "Long lonely months without our wives in sight. However, did we stand it? Good thing I get to go home to mine right now."

"Oh, get off of me." Cade flung his brother's arm off.

Garrett backed away, still laughing. "Breakfast at your place, Tobias? We'll continue the discussion then?"

With assent from Daniel and Jamison, Tobias nodded. He cast a glance at their youngest brother. "I'll tell Sarah to expect an extra guest."

"Thanks, Tobias," Cade said. "Do you, uh, think that Julep could stay with you tonight? When we left this morning, I wasn't prepared to explain to her—"

Mid-sentence, the lodge door flew opened and Sarah stepped out onto the dirt path, a spattered apron tied around her middle and a washrag in her right hand. She slapped Tobias over the shoulder with a smile then reached up to kiss his cheek. "What are you all discussing out here for? Come in and wash up. You're just in time for supper."

Alice tried to ease behind Daniel, who was of broader form than Cade, but Sarah noticed the movement and her expression paled. Her voice dropped to but a whisper. "Alice Ann. What...what're you doing here?"

Tobias took his wife's arm. "It's complicated, darling. Let's afford everyone some rest and discuss it in the morning. Julep's going to stay with us until then."

"Discuss what in the morning?" Martha appeared at Sarah's shoulder, her copper skin a silhouette in the twilight, but even so, Cade saw her lips press into a thin line. "Anwillik?" she called over her shoulder. Keep the children inside. We won't be long." Then she tugged the door closed and stepped into the street.

Her eyes narrowed as she took in Alice Ann's disheveled form. "Well, lands, I wasn't expecting you to be with them, yet, here you are. How long should we expect you? Have you time for supper or would that be too drowning on your dreams?"

Daniel stepped from between the two women, fingers running through his hair as he departed the confrontation. Cade groaned inwardly. So much for not dealing with this today.

Alice Ann's dark eyes met his, their corners soft and uncertain. Was she seeking an answer or was that what he wanted to believe?

Jamison's hand dropped on Martha's shoulder. "Now isn't the time. We all need a night of consideration before throwing too many accusations we might regret. Cade, go home with your wife. Talk this out. We'll see you for breakfast." He glanced at Alice Ann. "Both of you." Then he released Martha into Garrett's capable hands and turned to the door and his own wife behind it.

"What about Julep?" Martha asked Garrett.

"She's staying with Tobias and Sarah tonight."

Martha mumbled something else as they followed Tobias and Sarah inside, words Cade and Alice were both probably glad they couldn't hear.

They walked two lodges over, where a center wall divided his living quarters from Jamison and Coraline's. He and Alice Ann had shared the space before she left, so at least he knew she would remember it, even if their interactions within were now unfamiliar.

Once inside, he tugged off his boots and hung his hat and duster on the pegs near the door, allowing himself several deep breaths before finally turning back to his wife. She stood near the sofa, her head on a swivel, taking in all the new items he had acquired, such as Julep's toy box and a crocheted throw gifted from Martha two birthdays past. Martha had always been like one of the family, long before she married Garrett. After her role in rescuing Julep from Sterling's Theatrical, however, Cade had felt even more indebted to her. She acted as Julep's surrogate mother and he knew her volatile reaction to Alice Ann was due to her protective nature more than anything else.

"Are those Julep's?" Alice asked, nodding to the toy crate. He nodded. "When can I see her? Tomorrow?"

He licked his lips and swallowed hard. No sense putting it off. Julep would seek them out if he didn't make the first move. "Yeah, sure, I guess tomorrow."

"Do you think she'll be happy to see me?"

"There's nothing else she wants more," he replied honestly.

She gave a half smile. "I suppose I should be glad of that. It would be more challenging if she loathed me like everyone else does."

"She most definitely doesn't." He couldn't offer her any assurances on their other family members' feelings when their emotions were so plainly spilling from their lips. His hands came to rest on her shoulders and she looked up, her wet eyes shining in the lantern light, her lips moist. She dropped her hands to his waist, then wrapped them around his back, and clasped her fingers against his spine. He swallowed hard.

"Are you, uh, hungry?" he asked. "Would you like me to make some supper for us?"

"No, thank you. It's been a long day and I'd rather sleep."

"The, um, bedroom is through there."

Her half smile turned sly. "I know where the bedroom is, Cade. I used to live here."

Great golly, his face was on fire again, his heart about to explode from his chest. Her return was likely bad for him in many ways, but his heart clearly suffered the most. "Uh, right. Well, some of your things are still in the dresser and, um, there's an extra quilt if you're cold. I'll sleep on the sofa tonight."

She readjusted her grip, and her wedding band rubbed the ridges of his spine. She was still wearing it? How had he not noticed before?

If only his hadn't been stolen from him during his enslavement on the *Arletta*. Losing that ring had haunted him for months until he finally decided that maybe it was a sign to move on. As such, he hadn't replaced it.

But Alice Ann was still wearing hers...what was that a sign of?

"Are you sure you want me here?" she asked.

Oh, yes, he wanted her here. He shouldn't, maybe, but he did. Had she changed at all in their time apart? Was there any possibility for him to win her over? Or after they cured her, would she simply walk away again? His family seemed to think so.

Cade wanted the woman who had once smiled with such joy at their daughter's birth. The woman he knew she had the ability to be, if she but wanted it too.

His head dipped forward. Her shoulders pressed into his palms as she rose an inch to match his height.

Then, like a hammer banging on his skull, someone knocked on the door.

"Alice Ann!" Coraline called. "Alice Ann Lark, you answer the door this minute!"

"Thank the Lord," Alice gasped as she ran to answer it.

Funny, for how often he thanked the Lord, this time he was just annoyed. *Lord, your timing is the worst.* As he dropped himself onto the sofa, he thought he could actually hear God laughing.

7

Even with her sister's unfocused vision, Alice Ann still thought Coraline as beautiful as ever. Yes, her features were a little older, her dress more worn, but everything else was exactly as she remembered. Alice Ann threw herself into her sister's arms as tears welled within her. She wouldn't let them fall though. No, no. Let Coraline cry all she wanted—and she was crying indeed—but Alice Ann wasn't going to fall to pieces, especially not after the scene she had made back in the Ghost Forest. Losing control and running away only to faint into her husband's arms? Humiliating. Then almost kissing him just now, which complicated matters all the more.

What had she been thinking?

She'd been thinking that it felt good to be wrapped in his embrace. Four years of life lost between them, yet there was no less love in his eyes than there had been then. Evident distrust, yes, but not lack of love. And such desire, too; it made her shiver. Her current appearance held no amount of appeal, and yet he still wanted her. Either his marital commitments defied all logic of the flesh or he was simply as much of a pleasure-driven man as the rest of his fellows. Never had he seemed as such, so it must be something he saw in her alone.

A part of her—most of her—wanted him, too, try as she might to deny it.

Then Coraline had appeared with a knock from heaven, stopping Alice Ann from another mistake. How could she kiss Cade when she couldn't promise to stay here forever? She would go on their adventure, find the source, get her cure, but then...? Impossible to say.

She squeezed her sister tighter. "Oh, Cora, it is so good to see you!"

"How I wish I could say the same." Coraline laughed, but it wasn't bitter as it had so often been before Alice Ann's departure. Perhaps her sister truly was coming to terms with her condition.

Coraline eased back, holding Alice Ann's hands instead. "Tell me what you look like. Have you changed much?"

"Not at all," Cade offered from the sofa where he now sat. "Her hair's still about to burn down the town. Smile just as bright. Lovely as a painting." Alice Ann shot him a bewildered look, and he shrugged.

Unable to see her sister's soiled appearance, Coraline smiled at his words. "I am pleased to hear it. As soon as Jamison told me you had returned, I rushed right over. I don't even care what brought you back. The point is you've come and I'm never letting you get away again." She gripped her sister's hands as though to prove her point.

"You always did try to mother me."

"And I failed at it, time and again. So, this time, I'm going to convince Jamison to lock you in our cabin. Don't worry, we'll bring you food and you can read James and me books for entertainment."

"Who's James?"

Coraline's smile faltered. "Oh, that's right. You wouldn't know. James is our son. He's just turned three."

My nephew, Alice Ann thought. An entire person had been grown and taught to walk and talk, and she had missed it. She wondered if little James shared her sister's freckles or if he favored Jamison's dark hair. Perhaps both. Or neither.

She felt Cade watching her and forced a smile. Although her sister couldn't see, she could still hear it. "I do miss books. I didn't have those while I was gone."

"And that," Coraline said, "is the worst tragedy I can imagine. In that alone, you should regret ever leaving."

I wish I'd never gone, she wanted to say but restrained herself. Now that she remembered every detail of every conversation, how could she promise something only to recall her sister's distress when she shattered that promise later? It was better never to promise anything at all.

Her eyes slid closed, and she squeezed them tight. How could she continue living this way? Remembering every glance, every smile, every word, every...touch? How Cade had gazed on her moments ago, the way his lips had invited her in, how he had caressed her arms, his breath warm against her face. *Are you sure you want me here?* she had asked. The sound of those words would echo in her mind forever. Her brain hurt; blood pounded against her temples. Another memory moment jostled for an opening. She couldn't faint again, not in front of her sister, who couldn't see to help her.

Distraction, she must find distraction.

Her eyes popped open. "'As for me,'" she quoted, "'I am tormented with an everlasting itch for things remote. I love to sail forbidden seas and land on barbarous coasts.' Name the novel that's from."

"Oh, we haven't played this game in ages!" Coraline giggled. "No one here will play it with me."

"That's nonsense. Doesn't your husband read?"

"Nothing entertaining unless I suggest a title. Otherwise, it's all early Church Fathers. I'm afraid I don't recall the book you quoted, however. Is it Robinson Crusoe?"

"No. Here's another clue. 'There is, one knows not what sweet mystery about this sea, whose gently awful stirrings seem to speak of some hidden soul beneath.'"

Coraline grinned. "Ah, Moby Dick. It's been a while since I read that one."

"It is rather tedious, even with the sea faring. Now you ask me one." She heard Cade's soft steps move across the room followed by a chair drawn out at the table, the thin whir of playing cards being shuffled, and then laid out one by one, most likely for a game of Solitare.

Coraline had already begun her quote. "Happy, happy Christmas, that can win us back to the delusions of our childish days; that can recall to the old man the pleasures of his youth; that can transport the sailor and the traveler, thousands of miles away, back to his own fireside and his quiet home!'"

Childish days, pleasurable youth, sailors transported home. If only it was so easy to regain those things with but a bit of holiday merriment. If so, she would find a way to sail to Southeast Asia and live on Christmas Island forever.

"Dickens, of course," she told Cora. "*The Pickwick Papers.*"

"Correct." Of course it was. With Alice Ann's memory, she not only recalled conversations, but every word she had ever read. It really was exhausting sometimes, so much information in her head. But Coraline didn't know any of that yet. Only the Lark brothers knew about her Gift.

She playfully pinched her sister's elbow. "Are you even trying to trip me up? Think of a really difficult one."

"Hmmm...oh, I know! 'I am one who loved not wisely but too well.'"

Cade shifted in his chair, its uneven wooden leg tapping the floor as it had since being built. He flipped a card, its sound like an accusation, loud as a hammer against stone.

Alice Ann knew she had not loved wisely or well. Cade on the other hand had not been wise, but certainly loved her well. Was Cora purposely throwing stones with these quotes?

"It's from *Othello*." She grabbed Coraline's hand. "I think I've had enough of this game. Wouldn't it be nice to walk to the shore?" Eyes averted from her husband, she looped arms with her sister before calling back to Cade. "Don't wait up!" Then she pushed Coraline out the door and closed it behind them.

As they walked, Alice Ann avoided the spots others tended to congregate, especially the Lark brothers' homes and the Chinooks' central fire. She didn't want to see or speak with anyone else tonight. There would be enough time tomorrow and in the days and weeks to come, especially if they couldn't manage to decipher the compass. If they couldn't, much greater decisions would need to be made. For now, she needed her sister's arm, her ear, and her advice.

Stepping onto the evergreen-needle laden trail toward the shore, Coraline's fingers trailed the weathered rope strung from post to post along the path. Jamison had constructed it as a way for her to visit the ocean when she had no one to guide her or simply wished for time alone. The darkness of the forest enclosed them, long evergreen branches draping down from every direction. For the first time since Cade had approached her meager residence did Alice Ann feel hidden and almost safe. She could breathe a momentary sigh of relief and not worry about what to do next or if she would live long enough to see it accomplished.

"Have you heard from Mama or Papa recently?" she asked.

"A few letters since you've been gone. Mama's fingers aren't what they used to be, so Mercy's had to take on more of the laundry jobs along with the housework and the letter writing. Papa's doing as well as can be, but I suspect his age and disability are wearing more than our sister lets on. She said Southern unrest has also increased and eventual war is almost a certainty. I've had Jamison send them another letter asking them to come live with us, but I doubt they'll accept."

"Not so long as Papa's alive."

"No. It would be too risky for him to travel the westward trail. Remember how treacherous it was for us?"

"I remember." Coraline's first husband, Oliver, had been one of many who had died along the trail.

The forest opened atop the ridge, a slope of grass, rock, and driftwood leading down to the shore. Navy waves smoothed the sand's surface, the last rays of sunlight rippling in streaks of maroon and gold. About a half-mile down, Cade's schooner sat offshore, silhouetted against the vibrant sky. *Gratia*, he had called her. A beautiful name for a beautiful ship. The type of ship she had always longed to own for herself.

Her husband was a different man than she remembered. A wonderful man. Exactly the kind she had always wanted him to be. When she had backed down, he had stepped up and become the father Julep needed. Despite his inherent fear and fumbling, he had claimed her fishing business—*her* dreams—and made them his own, then succeeded where she had failed. He had built a lovely life in a place she had thought could only bring tepid pleasures. He was far more than her in every way.

Even if this adventure together went as planned, and they found the source, how could she stay? How could she find the daily strength to face him, while recalling every insult toward him in excruciating detail?

The day flashed in her mind when she had settled Julep in Coraline's arms and walked away. Even within her sister's empty eyes, Alice Ann had recognized her sister's devastation. She had watched tears roll down Cora's cheeks and saw her hold Julep tighter, the toddler asleep and snuggled in her lap. "This is the least selfish thing I've ever done," Alice Ann had told her, and at the time, she had truly believed it. Removing herself was supposed to be better for everyone. Now, she understood that, while everyone had survived without her, no one had thought it better.

If she had any desire to remain here, this time she must find a way to live with herself and her memories. But how? Tobias had lost his Gift by being shot, which was not an option she was willing to attempt. Otherwise, his brothers' Gifts had only grown stronger over time. If her memories continued to strengthen, based on Jamison's concerns, her head might literally explode.

What a mess that would cause.

Her husband's face filled her vision, the longing in his gaze when he had begged her to come away from the Ghost Forest, to be with him and Julep. "I forgive you," he had said, but would he if he truly knew all that she had done? She wanted to return his love wholeheartedly, without remembering why she shouldn't.

Tears dribbled down her cheeks, and she didn't wipe them away. Coraline couldn't see them anyhow. If she said nothing, her sister would never know—

"Are you crying?"

Alice wiped the back of her hand across each cheek in disgust. "How could you tell?"

"You're my sister. Some things don't need eyes to see."

"It's only that..." Quickly, she recanted the full story from Cade arriving at her shack to the details of her Gift to her fainting spell.

"What if we never find the source?" she finally finished. "Or what if we do, but it doesn't work? No one wants me here. We're supposed to meet for breakfast tomorrow and I know they'll tell me to leave. How can I ever begin to start over knowing I have no future?"

"Oh, Alice...I am sorry." Coraline squeezed her arm and for a minute, the sound of the ocean waves and the night forest surrounded them. It was soothing to hear that they were the same as she remembered from when she had lived here before.

If only Alice had been satisfied with settling like her sister had. Coraline had a happy marriage and satisfaction in the things she did despite her inability to see them. She had overcome the initial depression of losing her eyesight and become much stronger than Alice Ann had with two healthy eyes. Why couldn't Alice have been like that? If only she had stayed.

What then? Her Gift would have still developed and would still possibly be killing her. At least this way, if she died, no one would miss her much. They had already been living for years without her.

"It doesn't matter, Cora. This topic is for nothing. We should head back."

She turned from her sister, leading her elbow, trying to direct her steps, but Coraline stood rooted to the spot. Alice stared at her. She didn't want to ask. Thankfully, she didn't have to.

"What if..." Coraline murmured. She tapped a finger to her lips then gasped around it, her lips in a tiny 'o'. "What if there was another way to help your Gift without finding the source?"

"I'd love to hear it."

"Do you remember Gabriella Reed?"

"The woman missing on the trail? Clinton's wife? I thought she died."

"We all did, but she's alive, and she's here."

"*She is*? Where did you find her?"

"She was held hostage by a terrible man, Ashley Sterling, who owned a circus in San Francisco."

"The one who tried to kill Cade and kidnapped Julep?"

"Yes. One and the same. Sterling had a concoction he used to drug those he abducted. It made them docile, and it also made them forget. Clinton used it on Gabriella before handing her off to Sterling's men. Then Sterling used it on Martha once as well. It didn't affect either of them long-term, but perhaps..." She shook her head. "No, I could never suggest it."

"I suggest you do so anyway."

"Perhaps if the same concoction was administered to someone whose Gift is memory, it might remove those memories and therefore, remove the Gift."

"You want to erase my memory?" Alice Ann's voice rose. "I won't remember who I am."

"We don't know that. It might not remove all your memories, only some of them. Gabriella was under its influence for months and she could recall everything before that time." Coraline squeezed her sister's arm. "She knows how to make it. You could wipe away the past. Start over. Have a new life."

Like turning back time before she had made all her mistakes, before she'd almost made choices she could never reverse, choices she'd run away from rather than admit to.

She had hurt so many people, most especially her husband. Cade had said he wanted to win her back, but he wouldn't want her as she was. He didn't know the half of her story and she didn't want him to. If he did, he would hate her. She would expect him to because she hated herself. It was why she had left rather than face him for another day.

What if erasing her memory solved both her problems—curing these horrible memory moments and also granting her a second chance with her family? She remembered the minutes right after birthing Julep, when the three of them had snuggled close, such love in their eyes. For those brief minutes, she had believed...but then everything had changed so quickly, and afterward, whatever she'd once believed, she'd known could never be.

But what if it could?

She didn't deserve it. Not Cade, nor Julep, nor the love of her sister in this very moment.

"Cora," she said softly, "I've spent most of my life resenting you for always having our parents' attention, for bringing me out here, and stealing my dreams. But I..." She took a strong inhale. "I see now that I was wrong and I...I'm sorry."

Her sister smiled. "I forgave you a long time ago."

"I probably won't remember that tomorrow."

That forgiving smile faltered. "I know."

"And you still think I should try it?"

"I do."

With a sob, Alice Ann threw herself into her sister's arms. For a moment, they clung to one another, holding tightly to the sisterly affection so rare for their relationship. At least Cora would always have this memory, even if Alice Ann didn't. At least her sister would always know that, for one glimmer of time, their hearts had been on the same page.

Finally, with an unspoken agreement, they both let go.

Alice Ann swiped away her tears. "All right, Cora. Let's erase my memory."

8

Flashes of memory assailed Alice Ann's mind, breaking like waves against a ship, threatening to take her under. One after the other, first there then gone. She ran to keep up, to try to grasp them and hold on, but it was impossible.

Then one swept by and, finally, she gripped it tightly in hand. A day so dark and dismal as to be night, a squall along the coast of Larksong that had nearly claimed her life.

She ran out of the cabin she shared with Coraline and Martha, both women calling her name. It was dangerous to be out in the storm. Of course, she knew this but didn't care. Anger flared within her at the irritation of her family.

Ha, some family. The Lark brothers had just insulted her abilities and her fishing business. They'd told her it wasn't worth maintaining. That she was foolish to go out in such weather—to risk her life—just to collect a few oysters that wouldn't bring her much more than pennies.

Didn't they understand that she had Cade? He knew the weather better than anyone. He could come with her, show her what to do, bring her back when it became impossible to manage. That was his Gift!

Cade should have supported her. When she'd asked, he should have agreed. He claimed to love her. Why would he take his brothers' side?

"It's not a business, Alice Ann," he had said, then he'd tried to save face with that abysmal clarification: "My brothers think it's not a business."

Hmmph, what did he know? He was worthless at fishing and difficult to teach. Why had her parents sent her here? Now she was stuck here forever because she was carrying Cade's baby! Maybe he could be persuaded to leave once the baby arrived. She could show him that the wilderness was no place for an infant.

Slim chance of that. Plenty of women bore babies in the wilderness.

Well, she would figure something out.

"Alice! Alice Ann, wait!"

She half-turned, the wind slapping her wet hair across her cheek, raindrops slashing into her skin like pinpricks from her wretched sewing needles. Cade raced after her, devoid of jacket or hat, completely soaked from head to toe, his own hair plastered flat against his forehead.

He stretched out his hand to her. "Come back to the cabin."

"You know the weather. You can keep me safe."

"I do know the weather, and it isn't safe. Please," he begged. "Come back to the cabin."

"No. I have a business to run. If we don't have anything to sell, we lose out."

"I don't want to lose *you*."

"Then you should have taken my side."

She tore off along the ridge, away from the shore and through the trees. Conifer branches scratched her skin, spruce and cedar limbs waving low to the ground with the wind. Her bare feet slipped on the slick needles and she tripped, her hands barely breaking her fall. In her falter, Cade caught up. He grabbed her arm, only for her to shove him away. He landed in the mud, allowing her to create distance between them. She sprinted up the hill, her muscles ill-prepared and burning from the ascent.

She didn't care where she ended up, she simply wanted to escape from him and this town and all its rules. If Cade loved her, he would support her. He was just like Cora and their parents and everyone else—killing her dreams, ripping them right out from under her. She would show them all what Alice Ann Owens could do.

"Alice! Stop!" Glancing back, she saw Cade struggle up the hillside, breathing heavily as the wind threatened to push them both off balance. Below, the sea churned in thick midnight grey mountains. They must be nearing the top of the cliffs.

She had run herself right into a corner. Nowhere to go except back down the hill or leap from the cliff and pray she didn't hit the rocks. Neither seemed an ideal choice.

But her indecision had provided Cade the advantage. He grabbed her forearms and tried to drag her back the way they had come. As she struggled against him, she screamed words she knew would resonate, "I hate you, Cade Lark!"

His eyes bulged and as expected, his movements stilled. "You don't mean that."

"I do mean it. I've never meant anything more. I'm sorry I ever laid eyes on you."

She shoved him again, only this time, she needn't have bothered using force. At the same time she pushed, he released her and she stumbled backward. The pebbles beneath her shifted, causing her bare feet to slip on their wet surface. Immediately realizing the danger, Cade lunged for her, but she was already falling headlong. With a shout, she toppled over the cliffside.

"Alice!" Cade's screams were scooped up in the wind as she plummeted into the water. The impact tossed her over, and the current tore her like a ragdoll churned about on the angry waves. Thrashing, her fingers grappled for anything to hold. Her leg slammed into something and she screamed, but only bubbles expelled while water entered.

I told Cade I hated him, she thought. *Now, I'm going to drown and kill our baby, too.*

Another body broke through the sea, long legs and arms and hair flying all around her. She reached for her savior, but another riptide pulled her toward the rocks. As her skull slammed against the cliff face, her last thought was, *How terrible for Cade to watch me die.*

9

AUGUST 27, 1859
LARKSONG, WASHINGTON TERRITORY

Alice Ann bolted upright in bed, the sheet and quilt tangled around her, her heart racing. She remembered falling, hitting her head, arms scooping her up, then nothing. She had assumed the arms were Cade's, but perhaps not. Strangely, her head didn't hurt nor her leg, yet she had been certain she must have broken one or the other. Upon inspection, she couldn't find a single bruise. Not a bump or a scar.

Without a doubt, last night, she had fallen off a cliff. How she had come through the ordeal unscathed, she couldn't fathom. Perhaps Jamison's medicinal Gift was responsible and she would have one more thing to thank him for. And apologize for. So many apologies she would have to give.

First to her sister and Martha. They shared this cabin with her and must have helped her into bed afterward. Glancing around, however, she didn't recognize the room at all. Its walls were log-hewn like their cabin's but with crossbeams much higher above. A strung curtain separated a double bed and chest of drawers from the rest of the house. A worn pair of men's boots rested against the wall, a basket of handkerchiefs on the dresser. On the bedside table to her right sat a half-empty glass of water, a brown empty vial, and a Bible, well-read with many folded corners and moisture-wrinkled edges.

This couldn't be her cabin with Coraline and Martha, not if some

Bible-reading man lived here. Could it be Cade? Last she remembered, he shared space with Jamison in a cabin identical to hers. Maybe he had taken her to a stranger's home, except she couldn't recall any other settlers living nearby.

Still clothed in her nightgown, she slid from bed and searched the chest of drawers for something suitable to wear. When she opened the bottom drawer, she gasped. These skirts and blouses and undergarments were...hers. She did live here. With Cade? Or someone else? Why couldn't she remember?

Dressing quickly, she peeked around the curtain to find a large living space with a cold fire pit in the center and a hole in the ceiling above it. One side of the room held a square table and three chairs; the other side, a makeshift wooden sofa with thinly stuffed cushions, a rocking chair, and a chest. Beside that sat a wooden crate filled with what appeared to be children's toys: blocks, a miniature wagon, and stick-and-twine dolls with moss hair and Howqua shell eyes. In another corner crowded her familiar fishing tackle: three poles, a pile of netting, and a box of hooks, twine, and wooden bobbers. All to confirm that this must be *her* home, but what of the child to whom the toys belonged?

Alice Ann's hands splayed across her middle as she remembered. *She* was with child, only a few months along. Cade had been both overjoyed and nauseated. He had grinned, kissed her, and then thrown up on her boots. "What will my brothers think?" he had asked. "Mama didn't raise us to put the cart before the horse."

Disgusted, Alice Ann had wiped her vomit-covered boots onto the nearest bush. She'd folded her arms across her bosom, already tender and swollen with the first signs of motherhood. "Well, your mama isn't here, now is she? Neither is mine. We make our own decisions." But how were they to share such news with their Christian-to-the-core siblings? She could already imagine her sister's disappointment.

Well, what did Coraline know? She and Oliver had a Josephite marriage anyhow, vowing to never consummate and live merely as companions. What could she understand of true love or desire?

Cade's brother, Jamison, would be a similar matter. He had wanted to be a priest. He would lecture them up and down the

Washington coast until they both went old and grey.

However, as she now scanned the foreign room and caught sight of Cade curled asleep upon the too-short sofa, she concluded that this must be their home together. Surely, their families wouldn't approve of them living in sin, even if they were expecting. Did that mean they had married?

A golden band on her left hand sent a hiss through her teeth. Married indeed! But how? Had they eloped? Were they even still in Larksong? How hard had she hit her head that she didn't remember the wedding? Her stomach wasn't even showing her pregnancy, so it couldn't be too long after her accident. How long would Cade have needed to craft the toys in that crate? A few weeks perhaps? It was actually very sweet, him thinking of their child before he or she was even born. Although, she reasoned, also overly sentimental.

Rushing to the sofa, she jerked her husband's arm. "Cade!"

His eyes popped open like a frazzled jack-in-the-box, dark hair askew as the box's terrifying devil. He clasped her wrist. "Alice? What is it? What's the matter?"

Hearing his concern had her remembering every excruciating detail of their last conversation—or at least the last one she could recall. Rain pouring across her shoulders, his hair plastered to his ears, eyes wide and tortured as she screamed at him. She had said she hated him, that she wished she'd never laid eyes on him. Recalling it now, guilt flooded through her. And yet, despite her insult, he had still married her, was still here with her, crafting toys for their future child.

Then why weren't they sharing a bed? What else had she forgotten?

On impulse, she lay beside him, wrapping her arms around his waist, and kissing his neck. Startled, he jolted upright, but she wrapped herself tighter around him, resting her forehead on his solid chest. His muscles felt stronger than before, as though he had been hauling hay bales for months. But that task wasn't assigned to him. Had they indeed moved away from Larksong when they eloped? Maybe they had their own farm now. Without his brothers, hauling hay bales could be one of his regular chores.

Her nose crinkled. Had they given up their fishing business for the tedium of farm life?

That wasn't important right now. She could set him straight after she apologized.

"Cade, I'm so sorry. I wish we hadn't fought. I'm not sure of everything I said, but I didn't mean it. I'm sure I didn't. And I want to thank you for marrying me. You didn't have to just because we're having a baby, but you did, and you made our child toys. We're going to be good parents."

His hands clutched her arms. "What do you mean we're *going* to be?"

"When our child arrives. We'll figure it out together. Just please know that I don't hate you."

His demeanor quieted. The longest pause followed before he choked out, "Are you having another baby?"

Lifting her head, she stared at him, more frightened than before. What did he mean, *another* baby? Did they already have children? What more had she forgotten?

It was then that she noticed his appearance. His charcoal brunette curls were longer, nearly to his chin. His beard was fuller, long and wiry, and was it the poor morning light or were there wrinkles in his brow? Cade should be only twenty-one years old, yet his face had aged half a decade right before her eyes. Incredibly weathered for a man so young.

His tender eyes expressed uncertainty. "Are you with child?" he repeated. Every breath sounded of a dead man struggling to escape a tomb. He glanced away toward the box of toys. "I know we were apart for a long time. I shouldn't have expected you to remain faithful. Garrett told me to annul the marriage and be done with it, but I just couldn't, you see."

She sputtered. It was more words than she'd ever heard him chain together without stumbling, bumbling, or mumbling. With such confidence in what he spoke, despite his ragged delivery, and she should have been delighted at the change. But all she could think about were the words he'd said. They'd been apart? He wanted to annul the marriage? When had he talked to Garrett? His brother was in San Francisco. Wasn't he?

Pushing herself up, she rolled off the sofa, stood, and backed away. She clasped her hands to keep them from shaking. "I was never unfaithful to you. This baby is ours."

"That's impossible."

"I promise, you're the only man I've ever been with."

His eyes narrowed. "But you're telling me you're with child right now?"

"Yes, unless..." One hand cupped her lips. Her empty stomach curdled. "There are some things I don't remember. Did we...lose...the baby?"

"No. Julep's fine—what do you mean there are things you don't remember?"

Julep, she thought with a start. That was the name of their daughter? They had a daughter and Alice Ann didn't remember birthing her.

"How old is Julep?"

"Are you ill?" Cade tossed the blanket away and swung his feet around to rest on the floor—stockinged toes beneath a worn trouser hem. She glanced down at her own bare toes as she listened to his inexplicable answer. "Our daughter will be six in January."

Six? She had lost six years? "No. Tell the truth."

"I am."

"Stop it, Cade. I don't know what happened to you with the longer hair and the beard and the horrible jests, but it isn't funny. This isn't you, none of it."

"This is me, and I'm not joking. Are you?"

"No! But you must be, to seek revenge for all the terrible things I said to you. I apologized and you decide to make it a joke? You *are* a horrible person, and I can't be here another minute."

She stalked to the bedroom, ripping the curtain back only to pause with his soft reply. "I knew you would leave again."

Leave? She rubbed her forehead. That's right; earlier, he had mentioned they'd been apart for some time. How long? All six years of Julep's life?

His voice drifted from the sofa. "Why did you give us that whole song and dance about your Gift, if you planned on leaving the next day?"

"My Gift?" She turned and the curtain came with her, wrapping itself around her waist while still tethered to the ceiling. Its force grounded her enough to think straight. "Now you're speaking just plain foolish. You know I'm not Gifted."

"You said you were. You said it might be killing you. Now you're denying it?"

"I'm dying?"

"I hope not. I told you that yesterday."

"Yesterday, I fell off a cliff. There was a squall, and you and I fought, because I wanted to go fishing and you and your brothers said it was too dangerous. I fell off a cliff, and the last thing I remember is you diving into the ocean to save me. I hit my head and woke up here, and now you claim it's six years later. If this isn't a trick, then please, *please*, tell me what's happened to me."

As she spoke, Cade's face blanched paler and paler. He leaned into the sofa, hands to his knees, and stared at her like she might evaporate from sight. Maybe this was a horrid, horrid dream.

"You really don't remember?" he asked.

"No."

For a solid minute, he sat with eyes closed and face tilted to the ceiling. His breaths came so quickly, she almost ran for Jamison. Assuming Jamison was even nearby. She had no idea where he was. After six years, he could be anywhere.

She unwrapped herself from the curtain and let it fall. "Cade?"

When he finally opened his eyes, his words were somehow steady, although his expression was not. He didn't invite her to him or reach for her, and somehow, that was both better and worse. "You left me, Alice. Almost four years ago. You never said goodbye. You wrote me a letter and left it with Coraline."

"My sister's here?"

"Your sister who is blind. You handed her Julep and told her to stay on the shore until one of us happened to find them. Thankfully, we did before anything happened to either of them. But you were already far gone. No one saw you again until yesterday, when I asked

Garrett to locate you, so you could return our compass. It was an heirloom from my mother and was supposed to be the key to our Gifts. Unfortunately, so far, it's been another dead end."

He removed a tarnished compass from his pocket and held it out to her. Stepping forward, she let him place it in her hand. It was rather unassuming other than the design on its bottom side.

"Alice, you told us you'd failed at sailing. No captain would take you so you lived in the Ghost Forest in a shack rather than return home or ask forgiveness. You said you'd developed a Gift right after falling from that cliff, and from then on, you remembered every detail of every day in perfect clarity."

That meant she had her Gift now. She should be remembering everything, but instead she had forgotten everything. How could she have perfect memory one minute and within hours, lose it all? She had left her husband for years. She had abandoned her baby. Her sister had gone blind and she didn't know when. Worst, she had done all that and then failed at fulfilling her dreams, too. No wonder she had hidden away.

She slid to the floor as the world crashed down around her. Her life was gone, erased into smoke, into an existence she didn't recognize and didn't understand. The compass tumbled from her hand into her lap. Its arrow pointed north, always north, but she didn't know what that meant anymore. Her internal compass was spinning, the sails of her ship torn with the wind, and the helm ripped from her hands as the waves washed her overboard.

"I need Jamison," she murmured. "He can fix this."

"I'll get him." Without another word, Cade tugged on his boots and left her alone. Whether minutes or hours passed until he returned, she wasn't sure. She sat and stared at the compass, trying to remember, failing at that.

When the door burst open and Cade and Jamison entered, Coraline was with them. Like Cade, both Jamison and Cora appeared older. Unlike Cade, whose hair had lengthened, Jamison's usually shoulder-length hair now sat close to his ears. Coraline stared into nothingness, her eyes completely blank. Blind, exactly as Cade said. Alice Ann had known the day would come, but knowing hadn't prepared her for the grim reality.

That was when she noticed the wedding bands, one on her sister's fourth finger and one on Jamison's. "Are the two of you—" she sputtered. "Are you married?"

"We are." Jamison guided Coraline to sit at her sister's side. Alice Ann wrapped her arms around her and gripped her tight, refusing to meet her empty gaze. Its milky depths startled her to her soul.

There were so many things she couldn't recall about her own life; where had they all gone?

"Oh, Alice, my darling, I'm so dreadfully sorry." Cora held her close, smoothing her hair with gentle strokes. "You must be so frightened."

"Cade told you I lost my memory?"

"Yes, and..." She hesitated until Jamison cleared his throat, his expression livid. "You should read this. You told me to give it to you." Coraline placed a sealed envelope into Alice Ann's hands. Breaking the seal, Alice stared at the words, unable to believe they described her, although the handwriting was quite clearly her own.

Alice Ann,

Last night, you removed your own memory. Coraline helped you find the recipe and steal the ingredients from Jamison's stores. Don't be angry with her. She's more loyal than you deserve.

You're probably confused right now. I am, too. But this is the only way you're ever going to find happiness.

Trust me,
Alice Ann

Trust me? Alice Ann seethed at this other idiotic version of herself. Had she lost her mind? How was removing years of her life going to bring her happiness?

"Why would I do this?" she screeched. "No, I don't care why. Jamison, fix me right now."

Her brother-in-law snorted. "Sounds like the old Alice Ann is back.

What a delight. You read what you said. Your other self decided to choose another direction."

She gripped the paper in her fist, fear giving way to anger. "I don't care what this says. Give me my memories back!"

"I don't deserve this. Cade, she's your wife; you tell her. Meet us at Tobias's once she calms down." Then he took Coraline's arm, led her from the house, and slammed the door.

Alice Ann stood, waving the paper like a lunatic and feeling like one. "Unbelievable. Is this because he's afraid he'll remove my Gift like when he saved Tobias? He can go ahead. That's an acceptable loss." She didn't need to remember every detail. She could already remember everything from her conversation with Cade this morning and was exhausted from it. "Cade, go tell your brother to help me."

"No."

"Why not?"

His glare drove into her. He had left this room a worried man and somehow returned a hostile one. The vitriol in his tone was enough to step her backward. "Because," he spit. "I am the head of our family. You can't just demand things like you used to. And because there is literally nothing Jamison can do. He told me so."

"Can't?" she griped. "Or won't?"

"Can't. You made this choice, Alice Ann, and you're going to have to live with it." He looked away. "And it appears, so am I." He strode to the door and raised the latch before pausing, striding back, and retrieving the compass from the floor. "Meet me at Tobias's when you feel able."

"I don't know where it is."

"I guess you'll just have to figure it out, won't you?"

Then, for the first time she could remember, *he* walked out on *her*.

10

Tension permeated the walls of Tobias's cabin in waves so thick, Cade would have required a woodcutter's ax to break through it. Only the clatter of Sarah and Martha dishing out breakfast plates broke the uneasy silence between those gathered around the long spruce-hewn dining table: his brothers, their wives, and him.

Cade had breathed a sigh of relief when their friends Marie and Levi offered to keep Julep for the day. "That be a fam'ly affair," Marie had said when she'd learned of Alice Ann's arrival. "If ya need my opinion, well, I ain't never cared for how that girl treated any of ya, so best I stay out of the decidin'." The couple took all the Lark children, along with their own, for breakfast then to the shore for the morning. Only Josephine, the littlest babe, remained in a cradle near her mother's chair, Martha ready to nurse her at a moment's cry. On a day like today, all other chores could wait.

It was for the best. Despite what Cade had told Alice Ann last night, he couldn't justify introducing her to their daughter yet. Not until he figured out how to approach the new element in their already complex situation. How could he explain to Julep that her mother didn't remember her because she'd chosen to forget?

Also missing from their family unit were Josiah and Clary. About a month ago, after one particularly convicting homily by visiting Father Lionett, they, along with a few other circus folk, had decided to join the priest at Stella Maris Mission. They would begin their studies in preparation for the Catholic Sacraments this coming spring. While the Larks were sad to see their family members and friends move away, they also rejoiced in their decision. Not only did this step bring them closer to Christ, but it paved the way for more Native American conversions. If the natives experienced the Gospel from colored folks, rather than hearing it from the white men alone, they might take more interest. Cade deeply wished he could ask Josiah's advice today, but also admired the decision his friend had made.

The final link missing from their unusual family was Melvin, who when he'd been told of Alice Ann said, "I don't even know this woman. What concern is it of mine whatcha do with her?"

Cade jolted as Sarah set a tin plate of stewed spinach, fresh cut apples, and baked ham cutlets in front of him. The aroma set his mouth watering as he realized he hadn't eaten since breakfast the day before. His stomach hadn't the heart for it, and his heart hadn't the mind to inform his stomach that it was wrong.

"Is your wife joining us?" Sarah asked him as she set a second plate before Tobias seated at Cade's right. "Shall I prepare a plate for her?"

Cade glanced at the door again while everyone else stared at him. Where was Alice Ann? Only two chairs remained empty, Martha's and Sarah's. There would be nowhere for Alice to sit when she arrived, and Sarah must know it. Marie and Levi had taken the extra chairs to their house for the children, apparently taking more than they needed. Had it been intentional? Maybe. Maybe not. He shouldn't have assumed there would be a place set for his wife and brought an extra chair of his own. But he had left his conversation with Alice Ann in a huff and hadn't been thinking straight after that. He still felt as though he sat in a fog, clouds swirling through his brain.

He sighed, waving Sarah off. "Come to the table. She can make herself a plate when she arrives." If she arrived, he would give up his chair for her.

Once everyone had been served and seated, Jamison led them all in grace and then the clatter of silverware descended. For a solid fifteen minutes, it was all knives on forks and muted chewing with the occasional glass set back upon the wooden surface. The shuffle of feet beneath the table and readjustment of a napkin. Still, Alice Ann did not appear.

Then, Daniel set his silverware down and wiped his mouth with finality. "You all are going to have to broach the topic at some point as she's clearly not coming. Just have the discussion without her."

Eyes shifted around the table to each other and everywhere in between. Cade chewed the last of his ham which had smelled great initially, but now tasted like an old shoe on his dry tongue. At least, the meal had filled his belly and helped to somewhat revive his mind.

"Well, I have something to say," said Martha. "First thing's first. Coraline, what were you thinking? Erasing her memory? She doesn't even remember Julep. This complicates everything more than it already was."

Coraline's unfocused vision turned in Martha's direction, staring somewhere past her to the wall. "I was thinking that Alice Ann is still my sister. I know you're upset with her and you have every right to be, but for years, I've considered what I would say if I ever saw her again. I finally feel I can forgive her for what she's done. I want her to come home. I'm willing to give her a second chance. So, when she asked for my help—that she wanted those same things—she was so desperate to make amends, how could I refuse her?"

"But she doesn't remember telling you that!" Martha cried. She slapped a palm upon the table, jolting her chair backward with the movement. Its wooden leg nicked the edge of Josephine's cradle, causing the once-sleeping infant to wail in earnest. Martha bent for her, but Garrett placed a hand on his wife's arm.

"I've got her." He swooped Josephine up to his shoulder, rubbing her back as he paced the floor behind their chairs. Her resemblance to Garrett was so peculiar as to be astounding. Her father's dark thick curls sat close to her scalp, while wide charcoal eyes stared out from copper skin nearly identical to her mother's. The best of both of them.

He's a good father, Cade thought. He had considered that fact many times since their return from California, how much his brother had changed from his outrageous ways. But every time he saw Garrett with Josephine, the emotions of his own first days as a father also came flooding back, and he recalled how different his life had been compared to his brother's.

"How did you do it?" Tobias asked Coraline. "How did you erase her memories? That shouldn't be possible unless she took a knock to the skull."

Jamison spoke instead. "It's possible. Cora asked Rella for the tonic Sterling used to keep his circus girls sedated. Then she and Alice Ann stole everything they needed from my stores. For the most part, they're common enough ingredients, minus the ether I'm now out of and will have to special order." He sipped his coffee and stared at them over the mug's rim. "If anyone needs surgery soon, you'd better like it without sedation."

"Why isn't Rella here?" Garrett asked mid-stride. He turned, Josephine still bawling in his arms. "Shouldn't she answer for her part in this?"

Jamison waved him off. "We don't need more people involved. Besides, she isn't culpable."

"How could she not be? She gave them the recipe."

"I told her I wanted it to help me sleep," said Coraline. "When Sterling gave it to Martha, she was only out for the night. A few drops should have been enough to accomplish what I asked. Rella had no idea why I was really asking."

"Then why did Alice forget six years?" Cade asked.

"You know things always work differently for us Gifted folks." Tobias's expression held understanding, rather than the pity or derision Cade sensed from the rest of the room. "Being shot should have killed me, but losing my Gift saved my life. I think this did the same to her. It took her back to the start of her Gift. Maybe this is a new chance for both of you."

If Alice Ann truly asked Coraline to help her make amends, then she had also wanted to try to make their marriage work. Why hadn't she come back to the house and told him? Now, she didn't remember any of that. Whatever maturity Alice Ann might have developed was now buried beneath her forgotten memories. Was he kidding himself that there had ever been a chance?

Cade shook his head. He couldn't get his hopes up only to have them dashed. "She isn't herself. She's someone from years ago. I could have accepted this if she'd lost her memory naturally, but she did this to herself. She chose to erase her memories, and there's no chance to learn from that now."

"Why not?" Tobias asked.

Cade felt his fingers shaking and shoved them under his thighs. He glanced at the door, praying it would open, but it remained as it was. Not showing up to breakfast, choosing her own way rather than that of the family, was entirely indicative of the old Alice Ann.

He didn't want a wife who couldn't remember their wedding, birthing their child, or even that she had a child; who thought she was still pregnant and that Cade hadn't yet proposed. Her last memory was of their cliffside argument and that had been one of their worst. He had sided with his brothers, and she'd run off into a squall and the heart of danger. If Quea'Quim hadn't been there—the one who truly saved her—his wife wouldn't be, either. But their friend was dead now, and Alice didn't remember that he'd ever existed.

From the first day, everyone had told Cade to stay away from her, that she was toying with his emotions and would hurt him someday. They had been right. Even so, holding her in his arms yesterday, he could almost pretend that their marriage stood a chance. Now, any progress they might have made was gone. She couldn't remember any of the pain she had inflicted or any of the remorse it might have caused her to feel. They were both in love with people who no longer existed.

"We need to focus on what's most important," Cade said. "We need to keep searching for the source."

Garrett patted Josephine's bum, her cries dwindling to whimpers. "We'll search for it either way. Alice Ann's medical state isn't the scale by which we measure that decision."

"In a way it is," said Daniel. "Alice Ann's Gift could be killing her. We can't assume she'll be cured with a bout of forgetfulness."

"Precisely." Coraline's hands wrung her napkin upon the tabletop, her absent eyes flicking back and forth, trying to find her bearings. "Whether you like it or not, this was my sister's choice. She told me how she feared she had no future. She didn't want to die without becoming better than she was. Perhaps, my actions were misplaced, but I couldn't do nothing. Right now, my sister wants to be here."

"Right now." Jamison folded his arms and glowered, knowing full well that his wife couldn't see him, and likely why he let it show. "What about later? Cade gave her a choice. Come search for the source and once we find it, she's free to leave. Once she realizes she's cured, she may do exactly that. That girl's going to do what she wants to do. She's always been that way."

"Yes, I know, but—"

Suddenly, Martha released a sob. The sound filled the room and replaced her daughter's tears. She buried her face in her hands, such pain revealed with every upward heave of her shoulders. Sarah scooted her chair over to wrap her arm around her friend's shoulder.

Martha leaned into her. "I can't, I can't," she cried. "It's so hard to be here."

"I know," Sarah soothed. "You've done so much. No one expects more from you."

Garrett returned to the table, Josephine now resting peacefully against his shoulder. He inched down onto the seat and exhaled as the baby remained sleeping. Gently, he gripped Martha's hand. "Easy, darling. All this will work itself for good, you'll see."

"I don't see. Not right now, I can't, Garrett. For years, I've heard Julep talk about her mother, while I've been the one to care for her. Where was Alice Ann when Julep was in Sterling's circus? Where was she when he threatened to cut off her fingers? She didn't teach her to read or do sums. She wasn't there at all. Julep has a dream of someone so wonderful that I'll never understand. But I don't want her to lose it, either. Not even for my own selfish jealousy. But she's going to, Garrett. I love that girl and her momma is gonna break her heart."

Oh, Lord, could I have any more guilt piled on me right now? Cade was like the Roman Titan Atlas carrying the world and being crushed by it. Not only did he constantly question his decisions regarding Julep's welfare, but now he was responsible for the misery he'd heaped upon his sister-in-law. He had been the one to ask Martha if she would care for Julep while he set the fishing lines or tended the fields. She had seemed the most logical choice and he'd trusted her, but he had never considered how it might affect her if Alice Ann ever returned.

Because you never expected her to return, a voice inside him reasoned. No, the ramifications of such a dream were never realized.

Garrett caressed Martha's hand, his words extended to the group, but his eyes on his wife. "Alice Ann can't be trusted. I'm a walking talking example of forgiveness and people changing, but I doubt she will. We need a probationary measure in place—a safeguard—until we know we can trust her."

"And how long would that be, do you think?" Martha asked with a sniff. Her tears had lessened, but not ceased.

"For me, darling, probably never. For everyone else, eh?" he shrugged.

Martha's tear-filled eyes lifted, and the sorrow they held about knocked Cade from the chair. With stark realization, he realized his marriage had never been his and Alice Ann's alone. His entire family had suffered because of the choices they had made.

Pain grew in his sternum until the world he held upon his shoulders rolled down to land square upon his chest. He was pinned to the chair, drawing breaths without air, seeing without vision, hearing without sound.

"I'm sorry. I'm so so sorry. I just—I can't." Gasping for air, he shoved back his chair and fled the cabin.

11

Alice Ann reclined on the stream's grass-and-spruce-needle cushioned bank, her bare feet dipped in up to her ankles, and skirts bunched around her knees. Minnows darted diagonal paths to nibble on her toes, each turn making her smile. The forest breezed around her, conifer cones bouncing in the branches, thin rays of sunlight breaking through at irregular intervals. Completely at peace, unlike everything else right now.

This place reminded her of a spot she and Cade used to meet for secret rendezvous. To talk and kiss and...be...together. The memory of that made her smile, too. Despite him crying the first time they were together—tears of gladness he claimed—he had always been tender with her. She would never admit it aloud, but he had treated her like the most precious possession, as though when he held her there was nothing else he ever wanted to hold again.

Eventually, one of those encounters had led to a child named Julep and a wedding, although she couldn't picture either. Only the recollection of nights their family would have frowned upon, not the ones they would have blessed.

Her fingers walked her stomach as she tried to accept that the womb beneath it held no life. When she woke this morning, she had thought she was bearing a child. Now, that child could walk and talk and call her "Mama." But would she? Or would that child despise her for what she had done? How could she not after years of expressed hostility from her father and her aunts and uncles?

After Cade had told her to meet him at Tobias's, she had remained in the cabin for a while, paralyzed in indecision. Should she do as she had been told?—*No one told Alice Ann what to do!*—Then again, maybe it would be better to face the situation head on, accept their derision, and climb over to the other side of it. She would listen, but only on her terms.

Imagine her surprise when the town she entered wasn't the one she had left. The Larksong she recalled had been failing, but this one seemed vibrant and full of life. It wasn't even in the same location anymore. Long Indian lodges, each similar to Cade's, lined the path from his cabin into the center of town. Native Americans moved freely among them, each casting her a cursory glance before continuing on by. There were many other unfamiliar faces as well— different races and all ages. She wondered where so many had come from. She supposed six years would have provided ample opportunities for growth.

How much she had missed. No, she corrected, how much her other self had taken from her. Was this a new beginning or the beginning of a nightmare?

This is the only way you're ever going to find happiness, the letter had said. *Trust me.*

"I don't trust you, Alice Ann. If you're my older self, this proves humans only grow more daft with age."

With a rustle of branches, Cade crashed through the foliage to the stream, half ragged and heaving. He leaned over, hands on his knees as he drew deep shuddering breaths, and finally collapsed to the ground. He clenched his fingers in his hair and wheezed.

She remained where she was, flicking her toes in the water. "Still having those episodes, I see. What brought it on this time?"

"You," he shot back. "It's always you. Besides, you haven't a leg to stand on or a chair to sit in. I know you have these *episodes*, too."

Her brows climbed her hairline. First, he walked out on their conversation in the cabin and now, he was firing back outright hostility? And what did he mean, she had them, too? "I don't have these."

He looked up at her. "Don't lie."

"I'm not. Why do you think I have them?" For a second, they

stared at each other, then her brain caught up and a real tightness filled her chest. She didn't like it and wished it would go away. "I had one yesterday, didn't I?"

He nodded. "When we found you in the Ghost Forest, you began to panic and ran away from me before passing out in my arms."

"Oh, I see. How embarrassing." What a perfect pair they had become. She was as damaged as he. What trauma had she been through that could create such a reaction?

Cade laid back on the bank, one palm pressed to his chest, the other at rest upon his stomach, and both knees raised. He stared up through the branches as his breathing slowed. Flickers of light and shadow painted across his troubled expression.

"Better?" she asked.

"Not really. Why didn't you come to breakfast?"

"I found Tobias's house, but I heard you all arguing. Who wants to willingly swim into a riptide?"

Cade's brow softened. "They agreed to let you stay. There was some dissension, of course, but they agreed it's worth giving you another chance. When I left, they were talking about taking precautionary measures, whatever that might entail."

"It couldn't have been that simple or you wouldn't have run away as you did."

"No, it wasn't." He sighed and stretched one hand to drift in the water, just covering the tips of his fingers. "This reminds me of our spot back in the original Larksong. Do you remember it?"

She smiled. "Of course I do. That's where you told me you loved me."

"No, I didn't. I said, 'Alice, I...' and that was all I said. I was too afraid to say the rest. Too afraid you wouldn't say it back."

"But I knew what you meant. It was all there. That's why I kissed you."

"We did a little more than that, Alice."

My, had they ever. She'd kissed him, and he'd kissed her, and her skirts were above her hips before she realized that she'd helped to raise them. She still wasn't entirely sure if he'd been the one to push them past the limit or if she had. They'd just arrived.

"Do you regret it?" she asked.

"Me and you?"

"Yes. Don't you ever wish you'd stayed away from me on the trail? Found some normal girl who wouldn't break your heart?"

"No such thing. We all break each other sometimes, whether we mean to or not." He rolled onto his side, one arm folded beneath his head, blinking up at her through ebony lashes. "Some days I consider what life would have been like with someone else, but then I wouldn't have Julep, and I wouldn't have the life I do. Your leaving made me a different man. Not sure I'm all that better, just different. More like the husband you wanted, rather than the one you got."

It had taken her leaving and destroying their marriage for him to finally become the man she'd always wanted him to be? She supposed in that way, it had been good that she'd left. But then why hadn't she wanted to remember it? Why, when she found out, had she chosen to forget?

The minnows nipped her toes, and she wiggled them, scattering the fish into the waters. But they raced right back, undeterred by her actions, ready to accept her again without question.

"Tell me about Julep," she asked. "What does she look like?"

"She's beautiful. She has my dark hair and a few of your sister's freckles. She loves the water, and she loves to fish. She's adventurous, but also spiritual. Having had a chance to raise her...I feel so unworthy that God granted me such responsibility."

"She didn't make anything better? We weren't any happier?" If Alice Ann had left, how could they have been?

"Not particularly. Right when she was born, we had a few minutes together before everyone came in to see her, and I'm pretty sure that was the happiest moment of our lives. But after that, things became...well...they became more complicated between us. We weren't often happy, but if we had both tried, I think we could have been."

Her inner defenses shot up, a harsh rebuttal flying to her lips. How dare he put all the blame on her for not trying! But then she glanced at his expression, the pain behind his eyes as he turned away to stare out over the water, and she reconsidered. Maybe his words meant exactly what he said—if they had *both* tried. He blamed himself as much as he blamed her for their failures.

Scooting closer, she cupped his cheek within her palm, the warmth beneath his beard seeping into the coolness of her skin. He leaned into her touch, turning his head to press a kiss to her wrist. It was nice, being together in their place—or what represented their place now—without the opinions of their meddlesome families.

Then he glanced down at her arm and his eyes widened. He grabbed her wrist and pushed her sleeve up. There, painted onto the inner skin, was the black outline of a bird.

"When did you get that?" he asked, then shook his head. "I'm sorry. You wouldn't know the answer. You didn't have it when you left."

She *wished* she remembered. Usually reserved for unsavory types such as pirates and thieves, or occasionally for merchant or Navy sailors, tattoos weren't common to those in respectable society, and rarely on women. Hers didn't appear to be a criminal brand, nor a military one. Was it possible she could have taken to piracy for a time? The idea both thrilled and terrified her.

"What type of bird is it?" she asked.

"I think it's a lark." He ran his fingers over its curved lines, the creature's wings spread, its beak open in song. His gentle touch sent ripples up her arm. "Larks sing when they fly," he said softly. "Happy to be alive."

"That's what Martha always says."

"You remember?"

She gave a half smile. "She said that long before I lost my memory."

"You always did want to fly away from here."

"Then why a lark? Why didn't I choose some other bird?" If he was really and truly trying to woo her, there could only be one answer, whether he believed it or not.

When his fingers started to pull away, she flipped her wrist and clung to them. "Tell me what you're thinking, Cade. I don't remember. Help me fill in the pieces."

His thumb ran over the lark again, its pad smooth despite the manual labor she knew he daily endured. His eyes raised to hers and she remembered the first time he'd looked at her that way, as though he was afraid to. "Maybe it means that all the while you were flying away, you were also trying to find your way back home."

Without hesitation, she leaned in and brushed her lips to his. She expected him to reciprocate, to draw her up into his arms and devour her in passion like he used to. Like her brain remembered him doing on what, to her, had only been a few nights before.

Instead, he immediately withdrew, rising to his feet before their lips had barely touched. He folded his arms and left her sitting in the dirt, as though to offer her a hand up would be to inflict fire on his fingers. "Alice, please don't make this more difficult than it already is."

"It doesn't have to be."

"It does. It is."

"Why?"

"Because you changed the rules. I never figured you would come back. I didn't plan to look for you until I needed to find the compass. And when I made you that offer—"

"What offer?"

He drew fingers through his long hair, ran a palm over his bearded chin, speaking quickly. "I asked you to adventure with me to find the source of our Gifts. The compass is supposed to be the key to get us there, except we don't know how it works. But when I asked you to go with me, I think I was trapped in the moment. You actually being there, remembering how it was, wanting how it could have been—but that doesn't matter anymore."

"Why not? Don't you love me?"

"Of course. Although, I always doubted if you loved me."

"Come, let me show you." Casting him a saucy smile, she crooked her finger, beckoning him over, but he only backed farther away.

"Alice, we can't do this."

She swung her feet out of the water and pushed up from the hard ground. Slapping needles from her skirt, she stomped over to face him. With his boots and her bare feet, she stood almost half a foot shorter, forcing her to raise her chin to meet his eyes. "I don't understand. We're married, we have a child. I know we had our arguments, but you seem so confident now. You own a ship! Never in my wildest dreams could I have imagined it."

"Exactly, never in your dreams was I the man you pictured. It doesn't matter who I am now, because you aren't the woman you're supposed to be. You took your memory and stole the chance we had to reconcile. I don't know how to be with the Alice of six years ago because I'm not the man of six years ago. I can't pick up where we left off back then."

"What is the alternative? Divorce?"

"No. Catholics don't believe in divorce."

"Well, they sure as a clam curl don't believe in leaving your wife to rot either. So, either agree to be my adventurous husband or get rid of me. I'm certainly not sharing a home with someone who doesn't even want me there. You might as well take me back to the Ghost Forest."

"I would never take you back to that shack."

"Then you'd better dump me in the ocean, because I am not sleeping under the same roof with you." With a gutted screech, she spun on her heel and stomped off through the brush. Fury flashed through her, heating down to her fingers and toes. How dare Cade say he cared and then toss her off like scraps of chum. She would get her few meager possessions and then...what? None of her relatives wanted her, either. Well, Coraline did, but Jamison would hardly allow Alice Ann to stay with them. She'd sleep in the dirt until she could make her way out of here. She'd done it once, she could do it again.

"Alice!" Cade grasped her elbow, but she shoved him off. He tracked alongside her instead. "Please. You can stay in the cabin alone tonight. Julep and I will sleep on the ship."

"The ship?" she snorted. "Won't Julep suspect something's the matter, then?"

"No. We already sleep there on occasion. She loves being on the water. Sometimes, I'm afraid she has too much of your spirit in her."

Alice Ann paused, just long enough to meet his weary gaze. "Better to have too much spirit than to simply be too afraid. Go to your ship, Cade. She loves you as much as you deserve."

The accusation was heartless and untrue, but those were still the words she left him with. He'd walked out on her this morning, and now she would turn back the tables.

12

After hours of fuming, pacing Cade's living room floor, and quietly muttering arguments lest anyone hear from outside, Alice Ann scavenged a meager supper and dropped exhausted into bed. The sun's setting rays sank below the trees, leaving the cabin in long twilight shadows while she absently traced the outline of the lark upon her arm.

Had it hurt when it was painted? Who would have even indulged such a request? Did it mean what Cade said it meant, that some part of her was always trying to return home, even while flying away? But if that were true, if he believed she'd always wanted to come back, then why would he reject her now?

"I don't know how to be with the Alice of six years ago because I'm not the man of six years ago," he had said. *"I can't pick up where we left off back then."*

But that decision had been made by some other Alice Ann, not her. He couldn't blame her for that choice. She couldn't control her other self anymore than she could control the tides.

This decision was supposed to have made her happy, but what happiness was there in it?

Glaring at the lark, she wondered if she had any other tattoos. Quickly, she rolled from bed, unbuttoned her collar, and shimmied from her dress. Her eyes skimmed across her skin, her stomach, legs, and sides. Craning her neck, she tried to see her back, but could only make out the edges.

Nothing.

Relieved, she retrieved her nightgown from the end of the bed, pausing when her wedding ring caught on the fabric. She twisted the ring off to free the fabric and gasped. Another tattoo in the most minuscule lettering sat within the indent on her finger. Only two numbers: "5:5."

Well, what in the world did that mean?

Tattoos were permanent which meant this must have been something she'd never wanted to forget. But it was also something she had wanted to hide from others. What could 5:5 signify? A ratio, but of what? Five parts to five parts or did it mean five to five like 100% of something?

Was it a time with a missing number? 5:50 or 5:15? But why wouldn't she add the extra digit?

Maybe a musical time signature? It sounded odd to her but she was no musician.

Five feet, five inches? Her height? Why would she need to remember that?

What was it? Come now, Alice Ann, think.

Turning her head, she caught sight of Cade's Bible.

That must be it! 5:5 was a scripture verse.

She had tattooed scripture on herself? That seemed more out of character than the lark on her arm or abandoning her dreams to live in a marsh. She believed in God, oh sure, but she didn't think she needed to spend all her time with Him. She and the all-knowing Creator had a companionable relationship. He ordered the universe, and she ordered her own life.

Although, she must not have done such a good job of that lately. If she had, she wouldn't have left her husband and daughter for a life surrounded by dead trees.

Hmmm.

Slipping her ring back on, she snatched up the Bible and paused. Which book out of seventy-three would she have chosen? Quickly flipping through, she eliminated twenty books from Ruth to Jude as all contained fewer than five chapters. Which left fifty-three possibilities.

Ugh.

The Book of Wisdom? She certainly needed that. Flipping to chapter five, verse five, she read, "See how he is accounted among the sons of God; how his lot is with the saints." Hmmm, sainthood didn't seem to describe her.

Perhaps Proverbs or Sirach? "Trust in the Lord with all your heart, on your own intelligence rely not." Or "Of forgiveness be not overconfident, adding sin upon sin." She groaned. Either of those would make sense.

Maybe it was a love verse. She flipped to Song of Solomon and read, "I rose to open to my lover, with my hands dripping myrrh, with my fingers dripping choice myrrh upon the fittings of the lock." Um, no, she felt she could safely rule that option out.

How about Isaiah? He was an observant man. "Now, I will let you know what I mean to do to my vineyard. Take away its hedge, give it to grazing, break through its wall, let it be trampled." Sweet sassafras, she hoped that wasn't it. It sounded rather violent.

Ephesians? It had better not be that verse about wives being subordinate, or she would literally scream and who cared who heard her. Tentatively, she opened to the page and released a breath. "Be sure of this, that no immoral or impure or greedy person, that is, an idolater, has any inheritance in the kingdom of Christ and of God." No subordination there, although it was from the same chapter.

Suddenly, she smacked her palm to her forehead. "The Gospels!" she cried. "Of course!" Hadn't Jamison preached time and again that if you memorized only one piece of scripture it should be the words of Jesus? That narrowed it down to four.

Matthew: "Blessed are the meek, for they shall inherit the earth."

Mark: "Night and day among the tombs and on the hillsides, the demoniac was always crying out and bruising himself with stones."

Luke: "Simon said in reply, 'Master, we have worked hard all night and have caught nothing, but at your command, I will lower the nets.'"

John: "One man was there who had been ill for thirty-eight years."

Only one of those verses came from Jesus' lips: *Blessed are the meek for they shall inherit the earth.* She had never been good at that. Being humble, patient, and quiet? Hardly. She would call Cade those things, and she would also call him lily-livered. Nonetheless, Cade had created a treasured life with their daughter while she had ended up alone and penniless in a shack.

Maybe she needed to take an example from her husband.

It certainly would be nice to inherit the earth.

13

Lord, help me. I am so confused.

From across *Gratia*'s deck, the ship currently at anchor in Larksong Bay, Cade watched his daughter chase her cousin, Philip, in the throes of an imaginary adventure. Both brandishing wooden swords, they charged to the rail, searching the waters for the *Oblique*'s lost treasure. From what they knew of their ancestor's ship, there was no treasure, but Julep had gotten it in her mind that there could be and so, now, there was.

At least, she was enjoying herself as a child should, while Cade sipped his tea and stewed over the direction of his entire life. He leaned against the quarterdeck rail while Tobias and Sarah sat on the double step, both holding their own steaming teacups and the pot resting on a crate lid between them.

Tonight was the quietest *Gratia*'s deck had been since the day Cade had purchased her. In a spur of the moment decision, he had sent the crew into Larksong for the evening with orders to return by midnight. Having explicitly hired them to serve aboard ship, there weren't many opportunities for onshore merriment, and they had leapt at the opportunity. It might not have been the wisest captain's decision he had made, but it made the crew happy and allowed him private conversation with his brother. He trusted Tobias and Sarah's opinions as a married couple and it was those opinions he needed now.

When he had invited them out for after-supper conversation, he'd thought it might help get him the answers he needed. After the Larks' breakfast argument, it felt as though Tobias was the only person willing to support him. Daniel, too, except Cade didn't know his eldest brother well enough to feel he could completely confide in him. Meanwhile, Jamison and Garrett might, like him, not believe in divorce, but they also weren't bestowing a rousing round of applause on his marriage either. Jamison was as holy as they came. If he couldn't find hope for the situation, was there any?

Did Cade want there to be? He had dreamed of Alice Ann returning home and now she had. But she wasn't her. It was like sailing a ship into fog. No matter how many times you did it, you still never quite knew whether to expect smooth sailing or sea sirens. In the case of Alice Ann, it was both.

As I said, Lord, I'm so confused.

"Ahhh, Philip, look out!" Julep cried. She lifted her sword and tried to push her cousin behind her as she pretended to attack a monster as it sprang from the sea. Being the same age, however, Philip wouldn't stand for a girl rescuing *him*.

"I'll stop it!" He leapt forward, slicing through the air in triumph. "Now, let's kill him once and for all!" She ducked, and he swung his sword over her head, then upward in a final blow. They both peered down at the deck, where their invisible foe now lay vanquished. "We did it. We saved the ship."

Julep turned a wide smile on her father, aunt, and uncle. "We did it, Papa! We stopped the monster."

"Well done, my jewel. You're going to need that feisty spirit on our travels."

"I will, Papa. I'll protect you from anything. Uncle Tobias, may Philip have a snack?"

Tobias snickered, the chuckle of a father well-versed in children's fluctuating moods. Ever conscious of the trick Julep tried to play, he said, "If your father agrees, I do, too.

Cade nodded. "Go ahead. It's getting late, anyway. How about you and Philip settle on one of the berths and read until it's time for them to head home? Stay away from the stove; it's still warm."

The girl's eyes lit up, and she ran for the cabin ladder, dragging her cousin along with her. "I've got a really good story for us to read," she said as they descended. "It was one of Mama's."

With a sigh, Cade lowered himself onto the deck, one knee raised and his other boot on the step below. He set down his tea cup and ran both hands through his hair, the curls heavy between his fingers. "How can I explain to her what's happened with Alice?" he asked his brother. "You heard what Martha said. How can I shatter this childhood innocence she still possesses?"

"If being imprisoned in Sterling's circus didn't already do so, why would you expect this to?"

"Sterling was a stranger. This is her mother. It means more."

Tobias and Sarah exchanged a glance, another conversation completed in one look. That look was what marriage should be, knowing one another—trusting one another—well enough that no words were needed. All he and Alice Ann had ever had were words and often spiteful ones at that.

"Let's focus on finding the source," Tobias told him. "Everything else can fall into place around that."

"We don't have any leads, no clues to guide us. Where do we even begin?"

"We pray about it," Tobias and Sarah replied in unison. In that moment, Cade loved his brother and also kind of wanted to punch him.

With a final tug to his curls, he released them. "Is God going to give me a straightforward answer? I know he always answers us, but it usually arrives in an odd, convoluted way. Point in case, I never expected Alice Ann to be part of His plan again, especially not the Alice of six years ago."

"But she is," said Tobias, "and you can't change that, unless you want to send her away. Do you?"

"Everyone else does."

"That isn't what I asked. I asked, do *you*?"

Cade retrieved his tea cup, sipping it simply so he wouldn't have to answer immediately. The tea was cold and bitter, despite the blackberries he had crushed and strained within. A heaping teaspoonful of South Carolina sugar would have tasted great right about then. But what tasted great wasn't always good for him, and he knew it. He couldn't say if the Alice Ann of the Ghost Forest would have been a wise spousal choice, but he knew that the Alice Ann of six years ago wasn't.

"I don't know. I feel like Garrett and I switched places. He's grounded now with Martha and Josephine and taking care of the circus folk. I feel like I'm floating along, wondering if I should give this new past Alice a second chance, or if I should cut my losses and seek an annulment like he suggested once upon a time."

"It's unlikely you would be granted one," Sarah said. "Not anymore. Perhaps when Alice Ann was gone, but she's back now, and in her mind, she never left. As long as she stays, a bishop wouldn't consider your marriage invalid."

Tobias chuckled. "No, you'd be the lout who tried to leave a woman with a broken brain."

"Tactful, my darling." Sarah rolled her eyes and turned back to Cade. "Not to be insensitive, but he's correct. Leaving her now, when she doesn't understand why, would only reflect poorly on you. You need to allow her the chance to grow into the wife you need."

"I was only seeing faint glimpses of growth before she turned back the clock. You're telling me I have to wait another six years?"

"If that's what it takes."

"Ahhh!" he yelled into his teacup, sloshing his reflection in the water. A moment later, Julep's head popped up from the cabin hatch. "Are you all right, Papa?" Her wide eyes blinked slowly with concern. Like her mother's blinking up at him not so many hours ago, asking what the lark on her arm meant.

Maybe it means that all the while you were flying away, you were also trying to find your way back home.

He needed to give her another chance to prove herself. He needed another chance to prove himself as well. And he couldn't leave their daughter out of the reckoning. She was pieces of them both.

He smiled at his daughter. "Yes, Jules, Papa's fine. I was frustrated by something your aunt and uncle said, but it's fine now."

"Oh, good." Running across the deck, she leapt up the quarterdeck steps, tumbled to her knees, and rebounded in amazing fashion. She threw her arms around Cade's neck. "I love you, Papa." Then she was

STARS IN THE STORM

off again, hurrying back down to read with Philip.

Or to eavesdrop on their conversation. Cade would need to deal with that once Tobias's clan left for the night. He closed the cabin hatch and paused for a breath with his hand on the wood.

That little girl was his world, his whole heart.

When Alice Ann had left, he had allowed Julep to fill all the empty places within him. They hadn't fit as securely as before, but they'd helped him to move on with his life. But, in the same way man wasn't meant to be alone, God also hadn't meant to fill that loneliness with children, nor brothers or friends. Only a woman was man's perfect match, designed especially for him. Cade needed to find room again in his heart and his life for the woman the Lord had chosen for him. Their love had never been perfect, and never would be, but perhaps they had been granted a way to try again. If it all turned out the same, then so be it, but it would not be because he chose to slam the door.

Collapsing back on the quarterdeck, he swallowed the last of his tea. The cup clinked against the saucer as he set both on the deck and turned to Tobias. "Ok, brother, you're the master of wooing a woman who wants nothing to do with you. Tell me how you won over Sarah, and I'll do that with Alice Ann."

"Tall order," Tobias laughed. At the same time Sarah tutted, "I didn't not want anything to do with him."

"You did try to drive me away pretty thoroughly, darlin'." Tobias lifted her hand and kissed her knuckles. "But I knew I had you enchanted from the moment we met."

"I was married to Jackson Whitticomb the moment we met."

"That is not a denial."

"It's not an admission."

He grinned. "Call it what you will. You didn't get that baby in there because you found me hideous."

"Baby?" Cade leaned forward. "Are you telling me you're expecting again?"

Tobias started laughing and nodding and Sarah shoved him over. He fell onto his elbow and rolled onto his back on the deck boards, still in stitches. "You oaf," she groaned. "We said we were going to tell everyone together." Her face blushed prettily as her hand came to rest upon her middle. "Arriving in the spring. Philip doesn't even know yet."

Cade reached out to embrace her. "I'm happy for you both. I won't tell a soul." What would *his* wife look like all round in the middle and actually happy about it? Because of their poor decisions, he and Alice had restrained from telling anyone about Julep until she was four months along, and even then, Alice had never enjoyed it. The pains of childbearing had been nothing more than that—pains. In their house, complaints had been served daily with most of them directed at his incompetence.

Julep, on the other hand, loved her cousins. She would love a brother or sister, too. He could imagine her laying her head on her mother's stomach to try to hear the baby and laughing as the little one kicked her square in the face. Or how she would help stitch a baby-sized rag doll similar to the beloved Fee Fee her Aunt Martha had made for her. Perhaps Julep's joy could seep onto her mother.

What if this time it *could* be different?

"Stop smiling like that," Tobias said, jerking Cade back to the present. "Your arm is around my wife and your expression is unsettling."

Quickly, he extracted himself from Sarah and moved away. "Sorry. I was thinking about all those ways you're going to help me woo my wife, so she'll never want to leave."

"And you'll never want to let her."

"Precisely."

His brother's spirited grin bounced back into place. He rubbed his hands together and leaned in. "I know exactly the place to begin."

14

"Gotcha, ya little rascal." Alice Ann pried the wiggling trout off the hook and dropped it into the water bucket at her feet. Two more fish thrashed inside, sending droplets into the air and onto her skirt. At least, she would be able to contribute something to today's meals after yesterday's poor performance.

Tossing the line back into the waves, she peered past it and the other two lines buried in sand and secured between rocks at her feet. *Gratia* sat about a quarter mile offshore, her sails furled and deck quiet in the grey morning light. Somewhere on board, Cade and Julep readied for the day, perhaps him sipping coffee and she finishing the last bites of breakfast.

"She loves being on the water," Cade had said. *"Sometimes, I'm afraid she has too much of your spirit in her."*

"Better to have too much spirit than to simply be too afraid," Alice Ann had returned.

But she was also afraid, more than she cared to admit. Cade claimed her fear led her to experience fits of emotion similar to his, that she had experienced a mere day ago, but couldn't remember. Sometime between her fall from the cliff and her time in the Ghost Forest, they had manifested. What if she never remembered how they began or why?

91

Holding tight to the fishing pole, she let the waves and the wind and the salty sea air wash over her. With each breath, she listed off another event she *could* remember, rather than solely focusing on what she couldn't. By focusing on truths, perhaps it would help decipher the unknown.

"I am Alice Ann Owens"—she couldn't rightly say *Alice Ann Lark* when she didn't remember marrying—"and I love the sea. I long for adventure. I want the opportunity to sail. I used to sail with Papa in Charleston. Charleston is where I'm from. I should have taken over the family business, but Papa sold it to pay the eye doctor. Coraline helped me erase my memory."

No, she scolded. That last one wasn't a memory. She only knew her sister helped her because Coraline told her so. In reality, she and Cora had argued more than anything else. Ever since childhood, the Owens sisters were always at odds. Mercy was the caretaker, Cora the infirm, and Alice Ann's dreams forgotten in the mix.

Along the westward trail, being with Cade had occasionally made her forget all that. He had adored her and lavished her with more attention than she had deserved. Too much. Once they'd reached Washington, it had felt like he was smothering her, holding her in place like an anchor to the sea bed. Now, she longed to know what his hold was to this place, how she could find it for herself. Why he gripped his family so tightly and seemed content to settle when he could do so much more.

If only he would move out of his own way, he could be a sea captain and she his glorious first mate.

But no, she was supposed to be meek—patient, quiet, and humble. The tattoo on her finger said so.

One of her fishing lines pulled low to the water, and she leapt for it, dropping the pole in her hands to tug the opposite from its rocky anchor. Drawing the rope in bit by bit, she fought the fish's determined hold like she wanted to fight this 5:5 instruction from her future. Ugh, why did her other self need to choose *that* verse?

Maybe she had guessed wrong. Maybe it *was* the one about trampling down walls. Those could be the metaphorical walls she needed to break in order to find her dreams.

She released a bitter chuckle and bit down on her lip to maintain focus. She could almost hear Jamison's rebuttal. "Yes, of course, because Jesus's advice was always, 'Follow your dreams,' rather than to follow Him."

Couldn't she have both? Why couldn't her dreams be exactly what God wanted her to do?

Without warning, the fishing line snapped back, up, and out of the water, its now fishless hook flying in her direction. She screeched and spun sideways, but that only sent the hook directly into her raised forearm. It stabbed the flesh in a shock of pain and a trail of blood across her elbow.

"Cripes and a pair of crawdads!" She dropped the fishing pole then screamed some more as the pole's trajectory sank the hook deeper into her arm. "Is that my sign?" she shouted at the sky. "Is that my answer? If I can't be quiet and mousy, I get a hook in me? Blast it all." With a final slew of rather sailor-appropriate language, she dropped to her knees, teeth clenched against the pain.

"Lands, girl, what've you done?" Alice looked up as Martha rushed toward her, skirts held aloft in one hand. Her other tightened against the back of the infant secured to her chest by a swath of material. Brown baby eyes stared out in confusion.

"Whose child is that?" Alice asked.

"Mine, of course. Now, let me see that." Martha reached for her arm, holding it gently as she examined the wound. "Doesn't seem too deep, that's good. I can take out the hook, but Jamison should patch you up. Just hold still."

Alice Ann gripped the woman's wrist. "Wait. You had a baby? With whom?"

Martha's stare grew as wide as the baby's. "Oh. I forgot that you forgot. You wouldn't know. Garrett and I married. This is your niece, Josephine."

"Garrett? You can't be serious. That baby is black."

"And you can't possibly be that foolish." With a swift movement, Martha maneuvered the fish hook free from Alice Ann's arm, causing surprisingly less pain than she had expected.

"Did Jamison teach you that?"

Martha pulled a handkerchief from her sleeve cuff and pressed it to the wound. "No, Cade did. Hold that there. Let's get you to Jamison's."

After securing the hooks to the pole handles and dumping the water from the fish bucket, she hefted them both and headed up shore. Alice Ann hurried after her, the handkerchief pressed tightly against her wound. A faint circle of red already showed through the material.

"Why did you come down here?" she asked Martha as they passed under the threshold to the forest. Even though the day was overcast, the temperature still dropped significantly beneath the conifer canopy. Mud underfoot chilled her bare toes and for a moment, the only sound was the cool wind and the slap of dying fish within the wooden bucket.

"You did wrong when you left him," Martha said finally. "When you left all of us. I can't forget how you gave Coraline your baby and that horrible goodbye note to your husband. Their expressions broke my heart."

"But I don't remember doing that."

"I know, and I've asked myself, should I allow those grievances to fade in your ignorance? You might not remember, but we do, and I know the Lord asks us to forgive, but I have to pray for the courage every minute." Martha paused on the path. The fish had gone silent. "A lot of people in this town are hurting because of you, and we don't want any more false promises. Our lives are trying enough."

"My life hasn't been perfect either."

"I know that's true, but it could have been better, and Cade's could've, too. Even so, he's become a strong man. One of the best. Zealous for the Lord, a courageous father, stands by his brothers through anything. Since you left, he's kept your business afloat, and I helped him raise Julep. You might have had a dream, but when you get married and make a baby, you choose family over any girlish dreams you may have had. They're gone, you hear me? Julep needed a mother, and I gave her that. I won't have you coming in and ruining her life."

The woman's words stopped Alice Ann in her tracks. Martha

continued up the path while Alice Ann gripped the handkerchief tight to her wound. She couldn't remember this other version of herself, but it was the person she was destined to become if she didn't take control right now. Had she truly not considered the welfare of her family at all? What had she written to Cade? Martha said it was horrible. Why would she...how could she...Alice didn't understand anything anymore.

"Martha, I..." But that was as far as she ventured in her words or her thoughts for at that moment, she spied a small figure darting down the path from town, two nearly-black braids swinging and a smile as wide as the sea. Behind her strode Cade, hat brim pulled low upon his brow and expertly avoiding his wife's gaze.

Alice Ann's breath caught. Julep was unbelievably beautiful, exactly as Cade had said. With her dark hair and grey eyes, she looked like his female miniature. Only a few scattered freckles could be attributed to the Owens side, but those were shared with Coraline. Julep was closer in appearance to *Martha* than she was to her own mother.

Instead of introducing them, Cade took the fishing poles and bucket from Martha, allowing her to stoop for a kiss from her niece. When Josephine began to coo, Julep waved a finger at the baby and tickled under her chin. Not being able to suffer the familiar situation of which she had no part, Alice Ann turned to Cade instead. No matter how awkward it might be between them after yesterday, they needed to come to some conclusions. Already, she wanted to yell out that he was wrong without him uttering a word. But quiet she would be. Meek and humble, right?

"Good morning, Cade."

He nodded. "Good morning."

"So, that's Julep?" she whispered. "She's pretty."

"I told you she was."

Ugh, this is not going to be easy, she thought. *Future me, whatever were you thinking?*

"I figured you would still be on the ship. Getting her ready to go out."

"We rowed back early for breakfast with the family. I noticed you weren't there."

"No, I didn't feel up to it. I put out some lines instead." She held up her wounded arm. "One of the fish showed me its thoughts on being caught."

He stepped forward as though to examine the injury, then realizing his hands were already full, tucked his chin and whispered, "Are you badly hurt?"

"Nothing Jamison can't fix. I only wish the fish hadn't escaped."

"I know how that feels." His dark eyes rested on hers and something passed between them. Something different that she couldn't name and wasn't sure if she should allow. Was she the fish that had escaped? Did he want her back? Only last night he had mentioned divorce, or at least, some version of their separation. Now, his expression held a determined longing with no indication of retreat.

"Papa?" Julep's voice shifted their attention, finally breaking the spell when Cade looked away. Martha still had Julep wrapped tightly in her arms from where they crouched together. "Aren't you going to ask Mama to join us on the boat?"

Alice Ann startled to hear herself mentioned. "Julep, you know who I am?"

"Of course. Daddy told me all about you. You look just like Auntie Cora."

In reality, Alice Ann didn't look anything like her sister. Cora's hair was as brunette as Alice Ann's was crimson. They shared tastes in literature—and apparently brothers—but those were things one couldn't notice from outside.

"I'm very glad to meet you, Mama." Julep gave a small curtsy, polite as could be, all within the circle of Martha's arms.

Where had this obedient child come from? Alice wondered. Certainly not from her. How unnerving for her daughter to be this child rather than an unknown babe still inside.

"I'm very glad to meet you, too, Julep." *Now change the topic quickly*, her mind screamed. "You and your Papa are sailing somewhere soon?"

Cade shifted the fishing poles, setting their bases on top of his boot. He appeared as relieved as she for the introductions to be over. "I figured I'd take Julep down to Astoria for supplies and to sell off our latest oyster catch. I thought—well, Tobias thought and Julep overheard—that it might be wise to invite you along. You mentioned you lived in Astoria for a while, and he figured it could help you piece some things together."

Astoria was in a completely different territory, miles from the Ghost Forest in an opposite direction. "What was I doing there?"

"Trying to join a ship's crew. That's what you told me anyway, but you said no one would take you because you were a woman."

"That's absurd. I'm a better fisherman and sailor than half the men I knew back in Charleston. Any ship would be lucky to have me."

His lip twitched. "Yeah, that sounds like you. Apparently, they didn't feel the same."

"Or maybe it was your arrogance and colorful language they found off-putting," Martha muttered.

"*My* colorful language? If you had met any sailors, you'd know that my words sound like melodious bird song compared to their rank tales."

Julep broke into peals of laughter which caused Josephine to squawk and wriggle in her restraints. "Mama's funny. Mama, have you heard about the thirteen men in the rowboat? I'll tell it to you. There were thirteen men in a rowboat and they all said, 'George, tell us a story—'"

"All right, Julep," Cade cut in. "We can tell the rowboat story later. We need to get your mama's arm fixed up. Give your auntie and cousin hugs goodbye."

As Julep snuggled her cousin, Cade leaned into Alice Ann, his voice low. "The rowboat joke never ends. There's thirteen men forever trapped with George telling the same story over and over and *over* again. Don't ask her to start unless you have an entire night to spend."

Despite the awful prospect, Alice Ann giggled. "I've missed your laugh," Cade whispered. His smile was right beside her, his hands full of her fishing supplies and muscles taut as he carried them with ease. Their lips stood barely inches apart and an urge tugged inside her to press forward and close the distance.

97

Except she'd tried that yesterday and had been rejected. Better to not try again. Yet.

Instead, she watched as Martha brushed a stray curl behind Julep's ear and wiped a smudge from her cheek. Julep threw her arms around her aunt's neck, squeezing tightly. A spark of jealousy heated like a mound of thick gruel in the pit of Alice Ann's stomach, one she knew she had no right to feel. She had left, after all, with no apparent intention to return. But that was a decision her future self had made, not her.

"You be a good girl for your papa," Martha told her.

Julep nodded. "Course, Auntie Marta. If I listen to Papa, we'll be safe and sound on the ship."

"Exactly right."

Another pang of jealousy flared, brighter this time. Alice Ann stepped away from Cade, the wound on her arm pounding staccato with each heartbeat. He was supposed to keep them safe aboard ship? He may have learned to sail this past year, but she had been raised on the water. Her papa had taught her how to manage the jollyboat before she was five and by ten, she could haul in fishing nets right alongside him. Was Cade, with his passive whims, even capable of the assertiveness needed to command a ship and bring it safely into port? True, he had brought them safely home from the Ghost Forest, but he also had his brothers on board to help him. Plus, she had been there. Surely, she had been an asset as well.

She would sail with them to Astoria and if Cade failed miserably, she would teach him how to do everything a thousand times better. By the time they returned, Julep would say that Mama knew best on the sea. They wouldn't even need Cade in order to fish. He had always been worthless anyhow.

The unexpected vehemence of her thoughts left her reeling. She reached out to grip the rope guide strung along the path. Where had those feelings originated? Right now, she doubted his skill as both shipmaster and father and none of those memories seemed to match the man she'd spoken with yesterday or the one Martha had described this morning. Had she always been like this with him? Perhaps what the other women, and men, and everyone said was true. She *had* been a sour woman who disrespected her husband and paid no heed to her marriage vows.

To have and to hold, for better, for worse, for richer, for poorer, in sickness and in health. Keeping faith with each other in unbroken loyalty, in peace with God according to His will, and living together in mutual love. How could she remember the words of those vows, yet not remember making the vows themselves?

Although Martha never said a word aloud, her tense posture seemed to blast accusation: *"You promised unto death, Alice Ann. Why did you make such a promise if you couldn't keep it?"*

Except Alice Ann had been with child when they married. That much she knew, even if she could not recall the details that had led to their exchange of vows. Cade said he loved her. Yesterday morning, she woke up knowing she loved him, devastated from all the insults she had thrown at him upon that cliff. But that was the Alice Ann of today, not the bitter woman she had just felt inside her.

What had changed? Had the pursuit of her dreams truly been all that enticed her away from him? Or something far worse?

"Mama?" Julep's hand slipped into hers, startling her from her unexpected vehemence. Tender brown eyes gazed up at her. "You don't have to come with us if you don't want to."

She swallowed hard, trying to regain control. "What makes you think I wouldn't want to?"

"Because you had an accident and can't remember things. Papa said that's why you stayed away so long. You couldn't remember how to get back."

That's what Cade had told her? He hadn't filled her head with terrible lies about her mother? Or perhaps they weren't lies at all, but terrible truths. He peered out into the forest rather than at her.

"But we're going to help her, aren't we, Papa?"

"Of course, my jewel. Of course we are."

Somehow, Alice Ann found the strength to squeeze the child's hand. "Then how could I ever say no?"

15

Julep chattered the entire way to Astoria, directing Alice Ann's attention to this and that from *Gratia*'s rail. Knowledge of the surrounding wilderness flowed from her lips as easily as she had adapted to Cade's careful sailing instructions. Alice Ann learned right alongside her, astonished that her daughter was of such a quick mind. For still being months from six years old, she nimbly climbed the rigging and worked knots between her tiny fingers. Her strength was not quite enough to manage the helm, but with her father's guiding hands, she was able to help steady the ship along the coastal waters. What a fine sailor the girl was bound to become; it created a maternal pride in Alice Ann quite unfamiliar to her being.

Gratia's crew likewise surprised her. She had expected them to be much the same as the other sailors her father had known, or those she encountered with him in Charleston harbor—uncouth loudmouths. As a girl, she had always been able to tell them off or ward them off as to suit her attitude. Although something must have changed in her demeanor if her future self had been unsuccessful at securing a position.

Most sailors knew they needed to respect their captain's order or risk serious repercussions, sometimes to the point of being tossed overboard. Cade's crew was true in that respect. They listened to every command and were quick to follow through. Although *Gratia*'s size truthfully necessitated a larger crew than she held, they managed to be efficient with the men they had, despite not one being a natural-born sailor. And when Cade asked that they include Alice Ann and Julep as part of the crew, not one man complained. His story of her lost memory might have also sealed their lips, but if so, they refused to let on. Although Jones did watch her extra carefully whenever she reached for any part of the ship, as though her slightest touch might capsize them. Yet, he expressed no such concern when Julep climbed up to the lookout platform and stood with arms outstretched, pretending to be a bird. In fact, he chuckled.

"Don't take it too hard, Mrs. Lark," Winasie said when he caught her watching, a frown upon her lips. He extended her a grandfatherly smile. "Miss Julep has been running through that rigging for months now. It seems she's fearless from it. Once you learn the ropes, Jones will reconsider."

"And what about Thatcher?" she asked. The black man seemed barely older than herself and so far, had been prone to crooked smiles, as though he wasn't certain if she had earned them.

"Not sure he knows what to think yet. If you don't mind it, we're all trying to figure you out. Day one, when you came on board, it appeared you would turn *Gratia* into a hen frigate."

How dare he take her to be an overbearing fussy captain's wife? She was about to fling an insult of equal caliber when she remembered that she couldn't actually remember the first day she stepped foot on *Gratia*. Perhaps she had been rude and ill-mannered. Had she not, just last night, determined that her list of strengths did not include a humble temperament? Having grown up near the harbor, she'd heard worse terms than *hen frigate* and none of them kind. To her father's chagrin, she'd even thrown a few back herself. So, she supposed she could let this one pass.

"You seem different now though," Winasie continued, ignorant of her retrospection. "We all have bad days and the captain says the past few have been some of your worst. I imagine losing yourself would be hard."

What understanding and such unexpected kindness in those deep brown eyes. Yes, she thought, certainly nothing like most of the sailors she had met before. Or, at least, that she could remember. "Thank you, Winasie. I suppose I was having a very bad day."

He patted her shoulder. "No harm. I'd better get to my post. We'll arrive soon and the captain will want us to be ready."

Within the hour, Astoria emerged, the abandoned remnants of John Jacob Astor's decommissioned fort still standing. Dense forest formed a wall right down to the edge of several scattered buildings, every one visible without needing to turn one's head. A house here, a house there, up on the hill a church with a thin white steeple. A long wooden-planked pier ran out from the shoreline, allowing *Gratia* to anchor near two other schooners, both of similar size to their own, and several smaller fishing dories. Across from the docks, a lumber mill stood on wooden pillars above the water, stacks of fresh lumber being carried through its doors and scattered scraps discarded among the rocks below. Beneath that stood the familiar fish market where she and Cade had regularly sold their catch and traded for the latest news. The pungent stench of its rejected castoffs wafted from across the water, where several sailors, uncaring of the aroma, hefted full seafood barrels upon their shoulders.

Truthfully, the town wasn't much to speak of, although it had grown since her last visit about a month ago. No, she corrected, those memories happened over six years ago. Supposedly, she had been here many times since, including an extended stay during her years distant from Larksong.

"I wonder how long I was here before I went to the Ghost Forest," she said as they descended the gangplank. Julep's hand lay secure within her own and two sacks of oysters bounced upon Cade's back before them.

He glanced briefly over his shoulder, arms straining under the weight. "Not long, I imagine, otherwise, I would have seen you on one of my visits. Let's sell the oysters, and then we can ask around." Rather than head toward shore, he turned in the opposite direction, moving along the dock toward two sailors in conversation, both sporting lit cigarettes and serious expressions. If she didn't know better, she would suspect their wiry beards and twine-tied hair to be reflective of piracy.

Hen frigate, indeed. If Cade considered such audacious business partners, he needed a strong woman at his side.

She reached for his arm, holding him back. "You're not planning to sell to those ruffians?"

His brows shot up. "I am. They're not ruffians, just unkempt sailors. Had you actually gone to sea, you would have learned this."

The statement stung like a slap to the face, yet he continued as though he had said nothing wrong. Perhaps to him, he didn't think he had. "For oysters, I've found a few lucrative dealings outside of the market. These men will take our catch down to California and make a handsome profit."

"Do *we* make a profit?" she ground out.

"Yes, and if I negotiate well, a rather substantial one. Now, why don't you wait here with Julep while I handle the business?"

A dry chuckle escaped before she considered its implications. "You? I've always been the one to handle our dealings."

"That was before. Now you need to trust that I, the useless milksop, won't lose our money in bad deals." The way he said it implied he'd heard those words from her lips before and often. True, she had rarely thought him capable of anything...until she saw his ship and watched the way he sailed it. But sailing was one thing and business quite another.

"Papa, what's a milksop?" Julep piped up before Alice Ann could wrangle a reply.

Cade's face colored. "Oh, ah, it's a piece of milk-soaked bread."

"Then why would you be one?"

"I don't know, Jules. Your papa was trying to make a joke."

Julep shook her head. "You know you're no good at that."

"There are many things I'm no good at," he muttered. Stepping closer and drawing the scent of oysters with him, he bent to whisper in Alice Ann's ear. "Things have changed, Alice. Don't forget, you were the one who changed them." Then he stepped away with a tight smile at his daughter. "Julep, stay here and show Mama how we play Quiet Mouse."

"Ok, Papa, I will." As her father readjusted the sacks on his shoulders and headed for the sailors, Julep squeezed Alice Ann's hand. "We have to stand here real quiet like a mouse hiding from a cat. Whoever stays quiet the longest wins."

What a mundane amusement, Alice Ann thought. What Julep needed to learn was how to run a business, not how to stand still as a wallflower or dainty like a china cup. And what Cade needed was a business partner. That was what they'd both always needed, a common passion to unite them and to restore their failing marriage. It seemed impossible that these sailors wouldn't give her a chance simply because of her gender. If she met with them, they would see she was clearly the better negotiator, and Cade would understand exactly how much good she could bring to their partnership.

"Come, Julep. We can stay quiet just as easily standing over there."

The girl frowned. "You already lost the game."

"Let me try again then. I didn't understand the rules."

Her lip crinkled upward. "All right, but this is your last chance."

On quiet tiptoes, they followed Cade, stopping just short of catching up. He swung the oyster sacks down from his shoulders and plunked them at his feet. "Afternoon, Fröm, Bobber. How's the sea been for ya?"

Both men raised a hand in greeting, the one named Fröm releasing a line of smoke between semi-rotted teeth. Bobber wiped a hand on his trousers before extending it to grip Cade's. "Well, if it ain't Mr. Lark, back already. Seems like we just saw ya."

"It's been a couple weeks, but not too long, I agree. Came into town for supplies at the store, but got a couple bags of oysters to off load if you're agreeable."

"More than. Just making my way back from Portsmouth and didn't get anything worth spitting at from them louts. What'ya say, Fröm? Make him yer best offer and I'm gonna beat it. I need this load and you already got plenty in yer hold." Bobber chuckled. "Hehe, load and hold, made me a joke and didn't even choke."

Fröm rolled his eyes. "You can have 'em all." Then to Cade he said, "Fella's been takin' the old mother's milk again. There's no negotiating with him when he gets like this." Alice Ann wasn't sure what mother's milk referred to, but the man clearly wasn't all in his rights today, which could be to their benefit.

She raised her chin and stepped forward. "Best oysters on the

Pacific coast, gentlemen. Take it from the proprietress, won't find any better."

Fröm dropped what remained of his cigarette. "What's *she* doin' here?" he sputtered.

At the same time Cade released a distinctive groan, Julep tugged on Alice Ann's hand. "Mama, you lost the game again. You weren't supposed to talk."

"You keep playing then." She waved the child behind her skirts and stacked a fist to either hip. She may not remember her time in Astoria, but she could pretend well enough. Martha might think that Cade was flourishing, but likely she was being kind to ruffle Alice Ann's feathers. He would appreciate her ingenuity and be far more successful with her at his side.

"So—Bobber, I believe?—what will you offer my husband for these two sacks worth? Don't be stingy for I'll see right through a poor deal."

The sailors glanced at each other and broke into peals of laughter. Bobber even had the audacity to slap his knee and spit on the ground at her feet. She hopped back before his spittle splattered the boots she'd borrowed from Coraline.

"Lark, this's your wife?" Fröm cackled. "We didn't even know you was married. Did you know she was out here huntin' down ships once back when?"

Cade's face reddened. "You must have her confused with someone else."

"Nah, I'd remember her anywhere. She tried to join my crew—how long's it been—maybe three or so years ago. Might be pretty, but she sure ain't bright. I told her no captain wants a woman on board, but she just kept coming 'round, askin' and askin'. I said she should get herself home, unless she'd like to be hired for something else. Know a few fellas who could use another saloon girl to keep their customers warm."

Warmth flamed into Alice Ann as hot as Cade's ever deepening shades of crimson. "How dare you speak to a lady that way."

"You ain't no lady," Fröm laughed. "But you're right that you ain't no soiled dove either. If you're here to try joining my crew again, my answer'll still be no. It's yer attitude I can't abide more than you being female. Can't have a sailor who doesn't know his place."

"I could have learned."

"With that flamin' hair and such a pout upon your lips? Not likely. Odds are the crew'd toss ya overboard at the first sign of Poseidon's trident and blame ya for the whole affair. But eh, I told ya all this before. No sense hashin' it over again."

"True enough," said Bobber. "Now off with your wee one. We've got business to attend to." He beckoned for Cade to hand over the oysters for inspection. Still flushed to the ear tips, Cade removed three good-sized ones and placed them in the other man's hands. Bobber turned them over, then pulled a knife from his belt and cracked the shell. Alice barely restrained herself from yelling at him for trying without buying when he sliced off the slimy oyster and upended it into his gullet. Only Julep's sudden grip around her waist halted her actions.

Fröm selected an oyster and did the same. "I can't believe you married that one, Lark. The west sure does drive a man to desperation, doesn't it?"

In the end, the men agreed to a sum that seemed low to Alice Ann but which Cade appeared satisfied by. Then he took her elbow on one side and Julep's hand on the other and led them up the hill toward the small heart of Astoria.

Both unhappy and infuriated, she moved a pace ahead of Cade, tears stinging her eyes. "You could have said something," she spat. "You could have defended me."

"I told you things were different. I needed to make the deal."

She rubbed at her eyes, determined not to let tears fall as the sailors' cackles faded away behind them. "Women can't do this and women can't do that. Who gave them the privilege to decide what I'm capable of? It's so unfair."

His pace quickened beside her and Julep tripped to keep up. Gripping Alice Ann's arm, he eased her to a stop halfway up the hill. Sea grass and wildflowers waved along either side of the packed dirt road, a steady breeze off the sea mixing their pleasant aroma with that of chum. Alice Ann observed Julep watching them both and listening intently. Would Cade continue his charitable façade or finally berate her with his true feelings?

He nodded at the flowers. "Julep, your mama is sad about the things she can't remember. Could you gather her a big bouquet to cheer her up?"

"Of course, Papa!" As soon as she started selecting flowers, he pulled Alice Ann into his arms.

Her first instinct was to shove him away, but her second instinct quickly followed, that of wanting him exactly where he was, holding her close to his chest. "How can you mourn being kept from the ways of men?" he murmured against her cheek. "The things you long for anyone could do. But the thing you've already done is uniquely feminine. Don't underestimate the power that holds nor underestimate yourself."

"And what is it that I've done?"

"Julep. You carried her. She grew inside you and you brought her into the world. Only a woman can do that. I'm in awe of this beautiful child that only you could give me. At least, without you, I still had her."

"Me being a mother?" she scoffed. "That would have been enough for you?"

"Of course. Being a father gave my life unimaginable purpose. I wish it could have for you, too."

He watched Julep dash from flower to flower, carefully arranging each one into a colorful bouquet. When she caught her father's gaze, she rewarded him with an enormous grin before returning to her selections, her youthful ignorance once again a blessing.

"I probably shouldn't have brought her," he continued quietly. "She was already somehow spared the worst of that circus's indecency. No need to place her in harm's way again."

"Circus?"

He coughed. "Sorry, I forgot myself again. Julep was kidnapped and forced to entertain at a Gifted circus for nearly a year before my brothers and I were able to rescue her. Martha was held there as well. That was while Garrett, Josiah, and I were enslaved on the *Arletta*."

Martha hadn't mentioned that. Why would she leave out such an

107

important detail? Unless, like everyone else, she expected Alice Ann to leave again and felt such details didn't matter. "You were responsible for her when it happened?"

"I wasn't, no, but I understand why you'd think that. I did almost lose myself when I heard the news. I'd rather not relive it today." He shrugged. "Next time I make the trip down here, I'll make sure to bring someone who can tend to her while I conduct business."

"Couldn't I do it?"

"Do what?"

"Stay with Julep on the ship while you conduct business, as you said."

"You would *want* to?" Cade immediately stepped away, holding her at arm's length, chin tilted with concern. He didn't believe her, but why should he after her past behavior? She had startled even herself with this train of thought. She was the one who had bare feet for most of the westward trail and braids half done, frizzy hair all asunder. She, who didn't care for others' opinions and loudly touted her ability to be a crack shot, as good as or better than the men. Who had just tried to usurp her husband's oyster deal. So why was she having this homebody feeling now?

A more frightening thought intruded. Was this something she had actually wanted once? Before she lost her memory, had she desired the life of stuffy matrons like Coraline who, if her vision had allowed it, would happily tote babies around on either hip? There was something familiar in the thought, but no memories raced to fill in the blanks. It was simply a feeling she couldn't grasp or lay meaning to.

What if she tried? Cade wanted to win her over. Is this what would have worked?

It didn't seem likely, but perhaps...

Before she could answer, however, Julep danced toward them, excitedly waving her flowers and pointing at something up the road. Turning, Alice Ann observed a young man standing outside the general store, his neatly-trimmed beard and hair the same color as her own. White lettering stenciled his traveling case, "Frye Photography," and a sandwich board hung across his shoulders announcing, "Tintypes in under 2 hours!"

Julep clutched her bouquet between both hands and bounced on her toes. "Oh, a picture man! Papa, can we get one, please, can we?"

"I'm afraid not, sweetheart. There's a storm arriving in a few hours, and I'd like to be on our way before it makes landfall. We need to purchase supplies at the store. There isn't time for both." As he spoke, a thin flash of lightning fluttered far against the horizon, announcing the legitimacy of his words. However, Alice Ann had been on the water many times with her father during rainstorms and with a sky far blacker than the one above. As always, her husband was being overly cautious. Affording Julep this one luxury could divert his attention from Alice Ann's recent misdeeds and perhaps, earn her daughter's affection as well.

So, as Julep whined, "Please, Papa, please!" and tugged on his jacket hem, Alice Ann slipped her arm through Cade's and whispered in his ear, "Surely, we have a few minutes for a family portrait?"

"It isn't a good idea. The storm—"

Lightning flashed again across the ocean, this time with a slight rumble of thunder. Grey clouds billowed, yet appeared to be slow moving. At least an hour off by her calculations and likely to pass by within the photographer's promised two-hour timeline.

"Cade, your Gift is predicting the weather and you've chosen a steadfast crew. I trust you to sail us through any storm."

His eyes swiveled from his daughter to meet hers, completely incredulous. "You do?"

"Absolutely." And if not, she had full confidence that she could.

Julep continued to whine while simultaneously pulling on his hand. "Paaaapaaa, pleeese!"

He looked to heaven and released a sigh. "I can't reward this behavior."

"Then let me reward it," Alice Ann offered. "I'm a new mother. Pretend I don't know any better."

"Do you? Know better?"

She tapped a finger to her chin and gave a sly smile. "Hmm, you know what, Cade Gideon? I simply can't remember."

"Yet you remember my middle name just fine."

She planted a kiss on his cheek and smiled when he blushed collar to brow. "There are simply one or two things about you it would be impossible to forget."

16

When Cade had agreed to Tobias's suggestion for Alice Ann to visit Astoria, he had anticipated it might spark a few lost memories or provide some indication of her interactions during their time apart. Thanks to Fröm and Bobber, one of those goals had been achieved. More tentatively, he had also hoped their time together could provide an opportunity to become reacquainted as a family of three. It didn't have to be perfect—whose day was?—but he'd also never expected a disaster of monumental proportions. One that now risked their lives and their daughter's.

He could kick himself. He had allowed his wife's unexpected admiration to fog his thinking, and now they were sailing straight through a foul storm.

Before that, they had been having a pleasant time with the traveling photographer, Henry Frye, a kind Missourian eager to produce a perfect portraiture for their "smart little family." Cade must admit he fancied the idea of being a smart little family, too, if that was indeed what they were becoming. He cherished the delight on his wife and daughter's faces as they'd observed Mr. Frye develop the tintype. As their likenesses had begun to emerge, they'd laughed together, Julep holding Alice Ann's hand and she holding her pretty bouquet of wildflowers. His girls were having fun as a mother and daughter should, as they should have been for years.

"It's so pretty!" Julep had exclaimed upon being handed the two-by-four sepia photograph. "Look, Papa! Don't you think it's pretty?" She'd shoved the tintype under his nose and he'd gently eased it from her grip. Mr. Frye had indeed crafted a handsome picture. The three of them stood close together, Cade and Alice Ann behind Julep. His arm circled his wife's waist, she with either hand on their daughter's shoulders and his free hand atop hers. They weren't smiling and they didn't look happy...and yet, they didn't look altogether unhappy either. He could almost imagine them back in Larksong, as they were before Alice Ann had deserted them. Better than they were.

At that point, everything had seemed fine. A light drizzle began to fall, but if they returned to the ship straight away, Cade knew they could still outsail the worst of it.

Then Mr. Frye invited them to stay for supper.

"Thank you, sir, but no," Cade told him. "We need to return to our ship before the storm sets in."

"Oh, quite right, yes," Mr. Frye agreed. "I won't keep you then."

Alice Ann released Julep's hand to take her husband's arm. "But surely we need to eat?"

"We packed a hamper on the ship," Cade gently reminded her. "We need to be getting back."

"Oh, honestly, don't be such a ninny. It's barely damp out there. If we have supper here, we won't have to sail through the storm at all. It will pass us by."

More than anything right then, Cade had desired to keep his frustration in check in front of the photographer and especially Julep, whose attention now shifted between her parents with interest. "Alice," he breathed low, "the weather is my specialty. You should trust me on this." Hadn't she said earlier that she would? That she trusted him to lead them through any storm? Why was she fighting him now?

"You're a weather prophet, then?" Mr. Frye scratched his temple. "Met me more than a dozen of them. Never seemed to predict it quite right."

"I have a special knack for it."

"Yes," Alice Ann agreed before immediately dismissing him with, "But often your Gift leads to an overreaction, and we certainly don't want Julep to miss out, do we? I've sailed through storms with my father; you can trust me on this." She turned away and smiled at Mr.

Frye. "Thank you for the invitation. We accept."

"Wonderful!" the photographer grinned. "Right this way."

She reached for Julep's hand. "Come, Jules. We're having supper in a restaurant. Won't that be fun?"

"Yippee! I've never ate in a res-tant!" Their daughter practically dragged her mother away, not a glance spared for her father.

Not wishing to insult Mr. Frye's generosity, Cade had silently followed. With every step, he had felt his chest tightening and not only at the rejection of his child for a mother she barely knew. Caution encouraged him to scoop up his family and hightail it for the schooner. Why was everyone undermining him today?

Because, for almost the full twenty-seven years of his life, he had been the family peacekeeper who did what everyone said. They had always undermined him, and he had just let it happen. Except for one time when he'd punched the *Arletta*'s engineer to save Garrett's life.

But that seemed so long ago and far away now. That had been the action of a different man, a man enslaved, a desperate man without much else to live for. Now, he had a family to reconstruct and an estranged wife to make sense of. Despite his better judgment, Alice Ann wanted him to trust her regarding the storm. Maybe if he did, it would take them one step closer to where they needed to be.

But no, he had been wrong again.

By the time they finally boarded the *Gratia* and made it out to sea, curtains of rain fell thick as night, waves washing across the deck, and the sail flogging in the wind. Terrified, Julep huddled in the cabin belowdecks with only her rag doll for comfort, while he and Alice Ann screamed at each other and the crew tried to keep the schooner from capsizing into the sea.

"I can't believe you did this!" Cade shouted from the helm. He gripped it harder, rain stinging against his skin.

Alice slapped wet crimson locks behind her shoulders while clinging to the quarterdeck rail with the opposite hand. "I didn't do anything wrong!"

"You didn't do anything right, either."

"As though you did." A wave struck their starboard side and the ship lurched to port, sending Alice to her knees and Cade nearly toppling with the force. His muscles ached as he hauled the helm back to center and shouted for Thatcher to secure the halyard or they'd all go overboard.

A wave flooded the deck, narrowly missing Alice's feet as she stumbled up beside him. She gripped the helm next to his hands, and he attempted to shove her off with his shoulder. "Don't you try to assume this helm, Alice Ann Lark."

She didn't move. "Do you want to make it home?"

"I'm an able sailor." Earlier she'd said she trusted him. Was that just so she could have her way? Clearly, it must have been.

"Where's the proof?" she yelled.

"You're standing on it! Now, let me do my job!"

She glared at him, her demeanor cold as the rain that cascaded over them while he turned away and shouted orders to keep *Gratia* from foundering. Meanwhile, despite his own commanding tone, he was enduring memories from a similar storm on *Arletta*. He, Garrett, Josiah, and Melvin had barely escaped with their lives rather than a sword in the back or a bullet to the head. If not for the kind father and daughter they had encountered in Georgia, Cade might have succumbed to the subsequent fever that had knocked his feet—and his sense—right out from under him.

On *Arletta*, however, there had been a full steamship of combative men, while here there was but him, his wife, and a minimal crew. And thunderclouds. And lightning. And deep waters and darkness and sea swells and the risk of capsize and...and...and... He held fast to the helm while the flogging sails sounded like the fierce pounding of his heart.

Panic seized him then and screamed to find an escape. But they were on a fool's ship miles from land. He could either curl into a ball upon the deck and be washed overboard, throw himself over the rail and drown, or leave the *Gratia* to his wife and hide with Julep. After all, Alice believed she could handle it alone. He should let her prove it.

Except he didn't believe she could handle it alone, and she shouldn't have to.

Thick or thin, no matter whether she stayed or left him again, he was still her husband, and he loved her.

He didn't trust her, but he did love her. Even if she didn't love him.

That was the crux of it, wasn't it? Now that she had removed her memories, he was more afraid than ever to fully welcome her back into his life. If she didn't recall her time away—whatever hardship had led her to that rundown shack in the Ghost Forest, her failure as a sailor, the loss of all her dreams—that meant she was still the woman from before they'd married. Rough, selfish, more concerned with what she deserved than she ever was with him or them together. She'd never even told him she loved him before they married and rarely said it after. Had she said it to Julep? Or anyone else? He couldn't recall.

Now, perhaps, neither could she.

As he held Alice Ann's stare, he felt the tension lessen slightly in his limbs. Her wild eyes held anger but also hurt and confusion. Her emotional wounds gave her no right to inflict them back upon him, but understanding her hurt allowed him to come a little closer to knowing why she did.

Maybe it wasn't about one of them succumbing to the other's will, but both of them stepping forward. And someone needed to step first.

"Alice, take the helm."

Her chin lifted. "What?"

"You heard me. Take the helm."

"But—"

"Take it!"

Alice scrambled for the helm at the same time he released it, but the delay was enough to jolt the ship and knock him to the quarterdeck. Sputtering from a face full of water, he rolled up to his knees and grabbed for the gunwale before he was washed overboard. At the same time, Alice thrust the helm right, bringing them back around. He held on for dear life as the *Gratia* crested a high wave and a second later, he felt his Gift alert him to approaching danger.

"Alice, to starboard!" With barely time to spare, the ship crushed back onto the sea, sailing windward as a bolt of lightning arced into the water mere yards off their hull. Had he not given her control and refocused on his Gift, the jolt would have cut straight through them and Julep in the cabin below.

Keep her safe, he prayed. She was safer than any of them at this moment, but he knew how a storm could turn on its head.

"How do I even know if I'm going the right away?" Alice cried.

Digging in his jacket pocket, he tossed her the old Lark compass. "Use this! Head northeast!"

She grabbed the compass out of the air and flipped open the lid with her thumb. For two seconds, the needle spun wildly and Cade wondered if he had somehow broken it, but then it righted itself once more. Alice adjusted the helm accordingly, although her eyes remained on the instrument in her hand. Another shock of lightning burst to the west, followed by the resulting clap of thunder, but she didn't glance up or shift her weight. When the next wave struck, she rocked to the side and Cade only managed to stand and steady her before she tumbled over.

In this fashion, they slowly sailed northward and out of the storm. Bit by bit, the waves calmed and the angle of the rain became less severe. The crew were able to move freely once again, without imminent fear of going overboard. While Winasie relit the lanterns, Cade had Thatcher and Jones examine the rigging to determine if anything was in need of immediate repair.

Before long, Winasie ascended to the quarterdeck, positioning the final lantern near the helm. "Captain, all lanterns are lit and Jones says the mainmast appears unaltered. Thatcher is nearly done on the foremast."

"Thank you, Win. I'd like to head belowdecks to check on my daughter. Alice?...Alice!" Every muscle in her had suddenly tensed, as though she was frozen to the helm by some unknown force. Her eyes remained open, but unseeing, still on the compass in her hand.

Cade shook her. "Alice, what's wrong?" Was this her Gift again? He thought they had freed her from those "memory moments," as she'd called them. Or at least freed her from the black-out fits she used to experience.

She jerked, an aggressive twitch of muscles that had her hunched over the helm and altering their course. "Alice!" he cried. "Winasie, take the helm."

When Winasie reached for the wheel, Cade had to practically pry her fingers away from it as she stared without seeing. At last, however, she relaxed into his arms. He let his first mate take over navigation while his attention swept over his wife. "Are you all right?"

"Yes," she said, her eyes once again alert as she studied his face. "You, however, appear as though you've seen a ghost."

"Have I?" he croaked. "You went stiff as a board and your gaze glossed over."

"Hmm, well, that's new." She grabbed his arm as the ship rocked again, bracing herself against the rail. Then she stuck out the compass, showing him the geometric design on its back. She tapped on the center where jagged lines met the center sun. "I remember this. It isn't just a compass. It's a puzzle box. See these markings like lightning? They're directing us how to open the box. Right here in the center."

"How do you know about puzzle boxes?"

"Read it in a book years ago. Larksong is dull as tombs; I needed something to do."

"But in the Ghost Forest, you said there was nothing special about it."

She shrugged. "Maybe my future self didn't make the connection. It's amusing to think I'm more intelligent than myself years from now." She tapped the compass. "Or actually, it's rather sad. Do I become utterly brainless in the future?"

A crash of thunder deafened her last words, followed by a long roll of rumbling from across the sea. More lightning flickered a mile distant in the direction they had sailed from.

"Get on with your meaning, Alice, while we're still alive to grasp it."

"Interesting choice of phrase considering we need to harness the lightning."

"Pardon? We need to do what?"

"We need to position the compass so that when a bolt of lightning strikes, it opens the compass and reveals the puzzle."

That couldn't be the answer. If lightning struck the ship, *Gratia* would burst into flames and they would all die. Sure, he might learn the compass's secret, but what sort of reward was that? Was she insane?

Winasie's jaw hung agape, so he certainly thought so. "Why would someone make something so dangerous?" the native asked then, embarrassed, mumbled, "Sorry, Captain. Not my place to ask."

Cade waved him away. "No, it's the right question. Alice, what you're suggesting is too dangerous for any normal person to take on."

Alice Ann's expression lit in the lantern's glow, her wide grin confirming the level of her sanity—likely none. "Exactly, Cade," she laughed. "A normal person couldn't open this without dying, but *you* can. You know exactly where the lightning will strike, and can therefore open it safely. This message from your ancestor, Cade—it's meant for you."

For him? For too long, his family had considered his Gift to be the least useful of all of them. Jamison could save people's lives and Garrett could find them when they were lost. Tobias, while without a Gift now, had perhaps been the most talented of any of them once. Daniel always said he didn't fit in because he didn't have a Gift, but he didn't know that Cade often felt the same way. As though he wasn't good *enough* to be called Gifted. It had only been recently that his brothers had begun to see him in a different light. If Alice was right, however, his Gift had a greater purpose he'd yet realized.

"How did my mother know?" he asked. "When she gave me this, I didn't even know if I had a Gift."

"I reckon your mama knew far more than she let on."

There had been other secrets that his mother had taken to the grave: her affair with Josiah and the subsequent child conceived and later kidnapped by Sterling's circus. For over twenty years, that secret had been buried beneath his mother's death and Josiah's grief, until at last the truth could no longer be obscured. Could this be another example? Perhaps his brothers would be able to help him uncover the truth.

If he lived that long.

"Winasie, turn her around."

The native stared at him. "Captain, you can't consider—"

"I can. Take her back into the storm, Winasie. Thatcher, Jones!" he called up to his men as they checked the lines. "Prepare for another storm. I will lay aloft the mainmast."

"Captain?" Jones's brows furrowed. "The evening ahead looks clear."

"But the one behind us is not."

"Behind us?" Thatcher asked. "Why would we turn into the storm?"

"Trust me. I have my reasons." His crew waited for more, but Cade chose not to expand. He didn't honestly believe that his crew would mutiny if they knew the reasons, but in this instance, they would have a legitimate reason to do so. What he was ordering them to do was outright reckless.

Loyal to a fault, his men hurried off to do as they had been commanded. Cade felt like a lout for thinking that at least none of them had families waiting for them back home. Not like he did on this ship.

He took Alice Ann's hands and drew her aside. "You remember how I showed you how to lower the gig?" She nodded. "Good. You may need to help do so before the night is through. But right now, I need you to wait belowdecks with Julep."

"What are you going to do?"

"Exactly as I told Jones. I'll lay aloft the mainmast. Then I'll attach the compass to it and pray that when it's struck, it doesn't kill me. If it does, Julep needs one of us to bring her home."

A drizzle began to fall across her face as the wind howled anew. "Cade, don't be stupid." She whispered the words, but he could interpret the formation of her lips. He had heard the same from her many times before. Except this time, it almost seemed like she didn't mean it, or maybe that was his own "stupid" wishful thinking.

Before he could reason with himself, he kissed her quickly. A second at most, then he turned away. His ragged emotions could wait. He hoped.

Without looking back, he climbed the main mast. Nine minutes until the next lightning strike. He needed to get them into position.

Lord, I'm asking you for my life here, he prayed. *My life, my wife, my child, and my crew. But I'm their captain, so if I can only have one, take my life and give theirs to them.*

With the scent of the storm thrumming through his senses, he wrapped the wet line around his upper arm to secure himself to the mast and braced his feet on either side. Then with one hand, he held the compass against the topmost side of the beam and with the other, wrapped a coil of twine four times around it. *A puzzle box*, Alice had called it. Hopefully, not a death trap. He would dearly love to kiss his wife again.

His eyes swept the deck, but saw no sight of her within the rain. The cabin hatch was also closed. At least she had listened. Whatever happened to him, hopefully she and Julep would be safe.

"Three points to starboard!" he called down to Winasie, and he immediately shifted the helm. "There, there! Hold her steady!"

One minute until the next lightning strike, and it would fall upon the very mast he clung to. But he couldn't descend until the last moment. If the compass jarred loose, they would have to wait for another chance. He was tired of waiting, always waiting. For his wife to come home, for life to make sense, for his brothers to respect him, for his own foolish insecurities to stop controlling his life. This time, he wasn't going to wait.

At ten seconds remaining, he lifted his hand from the compass. It stayed where it was, flush against the wood, the wet twine keeping it in place. Another five and still it held.

Jones shouted something at him, but his words were caught up and ripped away in the wind. Gripping the line, Cade kicked off from the mast and swung toward the one opposite. A white bolt shot down behind him, bursting with a blinding glow. Disoriented, he slammed against the foremast and lost his grip. The wet rope uncoiled and slipped through his fingers, sending his body in a free fall toward the deck. His hands reached for purchase, knocking against the rigging and struggling to grip another line as it burned through his fingers, yet somehow managing to slow his descent. God be praised, he landed on a coil of rope, which still felt like falling onto a pile of logs, but thankfully didn't kill him. A half second later and the distinct tinge of char laced the air, but not the crackle of fire. *Gratia* remained intact, although he wondered if the same could be said for the compass.

"Cade!" Alice screamed. He turned his head to see her halfway out the cabin hatch, holding the door open with one hand and clinging to the ladder with the other, her expression clearly centered on a longing to run to him.

She wants to run to me, he thought. *How strange that we're married, and I never knew what that expression looked like before.*

Then Jones and Thatcher were kneeling on either side of him and he felt *Gratia* sway as she turned toward safer waters. Winasie hadn't received that order, but the native also knew that Cade had done what he intended to do. Considering the breath currently missing from his lungs, he wouldn't have been able to shout it if he tried.

"Captain!" Jones called. "Sir, are you hurt? What can we do?"

The wind was slowing now, the ship moving out of the storm once again. Cade lay still another few beats as the waves quieted.

"I'm all right," he told them. "Back to your posts."

Thatcher shook his head. "Captain, we can't leave you on the deck like this."

"Then help me belowdecks. My wife can tend to me."

The two crewmen exchanged a doubtful glance, but hauled him up anyway. With one man bracing each of his shoulders, they helped him hobble toward the cabin ladder. His left side ached from bicep to calf and would be bruised for a few weeks at least, unless Jamison had some way to set it to rights more quickly.

Alice dashed from the cabin hatch as they approached, dipping under his right arm to take him from Thatcher's aid. "I can manage," she told Jones.

"You're certain?"

"I'm certain."

He released Cade to lean on Alice Ann's strength as they took the first step down the cabin ladder, although the crewmate remained at the top until they had both safely descended. "Captain, I will bring word when we approach the bay."

"Or if we encounter anything else."

"Aye."

"Thank you, men." They nodded and closed the hatch behind

them, sealing out the wind and the dampness for the warmth of the cabin below. Alice Ann hadn't lit the stove fire—wise given how the ship had been rocking—but she had battened all the porthole hatches and stored any other objects which may have fallen. A single lantern swung light across the room in elongated shadows.

He directed her to his berth and she helped him sit, then lowered beside him, their shoulders pressed close together. He shivered in his wet clothes, the intensity of the situation finally beginning to wear off. He wasn't about to change out of them though with Alice sitting right there. They were married, but it just didn't seem...right.

On the adjacent berth, Julep lay curled asleep under her blanket, Fee Fee clutched tightly in her arms. "Did she sleep through the entire storm?" he asked.

"No. She was afraid through most of it. She fell asleep as soon as I told her you were all right." She studied him, her lips turned down and eyes analyzing. "Are you all right? The entire time I was down here, I thought you died."

"Would you have missed me? Did you...did you miss me?" He turned to look at her and her eyelids lowered.

"You weren't up there that long."

"I mean before, when you were...gone. Did you ever miss me?"

Her arm stiffened against him. "That's a stupid question. You know I don't remember." Then she stood and backed away, wiping her eyes with the palm of her hand. She spoke to the deck boards. "Why don't you get some rest? I'll go up top and see how the crew fares."

Once Alice disappeared up the hatch, he sagged back on the berth, and dragged the blanket over himself, face and all. He could change out of his wet things now, but his side ached and so did his heart. Beneath him, the ship swayed while his entire body shook with the shock of all it had endured. *Lord Jesus, must it always be this difficult?* He buried his face in his hands, waiting for what, he didn't know.

Who only knew how many minutes later, two tiny arms wrapped him from behind, a little body squeezing under the blanket beside him. Julep rested her chin upon his shoulder and nuzzled into his neck. "Papa, are you frightened? I was, too, but then Mama helped make me better. Maybe she can make you better, too."

His wife had willingly comforted their child? Why did *that*, of all things, make him want to weep?

He lifted his hands away to meet his daughter's thoughtful gaze. An errant lock of hair tumbled onto her brow and fell across her cheek. How thankful he was to be her father.

The sound of footsteps descending interrupted his thoughts as Julep batted the blanket away from their faces. Alice Ann at the foot of the ladder, the cabin hatch closed above her, staring at the compass in her hands. Its back lay open like the petals of a flower. Is that what she had been doing just now, climbing the rigging to retrieve it? How long had he been laying immobile in his lightning-charged emotions?

"Alice?" he croaked. "Is anything there?"

Slowly, she nodded. "A message: 'Thompson remains.'"

Thompson remains? Thompson was a common enough family name, but he didn't personally know anyone who carried it. And where did he or she or their relatives remain? If he knew that, would it lead them to the origin of their Gifts?

"I'm sorry, Alice. I don't know what that means."

His wife's gaze slowly rolled up to meet his, a strange faraway look in her eyes. "You should. I do."

17

Alice Ann inhaled slowly, then released the breath. She focused on the memory and the name of Thompson, trying to draw more details from her mind as she relayed them to Cade.

"It was July of 1853 when I heard the name for the first and only time, the same day we learned that my ancestor was one of the seven Gifted survivors of the *Oblique*."

"It was also the same day we married," Cade said. His expression brightened. "Do you remember?"

She shook her head. What she did remember was Tobias and Jamison and their wives in the Stella Maris Mission chapel, along with Martha. There had been another woman, too, a young widow named Anwillik, and her brother, Quea'Quim, both with long black hair and tanned skin that glowed cherry in the candlelight. The woman held out her hand in offering, a bracelet of white Howqua shells and blue glass beads jangling. Both were Chinook natives, although she wore settler costume while her brother did not.

"Anwillik converted to Christianity," Cade explained. "It was always a point of contention between her and Quea'Quim that she left the tribe."

Oh, yes, she remembered now. There had been many arguments over the white man's God that evening. It all began with the siblings' discovery that Coraline could speak any language and understand anyone, too, without even realizing that she could.

How could Alice Ann recall that but not the wedding itself or remember the words of the vows but not the taking of them? Nothing prior to being seated in the chapel hours later.

Or no, she corrected, she hadn't been seated. She had been lying down on a pew, her feet up on the bench like a heathen, irritated that she had been pulled out of sleep for something so ludicrous.

"Are you Gifted too?" Tobias had asked her.

"I'm not a freak of nature like you all," she had sniffed. *"My gift is life on the sea, and you can all thank me when you have supper on the table and you don't starve."* Fishing was easy. Fishing she could understand, whereas these Gifts were beyond anything she could hope to unravel.

She had known then that something was different about her, had been ever since she fell from the cliff. Her memory wasn't what it used to be; it was far superior than before. But there were also strange rememberings she couldn't quite grasp and which frightened her if she dwelt on them too long. The last thing she had wanted was to suffer the same heartaches and anxieties Cade and Cora did. The mere thought made her head hurt and her stomach knot tighter than an anchor hitch on her papa's boat.

So, while her mind had spun a colorful tapestry, her mouth had done what it did best—effectively belittled everyone and everything and caused one dramatic moment after another.

"Julep," Cade interrupted her story. "Will you please take Fee Fee down to the supply hold and bring back a few oranges?"

"But Paaapaa. I wanna know who Mama yelled at."

"I bet you do." He nudged Julep off the berth, giving a light swat to her bum. "Do as I say, and you can have a peppermint stick. I picked some up at the general store for a surprise."

"Candy before bed? I'll be verrry good, Papa." The two of them laughed together before Julep ran off, half climbing, half tumbling from the cabin.

"Are there really oranges in the hold?" Alice asked.

"Not a one, but it should keep her occupied for a while." He rolled onto his back with a groan, as he wrapped an arm around his stomach to his bruised side and closed his eyes. Slowly, Alice Ann sat beside him. "Tell the truth, Cade. How bad are you hurting?"

"More than I want to let on."

"You should rest then. The compass can wait." She moved to stand but he snatched up her hand and held her in place.

He peered at her through hooded eyes. "Stop avoiding the rest of the story. Why do you think I sent Julep away? Just say whatever terrible thing you have to say and be done with it."

But Alice Ann didn't want to tell him the rest of it, because she now remembered exactly what she had said and to whom and how awful each word was. Stomping about the chapel like an unrestrained child, she had yelled how Tobias didn't make the rules for her, and she could make greater decisions than her fish business without his approval. She had opened her mouth to tell him all about the baby, to really drive in the point that he had no power over her, when Cade's hand had covered her mouth and silenced her.

"Alice, don't," he had pleaded. *"You said we wouldn't tell them. Not yet."*

How dare he tell her what to do or say, think or feel. No one had control of the things she did except for her and her alone. A streak of rage had enveloped her, and she'd kicked and fought, yet somehow her husband had maintained his hold. She'd tried to yell at him, curse at him, shouting muffled insults until finally admitting to herself that he was stronger than he appeared. If only he placed that strength to good use. Imagine the impressive feats he could accomplish! But no, she had married the emotionally weakest of the Lark brothers and now bore his child, who was probably destined to become as equally pitiful or worse.

With a defeated sigh, she had stopped fighting, and Cade had finally released her. Shoving him away, she had literally spat at his feet. *"Cade, you're such a milksop. We deserve our moment in the sun, what precious little of it there is to be found. Go ahead and tell them. Unless you think we made a mistake."*

To his minimal credit, he had told them about her pregnancy then, quickly and in but a few words, before racing her out the door and delaying their siblings' disapproval for another day. Alice Ann hadn't felt proud of him in that moment, nor had she felt any of the emotions she suspected most expectant parents do. Wasn't she supposed to be happy? Wasn't she supposed to fairly leap to her feet to tell them? There were supposed to be hugs and kisses and laughter all around. Questions of what to name the baby and whether they wished for a boy or a girl. Even though many infants died, there was still that joyful future mothers prayed for. Most could overlook the possibility of grief for the hope of happiness.

Not her, though. She wasn't happy. Cade wasn't happy. Nor Cora, Tobias, Jamison, Sarah, or Martha. None of them looked on this occasion with hope, unless it was a hope that she wouldn't completely ruin the life she had. And that prayer had fallen on deaf ears. For reasons she still didn't understand, she had left all of them to be alone in the Ghost Forest. She had chosen to forget rather than remember what she had done.

But she shared none of this with Cade while aboard the *Gratia*. All this washed through her mind in the minute they stared at one another, rain-drenched and exhausted. She couldn't say those things to him. He likely remembered them already; better for her to pretend she still forgot.

"What I said wasn't important. It was Anwillik who shared the most important parts. She said that Thompson was her ancestor and one of *Oblique*'s sailors before they had obtained their Gifts. The *Oblique* stayed in the Chinook village for a week to restore their health and supplies, and during that time, Thompson fell in love with a native woman, Spaärk. He promised to return for her once he had seen his men safely home, but that rascal never returned. Like us, she ended up with an unexpected child to raise, except she raised him by herself. No one wanted the child. Her family and friends, the entire tribe, thought the baby was wretched. During one of the worst storms they'd known, they even foolishly thought it was fathered by a sea serpent and wanted to kill it. In the end, they showed Spaärk mercy, but her family was shunned for generations because of what Thompson did. Spaärk believed her lover was dead, but I believe he was a coward. If he had plucked up the courage to do his duty, all would have been well."

"He did do his duty," Cade said slowly. "His first duty was to his shipmates. He didn't know he left a child behind."

"But he knew he left a woman behind. That should have been enough to fight for, even if they didn't have a wedding."

"Hmmm," he murmured and she realized what she'd just said. She had done the same, left him behind rather than fought for them. She braced herself, waiting for him to say so. Instead, he simply stared at her. "So, this was your way of telling me you remember everything about our wedding day except our actual wedding?"

She jerked back, both relieved at the turn of conversation and confused by it. "No. This was a story about Thompson."

"It had an awful lot about us in it. Seems you can remember all the ways I failed you fine, but none of the promises I made."

"That wasn't the purpose at all—"

"It doesn't matter, Alice. That was a long time ago, and you're right, this story is supposed to be about Thompson. Let's focus on that. I should have remembered his name when he's clearly the key to all of this." He relaxed back into the berth, drawing the blanket closer around himself. "Tell me more of your theory. I can tell you have one."

"I do. If *Thompson remains*, that means he definitely survived the storm. He had to have been one of the seven Gifted who returned to the South. He broke his promise to Spaärk and left Anwillik and Quea'Quim's family forever distanced from their tribe. The proof is right here in this compass, and I think someone should make him answer for that."

"How do you plan to do so? That was over one hundred and fifty years ago. It's impossible he's still alive."

"If he's Gifted, why couldn't he be? You and your brothers and my sister and half a circus can do incredible things, so why couldn't someone live for an exceptionally long time, too? Look at the note, *Thompson remains*. He was the last one who survived from the original seven."

She knew it sounded absurd, but she could also see the consideration in Cade's eyes. A spark flared that hadn't been there before, one that considered yet another impossibility possible.

"You may be right. Let's say that the seven made a pact to never share where to find the source. If they were like my father and

Sterling, they would have wanted to keep the Gifts in their family lines. Anyone else wouldn't have been worthy. Assuming your longevity theory, this Thompson would be the only one left who knows where the source is and how to get there. Somehow, my mother must have discovered that information and hid it in the compass." He stared at the instrument in Alice's hands, now charred and clearly broken. "If you're right, then this really was made for me. I just don't understand how that could be."

"She knew you were meant for great things."

Cade placed his hand over hers, managing to only wince minutely, the compass cool between their touch. "Is that what you think?"

"I think you're getting closer. Keep trying and you may become the most accomplished sailor to roam the seven seas. Or at least the Pacific Coast."

He barked out a laugh, once again stopped short by his injuries. "Ugh, maybe the most bruised sailor rather than most accomplished.

"All the best sailors have a scar or two."

"Or a tattoo?"

She offered him a small smile. "Yes. Now, time for you to get some rest while I retrieve Julep from her pointless task. Tomorrow begins a new adventure."

18

Morning found Alice Ann on one of *Gratia's* bottom berths, snuggled beneath a woven blanket as sunrise glittered through the rectangular portholes across the cabin. Having returned to Larksong late in the evening, drenched to the skin and still recovering from the storm, she and Cade had decided to rest anchored in the bay, rather than return to town and face their family's inquisition. Those conversations were unavoidable, especially now that they had uncovered the key in the compass, yet they could afford to gain their bearings before facing them.

From the berth adjacent, Cade grunted and turned over in his sleep, curling closer against Julep snuggled beside him. Her lashes fluttered before she settled back in with a sigh, her ragdoll clutched tight between them. *Such a lovely portrait*, Alice Ann thought. Lovelier even than yesterday's family photograph.

The tintype remained tucked in Cade's satchel, where he'd stashed it for safekeeping, although she remembered every detail of the tan and ebony image. With Cade's arm encircling her waist and Julep between them, anyone might believe they were a whole, content, and functioning family, rather than the mess they truly were. Last night had triggered complex emotions, thoughts of hope and possibility, fears of those same possibilities coming to fruition. Cade had kissed her. True, it had been during a powerful moment when neither of them knew what may come; however, she couldn't erase the pleasure it awakened. Especially now, her Gift being what it was, she recalled the feel of his hand on her waist and the intensity within his gaze right before he pressed his lips to hers. The kiss had been quick, barely enough to consider on a normal day, but within the wind and rain and the looming threat of death...how monumental it had felt.

It made her wish for another. And another. And another. For all the days of her life.

Cripes and crawdads, she needed fresh air.

Slipping from the berth, she padded across the cabin, and after wrapping in her shawl, climbed the ladder onto the deck. A northwest breeze rushed across the wooden planks, chilly on her bare feet after last night's storms and the low-hanging clouds of the morning. It appeared as though more rain could be headed their way. Cade would know. When he awoke, she would ask him.

Maybe then, he would kiss her again.

Quietly closing the cabin hatch, she rose and nearly ran into Jones swabbing the deck, his bucket of filthy sea water set nearby. "Oh! Good morning, Mr. Jones."

He blinked at her. "Good morning, Mrs. Lark." Then he nodded and returned to swabbing the deck. Winasie, too, avoided her stare from where he repaired lines at the port bow while Thatcher sat high in the rigging, either unaware of her presence or pretending to be.

She wasn't naive enough to believe the crew didn't speak freely once the captain went below. Winasie had likely shared the reason for Cade's unusual orders yesterday and Alice Ann being the inspiration for them. Whether she had been correct or not, her suggestion could have led to all their deaths. Most especially, it could have killed Cade, left the crew without a captain, and she unlikely to be accepted into the role.

It pained her to see the burnt mast above, scorch marks down the mainsail like poisoned veins. She recalled how ominous the veins in Coraline's first husband, Oliver's leg had appeared the day he'd died, the snake bite sending scarlet death throughout his body. How might her life have been had he survived? Other than lacking the existence of her nephew, James, perhaps it would not have altered much. She still would have found herself expecting, still married Cade, and likely still left him.

But why? Her true reasons must have been unbearable for her future self to not have shared them. Whatever the cause, she must somehow keep it from happening again. She could do better. They would find the source, cure her Gift, and redeem where she'd gone wrong all those years ago. Her future self had thought that to be the best way, and she had always trusted herself more than anyone else. She needed to trust herself now.

Everything appeared better in the light of a new day.

Ascending to the quarterdeck rail, she slid her hands along the smooth wood, admiring its lacquer and obvious care. Beneath her feet, *Gratia* swayed peacefully, her anchor holding firm against each wave that lapped upon her hull.

Her breath caught as a pod of Pacific grey whales surfaced not far off the stern. Gracefully, they floated through the waves, headed south to spend the winter and birth their babies. Two at a time, they raised their long, tapered bodies to the surface, spraying water into the sky before their white and grey speckled forms disappeared again. They danced in rehearsed succession—*two-four-six, two-four-six*—as though their movements were a performance and she the eager audience. Every year since arriving in Washington—or those years she could remember—she had watched them migrate down in the autumn then back north with their little-yet-not-so-little calves in the spring. Each and every time, she stood in wonder.

Back in Charleston, whale sightings were less frequent, although she often spied dolphins from her father's boat. Papa had never treated her like a child while out on the water, at least not before he lost his sight and they exchanged the townhouse for a seashore cottage. He had been the one to send her west without a say. But, she supposed, if she had remained in Carolina, she wouldn't have sailed on a schooner such as *Gratia*. Her Papa's sloop only held one lone sail and room enough for two or three men. It was meant for local fishing, not overnight excursions.

Echoed steps brought her back to the present. She turned as Julep tumbled out of the cabin hatch and began to call greetings to each of the crew. First Winasie called back, then Thatcher from above, offering her morning hellos and wide smiles.

Jones paused his swabbing at her approach and leaned a forearm on his mop handle. "Morning, Miss Julep. Your papa still asleep?"

"Yep. He got hurt yesterday, so Mama says he needs his rest."

Jones glanced at Alice Ann without comment, but his stare was enough to shift Julep's attention from another awkward conversation. Her smile glowed brighter than sunrise as she ran over and slipped her hand into Alice Ann's, her opposite grip firm upon her ragdoll.

"Good morning, Mama. Fee Fee and I were wond'rin' whatcha doing out here alone?"

"Your father mentioned Fee Fee yesterday, too. Who is she?"

"My dolly." She held up the fabric-knot-haired doll in introduction.

"Ah, I see. Well, she is a pretty little doll." Alice Ann wondered who had made the creation for her. Even with obvious wear, the stitching was pristine. Most likely Martha, if she had to guess. Coraline couldn't see and Sarah's sewing had only ever been mediocre. Strange to think all four women were now sisters by marriage.

Martha loved Julep, exactly as an aunt should. No, as a *mother* should. And that little girl loved Martha. Alice Ann could tell from the moment the older woman had confronted her on the shore. Martha had cared for Julep when Alice Ann wouldn't, and that responsibility had created an emotional wound deeper than any fishhook barb. Even after becoming a mother to Josephine, she still felt responsible for Julep's well-being and clearly feared that Alice Ann would never be up to the task.

Alice Ann feared as much herself.

"Mama?" Julep jerked her mother's hand, waiting for an answer.

"I came up here to think. I've always found the ocean to be the best place to make big decisions."

"What kind of decisions?"

"Oh, just grown-up things. You don't need to worry about them."

"Like if you want to stay with us? I promise I'll be real good if you stay."

Alice Ann bit her lip. Julep's eyes were flooding and about to spill and she wasn't equipped to handle it. Quickly, she knelt and wrapped her arms around the child, drawing her in close. "Don't cry, Julep. Of course, Mama is staying with you."

"You are?"

"I am." *Please, don't let it be a lie.* Julep sniffled right against her ear, and Alice cringed as she felt moisture drip upon her cheek. *Was that snot?* she wondered in disgust. How did Cade deal with these sorts of things?

No, that wasn't the way to approach this. If she wanted to stay, she needed to get used to these motherly duties, no matter how disgusting. If she could clean fish and dress a deer, she could certainly deal with a little snot.

Julep's arms tightened around her neck. She sniffed again and more wetness—tears this time—moistened Alice's cheek.

Alice Ann drew away and peered into the girl's eyes. "Would you like to play a game?"

Julep wrinkled her nose, sniffling. "Is it the game Auntie Cora says you played when you were girls? The one with the books? That game's boring."

Alice Ann laughed, long and loud, then again when Julep giggled, her tears drying as quickly as they'd come. "No, not the book game. You're right; Auntie Cora does pick some boring stories." She gripped the girl's hand and lifted her to her feet. Together, they turned to the ship's rail and Alice Ann helped her climb on a crate so she could see the waves.

"I want you to look in the water." She pointed toward the western sky where the horizon remained periwinkle blue, the sun's rays warm against their backs. "Earlier, I spotted some whales. I bet if you search really hard, you just might see them."

"Oh, I love the whales! We see them every year when they pass by."

"Ah, but do you know why they pass by?"

"Papa says they're going on holiday."

Alice Ann giggled again. "Your Papa's very silly, isn't he?" Julep nodded, and Alice Ann shifted down onto the crate beside her, both of them searching the waters. "The truth is that the gentleman whales go south to find a belle."

"Like to ring for dinner?"

"No, not a bell, a belle, with a second 'e.' They sound the same but are spelled differently. It means a very special lady who the gentleman whale will buy flowers for then sit on the porch with and ask her to be Mrs. Whale."

Julep raised an eyebrow. "Is that true? Mrs. Whale?"

"In a way. It was my turn to be a little silly."

"You are silly, but I like it." She leaned against Alice Ann and sighed. Together, they sat in silence, watching the water, listening to the gulls cry and the waves lap against the ship's hull. It reminded Alice Ann so much of days fishing with her father that her chest physically ached. Now, Julep had that with Cade, and she knew how precious it could be.

She had underestimated her husband. Over and over, always assuming the worst, figuring there was no chance for him to grow into himself or become better. Yet he had. This child proved it.

Out on the waves, another grey whale broke the surface, spraying water from its spout. "Look, Julep!" she pointed. Despite apparently seeing whales every year, the girl still clapped and squealed in delight. Three more whales joined the first, another pod journeying south together.

Julep spun and called out to the crew, "Look! Say good morning to the whales! Good morning, Mr. Whale!" The crew laughed, Jones and Winasie hollering back their own greetings in unison before returning to their tasks. It sounded like Thatcher might have even grunted something, although he remained in his perch.

Once again footsteps broke her from her admiration as Cade ascended the cabin ladder, still slow in his movements, but appearing much improved. Immediately, the crew stood at attention.

"Morning, Captain."

He nodded. "Morning, men. Winasie, How fares *Gratia*?"

"Better than expected. Nothing to worry over, sir."

"I'm glad to hear it. Once you and Jones complete your current tasks, offload the supplies we purchased and take them into town. After dinner, I'm taking Mrs. Lark and Miss Julep ashore for a few

135

days, so make sure to return by then."

"Aye, Captain."

"Thank you, Winasie. As you were, men," he called across the deck then turned toward the quarterdeck and his family.

As soon as he saw Julep and Alice Ann, he seemed to relax. Shuffling over, one hand pressed to his injured side, he heaved himself up to the quarterdeck. "What are you ladies doing out here?"

"Papa!" Julep leapt off the crate and ran to her father, hugging him around the legs. She grabbed his hand and pulled him over to the rail. "Mama was showing me the whales! There was a whole school of them."

"I believe they're called a pod." He looked to Alice Ann for confirmation. She nodded.

"We saw a pod then, Papa, but not like a pea pod. These were a pod of whales," Julep said seriously and Cade could barely contain his laughter. Alice saw it twitch at the corners of his lips and his eyes, and she found herself admiring the way his long lashes fell when he blinked. Then they rose and focused on her, deep and considerate.

She focused instead on her clasped fingers. She wasn't prepared for those types of smoldering glances. He might be a different man from six years ago, but she was still the same, and she didn't know how to adjust to this new version of him yet. No matter how much she might have enjoyed that kiss.

When she peeked back at him, he was watching the sea. He had plopped Julep back to her bare feet on the deck. "Your mother showed me the whales once," he told her.

"She *did*?"

"Yes. There was a pod of them that time, too. A different kind than these. They were black and white; I can't remember the name. We were standing on the shore and she pointed them out to me and then she said—" He broke off suddenly and rubbed a palm across his scalp then down his face. He shook his head as though to clear it.

"What'd Mama say?" Julep asked.

"She, uh, she...said that whales are some of the most adventurous creatures for being willing to travel so far. Then she said that girls named Julep need to go gather their things so we can travel back home ourselves."

Julep frowned. "I don't think Mama said that."

"Well, she would have had you been there." With a pat to her bottom, he ushered her toward the ladder.

Alice Ann reached for his arm before he could follow. He stared at her fingers rather than her. "Cade, what did I really say? About the whales?"

He shook his head. "Alice, don't ask me this now."

"Please, tell me." When he didn't speak, she squeezed his arm. "Please."

Finally, his eyes raised and in them was that same pain she had seen in Julep's when her daughter had asked if Alice Ann would stay. "You pointed to the whales and said you were exactly the same. You both belonged out on the sea, and Larksong was simply a port of call on the way to somewhere better. Those were the last words you ever said to me. After that moment, I never saw you again."

19

"Forty-eight degrees, twenty-four minutes, fifteen seconds North by one-hundred-twenty-two degrees, thirty-seven minutes, forty seconds West. Just east of Deception Pass."

"You're sure that's where Thompson is?" Cade asked Garrett. He and Alice sat side-by-side on the sofa in Tobias and Sarah's living room with Daniel occupying his other side. The rest of the family sat scattered about, every chair being dragged from the kitchen around the stone fire pit, smoke rising from its center and out the roof hole above it. The only one currently standing was Garrett who paced behind them all, interjecting opinions and increasing Cade's growing anxiety.

Garrett stopped beside the sofa, peering down at his youngest brother. "Have I ever been wrong before?"

"Well, no, but—"

"Then trust me; that's where this guy is." With that, his pacing continued.

"You are certain he is my ancestor?" asked Anwillik. "He could be another man with the same name." Over the past three years, her English had greatly improved, to the point where she rarely required translation anymore. She now sat across from Cade between Tobias and Sarah and Jamison and Coraline, the native woman's agitated fingers clicking her bracelet's cylindrical Howqua shells together. Although she had never said, Cade suspected the trinket may have been a gift from either Quea'Quim or her late husband, Mo'wich. He had never seen her without it.

Her son, Tleyuk, sat cross-legged on the floor near the kitchen stove, silently reading *Uncle Tom's Cabin* while likely listening to them discuss his long-lost relation. Nearby, Julep and Philip read their school primers, part of Coraline's library brought from Carolina; James stacked his blocks; and Josephine lay on a blanket and gurgled. The adults had considered leaving the children supervised elsewhere, but there had already been too much separation over the past days. The children suspected something to be amiss, and it was better for them to hear the truth than craft fantastical worries in their minds.

The combination of Anwillik's shell clicking, Garrett's footsteps, James dropping his blocks, and Josephine spouting baby bubbles was like a slow wedge driving into Cade's nerves. He set his knee to bouncing to try to channel his energy but feared that only contributed to his emotional distress.

"Garrett's right," he told them. "If his Gift says this is the right man, then he's the right man. We need to go to Deception Pass and find out what we can."

"Deception Pass is a death-trap," argued Jamison. "Fr. Lionett says folks talk about its dangers from Seattle to San Francisco."

"It's no more of a death-trap than Cape Disappointment," Cade told him. "More shipwrecks happen there."

Jamison shook his head. "Only because more ships pass through the cape. You have to cross it to enter the Columbia River. No one's daft enough to go through Deception Pass when a safer route exists through Skagit Bay."

"It seems more sensible than testing dangerous waters," Tobias agreed.

Cade wasn't about to be put off. "Don't you think I could handle it? I was almost struck by lightning last night and lived to tell the tale."

Jamison and Tobias simultaneously raised their eyebrows at him. "I treated your bruises this morning," Jamison told him at the same time Tobias said, "I'd rather you not almost kill yourself again."

The storm *had* banged him up worse than Cade wanted to admit. His entire side was covered in black and blue bruises. Oh sure, he'd live, no doubt about that, and the outcome could have been much worse. He didn't need to tempt fate by purposely sailing his ship through dark waters simply to prove he could.

"Maybe it's better to leave well enough alone," Martha said. Her eyes followed her husband from the exterior wall to the bedroom curtain and back again. "The *Oblique* wrecked almost one hundred and sixty years ago. Even if Thompson was only a sailor's apprentice at the time, he would have to be more than one-hundred-and-seventy years old. Maybe he should live out his final years in peace."

"We can't do that." Alice Ann shifted forward in her chair. "The Chinook vilified this man. He promised to return and then he didn't, but we know he could have. His actions have affected every member of Spaärk's family since. He's still in the same area, why didn't he travel a little farther south and find her, unless he didn't want to? We have to ask him why he spent one-hundred-and-fifty-nine years acting like a coward."

"Strange for that sentiment to come from you," Garrett muttered.

"Maybe he couldn't find his way back," Coraline suggested quickly.

Garrett snorted. "He was a sailor. He would have been knowledgeable in wayfaring." He locked eyes on Alice Ann as he said this. She held his stare without comment until finally Anwillik spoke and drew their attention apart.

"It may not have been his doing. What if he did return and Spaärk was not informed?" All attention turned on Anwillik as she fiddled with her Howqua shell bracelet. "All my life, I was told how Thompson abandoned Spaärk. It was the reason our family lost honored status among the rest of the tribe. But if they truly believed Spaärk's child to be fathered by the storm serpent, would they not kill her child or send him away? Why allow an evil spirit to remain and taint the entire tribe?"

"Because they showed mercy?" Tobias offered. "The Chinook once burned this very town to honor their dead chief. To us, it doesn't make sense, but it did to them."

She shook her head, shells jangling. "No. I believe Thompson did return, but the tribe told him Spaärk had died in the storm. That was why our people finally believed her story and allowed her son to stay. They knew the child wasn't from the storm serpent because they saw his father with their own eyes. But Thompson was still a white man and white men were unknown to them then. All they knew was that white men came and afterward an earthquake and a great flood arrived. They were afraid. So, they lied to Thompson to save their daughter and the tribe. Even knowing the truth, however, they still considered my family's blood tainted."

"They couldn't go back on their judgment against you," Coraline said softly. "Otherwise, they'd have to admit to what they'd done."

"But how did our mother know about Thompson?" asked Cade. "Father never told her anything. He treated her like she was a child."

"She didn't know." Daniel said. "She had no idea what was in that compass. All she knew was that it was important."

Cade folded his arms. "And how would *you* know that?"

"Because I'm the one who figured out how to use it."

Silence fell, all the way to the corner where the children sat. Three sets of eyes stared at their book pages, none shifting across the lines. James sprawled on the floor, still stacking blocks, which chose that moment to clatter to the ground.

Cade jolted. "What do you mean, you know how to use it?"

His eldest brother flushed. He rubbed his chest as he circled his neck in either direction and finally stared out the hole releasing smoke into the sky. "Mother and I spent years trying to decipher it in preparation for when I would take over the plantation. She encouraged me to read maps and follow weather patterns, to build and doctor in addition to learning sums and ledgers alongside Father. He thought she was dimwitted, but she listened when he thought she didn't. Then she taught me what she'd learned. It wasn't easy, but we managed. We just couldn't test to see if my theory about the compass worked. We could only hope it did once we found someone with the right Gift."

Cade couldn't believe his brother had had this information the entire time and had chosen not to share it. "You didn't think this would have been good information to share before I was almost struck by lightning and fell off a mast?"

"At first, I didn't know you had the compass. After Mother died, I couldn't very well ask Father where it was, now could I? After he died,

I searched for it without luck. I figured it was gone, so why would it matter to tell anyone? Then when the truth surfaced, and I found out you had it, I resented that she had given it to you and not to me. I didn't think you deserved it."

"You lout!" Garrett grabbed Daniel by the collar, shoving him back into the sofa cushions. "You knew this entire time, over thirty miserable years, that you had the key to our Gifts and you kept it to yourself?"

"Cade knew, too. He had the compass and never told you."

Garrett paused, his chest heaving. He looked from Daniel to Cade, then muttered, "Round one to Daniel," and plunked himself on the floor, glaring into the fire.

"Enough." Jamison spread his hands on his knees and took a deep breath. "Our family's never been perfect, and we've all made mistakes. But we're together now and I want to keep it that way. We're all agreed we want to find the source?" Heads bobbed around the circle. "Very well. Then what's done is done and we move forward. We can't all leave Larksong, but we all have a right to learn about our ancestors. Obviously, Anwillik more than any of us since Thompson is her relation."

Anwillik nodded. "I would like to meet the man who formed my family. Tleyuk, come here, please," she called to her son, who immediately laid his book aside and moved to stand before his mother. She took his hands in hers. "As Christians, we do not follow the Chinook spirit quests; however, your uncle Quea'Quim always wished to see you do so. It would honor him to have you join this journey."

"Yes, Mama." She nodded in approval, said something in the Chinook Jargon that Cade couldn't understand, then Tleyuk moved to stand behind her chair, his hands firm against its back. He had become quite the young man over the years Cade had known him. Ever since Tleyulk had witnessed Julep kidnapped, he had become quieter in speech yet more emboldened in his daily work. At ten years old, he was on the cusp of manhood and determined to prove himself.

"If Tleyuk's going, I want to go, too!" Julep piped up. She leaned forward to tickle Josephine, who rocked on her back, holding her toes and blowing more spit bubbles. A quick tickle to her belly resulted in delighted baby giggles. "See? Jo wants me to go."

Immediately, Jamison countered with, "No, you're too young," when at the same time Cade said, "You're right. You should go."

His older brother's eyebrows rose. "You're taking a five-year-old to meet a stranger in the wilderness?"

"Tell me, James, is it worse than Sterling's circus or the storm last night?"

Jamison paused, then sighed. "Very well. Anwillik, Tleyuk, Cade, Alice Ann, *and* Julep are going—"

"Yippee!" Philip leapt from the floor, his book crashing to the ground, almost on top of Josephine. Martha dashed across the room, scooping the baby up before Philip's boots stomped her flat.

"Philip, sit down," Tobias ordered. "You are not going with them."

The boy glared at his father mid-dance. "But you're going."

"No, I'm not. It isn't responsible for me to be away from you and your mother for weeks or months. We don't know where this quest will lead."

"On an adventure, Papa, that's where!"

"Yes!" Julep cried. "Oh, please, Uncle Tobias, let Philip come."

"Sarah?" Tobias turned to his wife who stared at him as though to ask, *"Whatever could you want?"* He narrowed his eyes and jutted his chin at their son silently saying, *"Do something about this."* With every tilt of their heads and exchange of glances, Cade felt the pit inside him grow deeper. It was the same way he had felt with them on the *Gratia*. Tobias and Sarah knew each other, really and truly *knew* and understood the other person. They could communicate a thought without a single word. Jamison and Coraline had been like that too before she lost her vision. Even Garrett and Martha were growing in their connection, albeit not as strong yet, since their time together had been shorter.

Cade and Alice Ann had never had that. *Never.* Would they ever? True, he'd kissed her. Yes, they'd shared an affectionate moment. They'd almost died together in the storm. But did that mean they were sailing in the right direction or were they as off course as they'd always been? Her forgotten memory meant a clean slate, but what about when all those memories returned? When she knew why she'd wanted away from him in the first place, would she choose it again?

He glanced at her seated beside him and she returned a crooked smile. She reached for his hand and held it, giving a slight squeeze to his fingers. But what did that mean? He couldn't decipher her expression anymore than he could read Jamison's medical textbooks.

"I think you and Philip should go with them." Cade's head snapped back to Sarah at her statement. Tobias's jaw hung agape, a tick visible at the edge of his lips.

"Excuse me, darlin', but you think we should do *what*?"

Sarah rested a hand on her husband's arm, even though he now appeared to want to smack her with it. Maybe Cade had overestimated the understanding between them.

"Tobias, you need to go with them," she said gently. "You have a chance to restore your Gift and I worry that if you don't take it, you will always wonder if you should have. Spending this time with Philip will be good for you both."

"I can't leave you, especially not..." His eyes flicked down to her middle then back to her eyes again. "As things are right now."

She smiled. "We'll be all right. I have an entire town to help me."

"And she'll have me," Jamison said. "You made me Larksong's political leader and God made me its spiritual leader and physical healer. Those are more important duties for me right now, and with Anwillik going, someone needs to look after the Chinook as well."

"Then I shouldn't go either," said Garrett. He poked at the fire's stone circle with his boot toe. "When I brought Sterling's performers here, I promised to care for them and help them find a home. They need me and Martha now more than ever. What would they say if I disappeared so soon after giving them their second chance?"

"That you've sought a life of piracy to take vengeance on the *Arletta*?" suggested Daniel.

"Truly tempting but no. Unless..." Garrett raised an eyebrow at his wife who shook her head. "Sorry, brother. The old lady says I have to stay home." Martha rolled her eyes and tsked. He grinned up at her. "I love you."

She smiled. "I know you do."

And the relational punches continue, thought Cade. How had his most disastrous brother managed to create a satisfying marriage and Cade, who had always played life cautious, felt like he was climbing a mud-covered embankment?

As though in response, James grunted from the corner. He dropped his blocks and released the tell-tale sound of a now-loaded diaper.

Jamison groaned. "Always at the worst moment, eh, James? I say, that child is never going to use the pot. I better change him." He started to stand, but Martha waved him back down.

"I'll take him. Josephine probably needs a changing, too. You stay and keep order to this conversation." Securing the baby against her chest with one arm, she took James's hand with the other and ushered him out the door.

"So, I'm going?" Philip asked.

One final look passed between Tobias and Sarah, and he sighed. "Yes, it seems we're both going."

"Yippee!" More dancing and cheers commenced between him and Julep before they both ran back to their reading corner to whisper about plans for their upcoming adventure.

Once more, Jamison listed off the travelers: Anwillik, Tleyuk, Cade, Alice Ann, Julep, Tobias, and Philip. "Anyone else? How about you, Daniel?"

"Me?" Daniel pointed at himself and Garrett rolled his eyes.

"No. The other fella named Daniel in this room. I say, you won the first round, but your inane questions are going to even the score."

Daniel frowned. "After all that's happened, you honestly want me to go with them?"

Garrett snorted. "We all do. We've had to listen to you moan about your self-imposed mediocrity since we were born. You're going to help find the source of our Gifts, you're getting a Gift, and then you can shut up about it."

"Umm, all right."

"Good. Great. Dandy. Daniel's going. Jamison, please proceed."

"And with that delightful commentary," said Jamison, "I believe we have our travel party. We'll need the rest of the day to prepare, but first—"

"Jamison, wait." Coraline stood, hands outstretched. Carefully counting her steps, she made her way across the circle, Garrett reaching for her hand halfway to direct her around the fire. She stopped before Cade. "Alice Ann?"

"Close." Gently, he took her hands and placed them into Alice's. She stared toward her sister's face yet focused somewhere past it.

"Cora?" Alice asked.

Coraline shook her head, squeezing her sister's hands. "I'm sorry, Alice Ann, but I don't think you should go."

"But I have to."

"Must you? You're making new memories without fainting. That means you're getting better. Erasing your memory worked. You don't need the source."

"We don't know that for sure. My symptoms could come back. If we find the source, I can remove this Gift completely."

"How do you know these memory moments are actually harmful? Cade and Garrett have lived with symptoms of their Gifts for decades—headaches, nausea—and they're fine."

"That we know of," Garrett cut in. "We don't know as much about our Gifts as we would like. That's apparent from all the lies we were told by our father." He counted off on his fingers. "Women aren't Gifted, Gifts don't work on each other, all the other Gifted are dead. All of those 'facts' ended up being a crock of pig polish."

"It's just—" Coraline's voice broke and she pressed a fist to her mouth. "I'm afraid that if you leave again, you won't come back."

"I will," Alice told her. "I want to be here."

"You do?"

Gently, Alice Ann cupped a palm to her sister's cheek. Even though Coraline couldn't see her, Alice still met her eyes. As though, through that moment of contact, she could convince her. "I think my future self might have learned something out in the forest. I promise you, this is what I want."

Could Cade believe her words, trust them? After they completed their adventure, would she still wish to stay? Or would another taste of life away from Larksong reinvigorate her wanderlust? Was she still that whale, here for a season, but then gone in the next?

The rest of the room stared openly at him, expecting some reaction. To whoop and holler with joy? To sputter with disbelief? He couldn't tell what they expected, but their expressions all said the same: not one of them fully believed her. Although, he did receive an encouraging smile from Tobias and Sarah. At least one brother remained on his side.

Alice and Coraline embraced one another, Coraline's eyes closing tight around her tears. "Let this be a new start for you, dear sister, to see what was and choose a different path. I'll pray you and Cade don't lose sight of that."

"You should come with us. The source might be able to cure you, too."

"No, I have my life, and most days, I'm at peace with it. You have your own path to follow and this time, it doesn't involve me." Then she smiled. "We never did well when I tried to be your mother. I'd much rather be your sister and your friend."

"I'd like that, too."

Alice Ann helped Coraline back to her chair and then sat at her sister's feet, her bare toes sticking out from her skirt hem and her copper braids frizzy from the humid Washington air. The scene reminded Cade of the girl back when, the one he fell in love with before he knew any better.

The day they had met, he had given her a tour of Larksong Plantation's grounds while Jamison showed Coraline the library. Alice Ann had leaned against the fence, staring out across the rice paddies, then void of field hands. "It's so...boring," she had complained.

"Well, it is rice."

"I know, but—" She had spun to face him. "It's good you're leaving. Now you can find something better."

In that moment, he'd foolishly believed he already had.

The morning after their family meeting, as Cade stood on shore surrounded by family, the *Gratia* supplied and ready to sail, Jamison gathered them together for one final prayer before departure. Like most days in Washington, today was grey and cloudy, but without rain, providing an optimism to the journey. Melvin, Marie, and Levi were there as well as the Harper children, all fully supportive although the latter somewhat disgruntled that they couldn't join them. From Martha holding baby Josephine to Julep, Philip, and Tleyuk to the adults, no one was forgotten a farewell.

"Lord," Jamison prayed, "protect our family. Give them safe travels. Whatever they may find, or even if they find nothing, help them remember they are held within Your arms. Just as you calmed the sea, calm all apprehension in their hearts, for You walk with them wherever they go. I now ask that each of our travelers adds their own part to the prayer, whatever the Spirit places on your heart."

Tobias spoke first. "Help me to journey beyond the familiar and into the unknown."

Alice Ann stood next in the circle and Cade tensed, wondering what she would say and if it would be appropriate. But when she spoke, her words surprised him. "Give me faith to leave old ways and break fresh ground with You."

Leave old ways...Break fresh ground. How they needed that in their marriage, needed that in their lives. How he needed to cast his doubts aside. "Jesus," he prayed. "I trust You to be stronger than each storm within me. Help me know that all my days, even now, are in Your hands."

Then Anwillik followed with a sweet, "Tune my spirit to the music of heaven, and make my obedience count for You."

Finally, it was the children's turn. Now that Cade knew his wife wouldn't say anything unbecoming, he worried that his daughter might. But Julep simply hugged her rag doll and whispered, "The Lord is my shepherd," while Tleyuk continued, "I shall not want."

When it came to Philip next, he extracted his hand from his mother's and wiped it on his pants before saying, "God makes me lay in the grass, and sometimes it's itchy, so I pray he brings me a blanket to sit on."

They all chuckled and concluded with a resounding, "Amen."

"Oh, Philip," Sarah sighed while her husband laughed.

"Excellent prayer, son," said Tobias. "You must have inherited that poetic wit from your mother."

Sarah glared at him. "Rascal."

"You married me."

"And for that I am glad." Then she kissed him while Philip pretended to vomit on his boots.

Cade said goodbye to his family, one by one. Embraces were exchanged, kind words and haranguing ones, too. Even a few tears, although Coraline mostly maintained her composure. This was the moment he had waited for since his mother had placed the compass into his hands at the age of six and told him to keep it safe. What would they find when they located Thompson? What would it mean for all their futures?

Purposely saving Garrett's goodbye for last, Cade pulled his brother away from the rest of the group. "Are you sure you don't want to come? It seems wrong for me to travel without you now."

"Aww, I always knew I was your favorite brother."

"Only since the *Arletta*. Don't tell the others."

Garrett playfully shoved Cade's non-injured shoulder, although it still caused enough discomfort that he didn't attempt to return the favor. "Chin up. It's a good opportunity for you to know Daniel better. See if we should keep him around or boot him out."

"You're hilarious."

Garrett grinned. "Funny, you think I'm kidding."

20

SEPTEMBER 1, 1859 — TWO DAYS LATER
THOMPSON'S ISLAND, WASHINGTON TERRITORY

"See anyone?" asked Daniel.

"Not yet." From *Gratia*'s bow, Cade peered through the spyglass, its lens affixed on Thompson's Island. He scanned the forest for signs of humanity; however, hundred-foot cedars right down to the rocky shoreline blocked his view. A hawk flashed across his viewfinder, swooping low into the lush undergrowth to catch some rodent or another. Waves lapped lightly against *Gratia*'s hull, but not a soul emerged to greet them, the only ship in the bay.

At least they had supplies aplenty if this entire effort was for nothing. Having no way to know how long their quest would take or what they might encounter along the way, they had docked for a day in Port Townsend to purchase up to a month's supplies. If, after speaking with Thompson—assuming the man was indeed there as Garrett had said—they decided more supplies were necessary, they could return south to purchase them before setting out for the source.

For this moment, however, they needed to find Thompson or all else was moot.

"Let's try the other side of the island," Cade told his brother. "Have Alice Ann bring us around south."

"Right away." Daniel went aft to the helm where Alice currently stood as helmsman. Meanwhile, Tobias waited with the crew to hoist the sails at Cade's command and Anwillik remained belowdecks with

150

the children.

"Hoist sails!" Cade felt the ship pull to port as the crew followed his orders. *Gratia* sliced smoothly through the water, drawing closer to the shore, yet keeping enough distance not to ground her. He swung the spyglass across the tree line, at first not seeing anything, but then...yes! There was something! With the island's next curve, the forest thinned to reveal a red-cedar-hewn canoe at dock and a matching cabin only forty yards or so up shore.

Cade had expected something similar to where Alice lived in the Ghost Forest; however, Thompson's home appeared sturdy and well-maintained. Only one story, the foundation spanned in three separate extensions from a main rectangular lodge, each with sizeable windows—where had he found glass?—and stone chimneys. Thick white chinking filled the space between logs and, although difficult to decipher from this distance, it seemed he had even applied some type of pitch to seal the roof. A double-rail fence enclosed a chicken coop and two goats on one side and separately, a garden ripe with all manner of vegetables on the other. Crouched in the garden, a plump dark-haired woman harvested potatoes. That obviously couldn't be Thompson. A relation, maybe? Or perhaps someone completely unconnected and they had reached a dead end after all.

He lowered the spyglass and returned to the helm. "Well?" Alice asked.

"There's a woman gardening. Short in stature, perhaps fifties in age. Doesn't seem to be a threat, but I'll have Thatcher hoist a white flag to be safe. Bring *Gratia* in another quarter mile. We'll drop anchor and take the gig in."

Another three-quarters of an hour later, the Larks were crowded in the captain's gig, while the crew remained aboard the schooner. The children bounced on the wooden benches, unaware that excitement could sometimes mean danger. The adults had voted to bring them ashore rather than leave them behind with the crew, but as with many decisions, Cade was starting to reconsider his vote.

Especially when a man emerged from the house to join the woman on shore.

The problem wasn't that the man appeared threatening. It was that he didn't. His smooth, shoulder-length white hair glistened in the sun, as though it had recently been soaped and oiled. The shirt he wore was oddly pristine, its color far too white for one living in the wilderness, whom Cade assumed had built his own home and cared for his own land. If Cade guessed at his age, he seemed mid-seventies and fit as a fiddle. He reminded him of an aristocratic Southerner in polished balmoral button boots and tied cravat, a permanent smirk upon his lips as he literally looked down on everyone from his extended height. Except this man wore riding boots rather than balmorals and suspenders in place of a cravat. No standard rifle to be seen. No weapons at all. Not a pistol, not even a woodcutter's ax. As the Larks' gig approached, he strode toward them, hands loose at his sides, seemingly without a care in the world. Even the woman, while set back a pace, appeared unconcerned with the strangers' arrival.

Cade's hands began to tremble, so he gave them something better to do, lest they get out of control. He stood, throwing his leg over the side into the knee-deep water, and with Tobias's help, dragged the boat ashore. They wedged the bow between two substantial rocks and tied a line to one before helping the rest of their party from the boat.

When he lifted Julep, he gave her a firm stare. "You and Philip keep close to Tleyuk, then all three of you stay behind us. You listen and do as we say exactly, understood?" Thankfully, she didn't question him, but nodded and took Tleyuk's hand. "Thank you, Jules."

Wind whipped off the water, first in one direction, then another, similar to Deception Pass's cross-currents not so far away. Even now, they could see the opening to the pass, the tall cliff walls bearing down on either side, the evergreen trees growing straight out from the rocky face. With the children fixedly behind them, Cade, Alice Ann, Tobias, Daniel, and Anwillik hiked up the incline, meeting the man and woman at the top of the ridge.

Now that they stood closer, Cade observed that the woman came from Asian descent, her tapered eyes, beige skin, and silver-streaked ebony braid indicative of the far east. Despite having worked in the garden, her calico dress was nearly pristine, the hem a neat line compared to the many tattered skirt hems in Larksong. Only a few smudges soiled her white apron and, had he not witnessed her digging potatoes, he might have believed she never worked at all.

How could that be, out here on the frontier? Everyone had to haul their own weight, especially those who lived on a homestead alone. Not even children were excluded. No one who strained under a day's work was spared substantial sweat and toil. Based on the Chinamen he had seen in San Francisco, they were pressed even harder into their work, often underpaid and ill-treated. Was that how this woman had arrived here, as Thompson's fancy girl? Assuming this man was indeed Thompson.

"Greetings." Cade raised a hand, quickly dropping it behind his back when he noticed it still shook. "Are you Mr. Thompson?"

The man produced a warm smile, but his eyes remained wary. "People don't stop on this island. They go around."

"We'll be on our way soon. We only need some answers first. We believe one of our family was with a man named Thompson on the merchant schooner, *Oblique*. We're trying to find him or his ship."

He tilted his chin. "The *Oblique* sank over a century ago."

"Yes, but we have reason to believe this man is still alive. You know of the ship, so then do you also know of Thompson?" Tobias asked.

"I go by Linus Wheatley and this is my wife, Mei. We have lived on this island for many years and have had no visitors for nearly as long. I do not know what business you intend with Thompson after all this time, but the man you seek is not a man who wishes to be found. Leave him at rest and take your troubles away from here." He swept a hand toward the garden as he turned away. "You may take some food as you go. I do not like to see any man go hungry. Come, Mei."

Food? How would they find Thompson or the source with a few potatoes? He and Alice hadn't sailed into a storm and nearly died to lose their only lead. Coraline had thought her sister to be well without the source, but what if she was wrong? Alice Ann had said she wished to remain in Larksong. If so, how could he accept the possibility of mere months with her, rather than the lifetime he had worked so hard to find again? He wanted that lifetime.

"Please, sir, wait." He dashed forward to cut off Mr. Wheatley's path back inside. "We're from a town populated by the *Oblique*'s descendants. Hundreds of people deserving of answers that no one else can give but Thompson. We don't wish to interfere with your life. All we want is his location and you'll never hear from us again."

The man paled. "What did you say your name was?"

"I didn't say. My name's Cade Lark. These are my brothers, Tobias and Daniel, my wife, Alice Ann, once of the Owens family, and Anwillik of the Chinook. Our children's names are not ones I wish to give until I know we can trust you."

"No, Cade. If trust is to be made, it must begin with us." Anwillik's fingertips came to rest on his arm, her gentle brown eyes meeting his with a confidence he didn't feel. "Was there not a time when your people needed to learn that same lesson from mine?" She offered him a reassuring smile before extending both hands to Mr. Wheatley. "I am Anwillik and this is my son, Tleyuk. We are the grandchildren of Thompson and Spaärk. For generations, my family has been tainted by the sins of our grandparents' past. Children of two worlds yet feeling as though we belonged to neither. We have no desire for vengeance but merely understanding. To know why."

"Spaärk was your grandmother?" Mr. Wheatley asked.

"Great-great-grandmother, but yes. It is said she never forgot the man who made her a mother. She believed a great ship carried him away, but it was the storm spirits who bound them forever."

This was new information to Cade, part of the story he had never heard. Anwillik, being a Christian, could not possibly believe her grandmother's story to be true, but that didn't mean Spaärk wouldn't have believed it with all her being. Whether it was true or fabricated for effect, immediate recognition emerged in Linus Wheatley's eyes. He, too, reached out a hand as though to take hers, but then let it fall back to find his wife's. Mei barely caught him before his knees gave way and he tumbled to the ground.

Cade rushed forward to support his other arm and together, they maneuvered him through the cabin door. They settled him on the sofa, the furniture piece surprisingly cushioned and its wooden arms freshly polished. In fact, the entire room was more akin to a parlor with mopped wood-plank floors and starched curtains. Decorative seascapes adorned the walls leading to a stone fireplace with a wooden mantel.

The unexpected extravagances reminded Cade of a less-lavish version of Ashley Sterling's office, and he shuddered.

"Tleyuk?" he called. "Please take Julep and Philip outside to play. Leave the door open and stay close to the cabin, no distance farther than the gig."

"Yes, sir. Come on, Julep. Philip, you can choose the game."

"Yipee!" the boy shouted as he ran for the door. "It's boring in here anyway."

Julep, however, pouted the entire way outside. "Not fair. Everything fun happens without me." Her little lip stuck out farther than the San Francisco pier, causing Cade to sigh. Her adolescent years were going to be something to behold.

"Well, she certainly does have my sass," Alice Ann muttered. She had snuck up beside him and now leaned in close, almost causing Cade's mind to unfocus from the task at hand. Almost. The children were gone and time was of the essence.

"All right, Mr. Wheatley," he said. "Be straight with us. You're actually Thompson, aren't you?"

With the man's emotional reaction to Anwillik's heritage, he had made such admissions unnecessary; nevertheless, the words must still be spoken. No one seemed surprised, not even Mei. She rushed to fetch her husband a glass of water while Anwillik lowered herself to the sofa beside him, hands carefully folded in her lap. "Please, tell us. Are you my great-great-grandfather?"

Mr. Wheatley's fingers slipped from his hair, down his face, then his neck. He seemed to fold in on himself, all fight to retain secrecy released in the curve of his shoulders. He nodded slowly. "I was born Linus Arthur Thompson, second mate of the *Oblique*. Cursed with this long life, a hell on earth. Mei is all that makes it worth anything." He accepted the glass his wife handed him and drank greedily. After a drawn exhale, he handed it back and collapsed into the sofa, head in hands, flowing white hair tousled about his shoulders.

"You aren't cursed. You're Gifted," Alice Ann told him. "As are many from our town. Not Gifted with longevity but still able to do the most extraordinary things."

"Or were," Tobias interjected. He and Daniel stood near the open door. "I lost my Gift a few years ago, and Daniel claims to never have had one, although he's more intelligent than probably all of us combined. He was the one who figured out the puzzle that brought us to you."

Daniel flushed at his brother's praise and mumbled a nearly incoherent, "That was hardly the way of it." From outside floated the distinct sounds of the children playing tag, a strange juxtaposition to the seriousness within the cabin.

Thompson exhaled a miserable muttered laugh. "Not cursed, yet day after day, trapped and unable to ever move on? To watch Mei die someday, yet I always remain? That is not what life was meant for. And no, before you ask, I never tried to take my own. I may despise my being but death is in the time of God alone. For some reason, He has chosen to leave me here."

"Perhaps it was so we could meet." Anwillik toyed with her bracelet, white shells and blue glass beads spinning around her wrist. "Why did you break your promise to our grandmother? Our family has lived for generations in grief from what you did."

"That was not the way of it. I did return, but a life with Spaärk was not meant to be."

She exhaled, her shells jangling as one hand rose to her chest in relief. "The tribe sent you away. I knew you were not the villain you must seem."

"Again, you are mistaken. It was Spaärk who sent me away."

"But why? All my life, I heard how you abandoned her. All she wished for was your safe return."

"Do not blame her. She truly was innocent in it all. I am ashamed to say that initially, I did not plan to return for her. After the *Oblique* wrecked, I was thankful to be alive and weary of all we had endured. At first, I did not think on her much. What we had done had been impulsive, and I believed we were better apart. But as time wore on, thoughts of her tormented me night and day. Eventually, I could stand our separation no longer. I packed a bag and purchased ship's passage to California followed by a long journey northward on foot.

"When I located the Chinook, there was hostility from the tribe. They wished to kill me. It was Spaärk's husband who saved my life—yes, she had married in my absence. Her husband knew of me and what we had done. He had defended my son and agreed to raise him, but sided with the tribe that my son's descendants would never have equal status. He had even offered himself to death if her son turned out to be that of a storm serpent—as absurd a notion as it was. For these reasons, Spaärk was bound to him. She would not leave him, nor did I expect her to. Her husband was a far better man than I.

"Unwilling to return home, I returned to the *Oblique*. I wished to remain close to where so many of my crewmates had died and close to Spaärk and my son, even if I could never be part of their family. This island seemed the perfect place to make my home. It was not until over a century later, when I investigated nearby Strawberry Island, that I discovered Mei hiding there. She had escaped from Chinese slave smugglers, bound for the Yukon mines. It took her a while to trust me, and our language barriers were difficult, but eventually, we found a love far greater than I ever expected."

"Where are your babies?" Every person in the cabin jolted, heads whipping toward the open door where Julep stood, hands fisted on her hips. "When people get married, they have babies. Where are they?"

That child really did eavesdrop at the worst times. Cade had no idea how to break her of the habit, but when all this was done, he was going to sit her down and teach her some manners.

"Julep," he scolded. "That's not polite to ask. Now, go back outside and play."

Tleyuk rushed up and shoved her shoulder, pegging her with a victorious grin. "I win!"

She shoved him back and stuck out her tongue. "I don't care 'cause now I have time to hear about Mei's babies."

"Julep!" Cade and Alice Ann both said as one. If they weren't surrounded by people and the air so charged with tension, he would have seriously kissed her in that moment. Few traits looked better on a woman than responsible motherhood. Or perhaps, nothing looked better to *him*.

Mei waved them off with a reassuring smile. "I do not mind. Enough time has passed that I am at peace with mentioning it now." She leaned in to meet Julep's question. "You are right, dear one. I used to have two children, sons ages ten and twelve, Tao and Lin. Along with their father, my first husband, they were the joy of my life. But the slave ship took them from me. Each one passed on from sickness before we crossed the ocean. On Strawberry Island, the ship abandoned me, said they had no use for me anymore, and there they planned to let me starve. I cannot explain why it was, except that I found comfort with Linus. By then, I was too old to have more babies."

"How terrible!" Julep exclaimed.

"Yes, dear one. It was." She gazed at Tleyuk then with such sadness, as though she could see the faces of her sons within the native boy. Then once again, her expression rose and she waved them away. "I believe there's another dear one calling for his turn."

Sure enough, Philip's frustrated cries could be heard outside the door. Julep and Tleyuk scampered off, eager to win the next round.

"You have beautiful children, but why would you bring them here in the midst of strangers?" Mei asked. "Our life is not a dream children would wish to pretend at."

An apt question, Cade thought. How to explain to this woman that, at least for his part, he had brought Julep to help save his failing marriage? "I can only say that they are the reason we are here—to preserve our family. My wife has suffered physically from her Gift, and I worry that eventually those symptoms may be her end. The *Oblique* is the source of our Gifts, and we believe it could take them away."

"So, you want me to tell you where the ship is." Thompson leaned forward, elbows on his knees and index fingers pointed outward. His lip curled. "Then those of you without Gifts can receive them and those with Gifts can lose them. It all seems so simple, doesn't it?"

"Isn't it?" Cade asked.

"No."

"No?"

"If it were, do you honestly believe I would still be here? I would have removed my Gift long ago and be dust in the earth by now. I am sorry to disappoint you, but the *Oblique* is not the source; she is merely the conduit."

"What do you mean?"

Thompson observed him another moment, the two men in a standoff, waiting for one to move. Decades of thought shifted behind the older man's eyes, contemplations he sifted through to decide what to say and what to hold behind. His words came slowly at first then quicker as he fell deeper into the story. "The *Oblique* was covered by a landslide during the storm, trapping me and many of the crew inside. Soon after, my mates began dying of their injuries. Then one day, starved and in a delirium, one of my mates took an ax to the hull, chopping like a madman. It turned out that behind that hull was a cave. The ship had wedged right into it. Had we known, we could have escaped weeks ago. Our mates might not have died or at least not as many as did. We escaped into the cavern, then followed a series of passages to what we discovered as the source. I could probably draw you a map of the path, but I don't remember the exact ending location, only where we began."

"Then take us to the *Oblique*," said Tobias. "We'll follow the same path you did."

"I told you, she is covered by a wall of mud. It was only by sheer luck that she landed at the mouth of that cave and we were able to break ourselves free."

"We'll dig her out," Cade insisted. "There are shovels on board the *Gratia*. We'll work at it, no matter how long it takes."

Thompson's brows rose. He and Mei exchanged a look. "You're going to excavate an entire ship?"

"Why would we need to do that? We only need a hole large enough to climb inside and gain entrance to the cavern. All you have to do is show us her location. You said you live nearby, did you not?"

"I did—"

"Then it will be no inconvenience to you," Cade told him. "Please, for my wife if not for yourself. If you come with us, the source could help you, too."

The older man appeared to want to dismiss them without further consideration. He tapped his fingers together and stared at his toes, then toyed with his hair in that annoying way belles flounce their curls. Why was he fighting this? Didn't he want to rid himself of his Gift as much as Tobias wanted to restore his? If they worked together, everyone could have everything they wanted.

Finally, Thompson nodded. "Until Mei sees heaven, I have no desire to leave; however, I will take you to the ship."

"You will? Thank yo—"

"In two weeks' time."

"Weeks?" Tobias practically shouted. He rounded the sofa to face Thompson head on, but Cade grabbed his arm and held him back. "Easy, Tobias."

"But he said weeks!"

"I did," Thompson nodded. "I assume that once you find the source, you will not return to my island. Is it not right for me to know my own descendants before you take them from me?"

"He's right." Anwillik raised a hand between them, pleading with Tobias directly. "Please listen. You should go, but I should stay. The source relates to your Gifts of which I have none, but this man is my flesh and blood. To him, I have a connection. Soon enough, we will return home, and he will remain here. Is it not right for me to learn what I can of my ancestor before that time comes?"

Tobias shook his head. "We cannot leave you alone with them. If they harmed you, your tribe would tan my hide or scalp me—"

"The Chinook do neither of those—"

"But they are still strangers and what of your son?"

"Tleyuk is nearly a man himself. I will allow him to make his own decision, but I suspect he will choose the more adventurous path. I will be well on my own."

Thompson and Mei were clearly hurt by these discussions, but could they truly blame them? The couple didn't know all the Larks had been through in recent years: being betrayed by a neighboring tribe during the Puget Sound War then enslavement under Sterling and on the *Arletta*. The Larks held their family in tight regard, but strangers had to earn that trust.

"I'll stay with her." Daniel stepped forward, looking around to each of them, and finally resting on Anwillik. "I'll stay here with you. I'll make sure you're safe with them."

She reached out and gripped his hand. "I cannot allow you to do that. You would miss your chance at a Gift."

"I have lived my entire life without a Gift and done few things worth earning one since. It won't make a difference whether I have one now."

"But this time will help you know your brothers better. You have been distant from them for too many years."

"Yes, that is true, but I think..." He inhaled then rushed ahead. "I believe I would like to know you better, too."

Anwillik flushed, her eyes misting over, while their family watched on in silence. Well, except for Mei. She gave a stifled squeak which only seemed to cause Anwillik's discomfort to grow. She dropped Daniel's hand, but to his credit, he didn't sit down nor back away. Rather, he stared her down, almost in challenge.

"Give me a chance, Anwillik. Let me earn your trust as well."

Could it be that Daniel was in love with Anwillik? He hadn't known her more than a few months, but it didn't take long when a match was right.

Or when it was wrong, Cade thought. Perhaps especially when it was wrong. He had been attracted to Alice Ann from the moment he'd laid eyes on her and had fallen in love with her not long after that. It hadn't been until the westward trail that they'd acknowledged those feelings, but once they had, they'd tumbled into them fast and hard. Too hard. Like a landslide burying a ship and killing her crew.

But Anwillik and Daniel weren't him and Alice Ann. They weren't children playing at adult romance. Daniel had been abandoned by a fiancée, Anwillik widowed by a husband. Daniel had led a plantation, Anwillik, a tribe. They were already knowledgeable in the ways of life. Since childhood, Daniel had wanted a Gift, but what he had needed was someone to understand him.

It was all any of them needed, really.

Giving up that chance professed more than any spoken declaration.

Anwillik's eyes met Daniel's, her voice low. "I would like you to stay with me." Daniel smiled, then Anwillik smiled, and then he lifted her hand and kissed it. They both blushed and laughed and Cade couldn't decipher the strange sensation wrestling within his gut. If his brother, at nearly forty years of age and with many mistakes under his belt, could find a woman to adore, perhaps there was still hope for him and Alice Ann.

Somehow, Daniel managed to tear his gaze away and back to Thompson, his expression serious once more. "If Anwillik and I remain here, you know that my brothers will return for us. I still plan to help them dig out the *Oblique*, but you have my word that I will not go a step farther. Is that enough assurance to provide us with the ship's location?"

"It is." Thompson dusted the lint from his trousers and smoothed his hair. "Tomorrow, I will take you to the *Oblique*. Head back to your ship, inventory your supplies, and sleep well. For tomorrow, you dig."

21

Gratia's gentle sway should have rocked Alice Ann straight to sleep that night. It certainly had everyone else in the cabin. Alice Ann and Cade were on the bottom berths, Anwillik on top, and Tobias, Daniel, and Tleyuk had taken hammocks in with the crew. Cade had offered Tleyuk the fourth berth, but the boy insisted he was old enough to stay with the other men. Had he been hired on another ship's crew, at ten years old, he wouldn't have received any special treatment. Meanwhile, Philip and Julep, silly children as they still were, had draped a quilt over the cabin table and slept underneath, laughing and whispering long past Cade telling them to settle down.

No one had asked Alice Ann if she wanted to share a berth with Cade, not even Cade. She wasn't sure when he would or if she should. They hadn't spoken of it, and Alice Ann didn't wish to cause another rift unnecessarily by being the first to mention it.

Sometime after midnight, she abandoned sleep, dressed quickly, and climbed up on deck. Thatcher was on watch at this hour and roosted in his preferred post halfway up the foremast. Behind him, stars peppered the night, constellations dancing beneath a black and brooding sky. Cepheus waltzed with his wife Cassiopeia and Pegasus flew after Pisces, while the sea monster Cetus threatened them all. Her father had taught her of the constellations, said it was imperative for any sailor to know. After he went blind, some nights, she had tried to describe the outlines from the cottage window, but he hadn't been interested anymore. That life was behind him. Yet, he always seemed to have enthusiasm for Coraline's nightly readings. Without fishing to bind them, Alice Ann had felt like little more than a stowaway in her father's heart.

Similar to Daniel with his brothers. Now, he had given up his one chance at a Gift to be with Anwillik. Would Alice Ann be willing to make such a sacrifice for Cade? If he asked her to give up her fishing business to be with him, to let him take the lead, would she be willing to comply? He was the captain of this ship, but did that mean he must be the captain of her life? If he loved her, would he even ask?

Meek and humble, meek and humble, she reminded herself over and over. Almost constantly these past few days. It wasn't in her nature to be the timid creature. She was more akin to a bobcat, snarling at everyone and making them wonder when she would pounce.

"Gnahhh," she grunted in frustration. What if she took the gig and rowed away in the middle of the night? No one would come after her; no one was looking for her right now—

"There you are. I was looking for you."

"Ahhhh!" She reeled around, swinging a fist which Cade narrowly ducked. He leapt out of the way to avoid her boot and fell over a coil of rope onto the deck. Rolling onto his back, he threw his hands up. "Alice, easy! It's me. Only me."

"Well, *only me*, you scared me to death." She slapped her folded arms across her chest and watched him haul himself back over the coil.

"Captain?" Thatcher called down. "Is there trouble?"

Cade waved him away. "At ease, Thatcher. We're fine."

Alice Ann returned to the rail before he could force another soulful expression upon her, as he had been doing with ever increasing regularity. "What are you doing out here at this hour anyhow?" he asked her.

"Same as you, I imagine. Not sleeping."

He joined her at the rail, forearms flat upon the gunwale, standing so close his shoulder pressed against hers. Tingles shivered through her limbs and she wasn't sure if she was allowed to feel them or not. She certainly wanted to.

"Are you worried about tomorrow?" he asked.

"No. That will be whatever it is. I was thinking about Daniel and Anwillik."

"I know. What a surprise. I'm happy for them. It's about time my brother became decent folk, and Anwillik is a treasure."

In the darkness, it was difficult to interpret his expression or the meaning of his words. Anwillik was certainly beautiful with exotic features and a pure heart. She served Christ rather than the native spirits, and her son and Julep were the best of friends. Alice Ann couldn't have blamed Cade if, in her absence, he had found his way into Anwillik's arms.

Alice Ann rubbed a tear away as it dribbled down her cheek, offended by her feeble heart. What was happening to her?

Cade's arm came around her and she leaned into him. "There's nothing to fear," he assured her. "We'll find the source and cure you."

"I'm not worried about that."

"No?"

Surprisingly, she wasn't. She hadn't had a memory moment since her other self removed her memory. The memories that had returned afterward had arrived without fainting, headaches, or other extreme symptoms. She knew they needed to find the source, if only to put everyone's minds at ease, but that seemed low on her list of concerns compared to the rest of her life.

"No," she assured him. "I keep thinking about everyone else. How Thompson and Mei both lost their loves and their children in different ways. Mei never wanted to leave her family, but they were taken from her. And Thompson did leave, then wanted to return, but it was too late." She peered up at him. "Is it too late for us?"

She braced herself for either his familiar cowardice and no response or his newfound courage and a scathing affront. Either seemed possible right now.

Rather, he pressed a kiss to her forehead. "You still enjoy adventures?"

"I suppose so."

"Then come with me to the mainland. I want to show you something."

"In the middle of the night? Won't Thatcher question where we're going?"

Cade shrugged. "He answers to me, not the other way around."

"Intriguing. Where are you taking me?"

"Surprise." He held out his hand, palm up. "I guarantee you'll love it."

After beaching the gig within *Gratia*'s sightlines, Alice Ann and Cade climbed the rocky ridge and into the exotic rainforest. They wound through trees of spruce, hemlock, and maple, their lanterns swinging shadows across dense Spanish moss draped in thick curtains from their limbs. Ferns held branches as tall as children and vines wound up trunks like snakes. Moisture clung to her skin as Cade helped her over a decaying log, its hollowed-out center heady with the scent of fresh earth. The farther they walked, the more wildlife echoed until they were immersed in chirps and clicks and the flicker of wings. A slight growl sounded to their left like a cat purring low in its throat.

"What was that?" she whispered.

"I'm not sure."

She imagined he would shrink back with his usual timidity, but he simply squeezed her hand and pushed a branch aside with the bottom edge of his lantern. She caught the brightness of his smile, firelight dancing in his eyes. "Don't worry. It's not much farther."

"Then what happens? I'll be eaten by whatever that creature was?"

He laughed. "Not if you keep a hold on my hand."

Another hundred feet and they pushed through a patch of fronds onto the curve of a river, its water reflecting a million twinkling stars in the sky above. The trees came nearly to the edge of the water on its opposite bank, creating seclusion within the already sheltered forest. Setting their lanterns on the soft moss, Cade led her down to the water and past its edge, until it covered her bare feet and the tops of his worn boots. Autumn hadn't yet fallen, and the water remained warm against her skin, her skirt hem stuck to her legs, and silt soft beneath her toes.

She squinted into the night. "What is it you wanted me to see?"

"Just wait a couple minutes."

Two minutes passed then three. Then, just as she was about to complain again, the sky exploded.

She screamed as the darkness lit with an array of color, bright as daylight yet appearing nothing like the sun. Shimmering waves of emerald, violet, and a vibrant shade of pink she had never seen and had no word to describe. The air seemed to crackle in its intensity. Bold yet with a graceful gentleness, like nothing she had ever experienced. Beautiful yet terrifying.

She gripped Cade's hand. "What's happening?"

"Nothing to fear. It's only a geomagnetic storm."

"A *what*?"

"A geomagnetic storm. This is a particularly large one; usually they're more localized, but people'll be able to see this all the way back to Charleston if not straight to Mexico."

"But what is it? The sky looks like it's on fire."

"It sort of is. It's caused by a solar flare. Basically, part of the sun explodes."

"And that's not a reason to worry?"

"Not for us. The telegraph companies won't be pleased when the flare's electric current knocks out the lines for a while, but we don't have those around here anyway."

"You're pulling my leg. Electric in the sky? But where's the lightning?"

He laughed again and squeezed her hand. "This storm doesn't need lightning."

The aerial waves continued to shine and glisten, wild colors rolling across his expression. His eyes turned up to watch them, wide and full of joy. Reminiscent of Julep's although the two stood years apart. "This is what my Gift does, predicts this. Usually, I feel like it's small potatoes, what I can do. But then something like this happens and I can't believe I have this ability. It's why I came outside tonight. I could have watched it alone, but you were already awake and I thought...well, it seemed like it would be better to share it with someone prettier than Thatcher." Turquoise waves rippled across his features, so much older than he should have been in her mind, his full beard reminding her that they had truly left childhood behind.

Easing closer, she pressed her free palm upon his sternum, warmth seeping into her splayed fingers, his heart pounding beneath their touch. Her eyes met his. "Cade, will you... Do you think you could...?" Why was this so difficult to ask? She just needed to say it. "Forgive me for leaving and erasing the memories we had. For all the wrong I've done to you. I know it's a lot to ask, but please, Cade, don't you think you could?"

His hand released hers to cuff the back of his neck. "I...Alice...it is a lot to ask."

Fear gripped her. She didn't want to go back to the Ghost Forest after they found the source. She didn't want to be alone. Why had she thrown her life away? If only she could remember. If this family had become as wonderful as she had seen over the past week, for what possible reason would she toss it aside? Yes, the sea had always called her name. Yes, she desired a fishing business, but why should it overshadow everything else? Especially when it was near to impossible for a woman to find her place on a sailing vessel. No one had wanted her when she'd tried, so why hadn't she gone home? Was her pride so great that she couldn't beg for forgiveness?

Well, she was begging now.

"Please." She lifted both arms to wrap his neck, her fingers trailing within his curls. This time, it wasn't for show or to be tempestuous. She genuinely meant every word she said. "Cade, I love you."

"Do you?" he asked, and it was with great remorse that she realized he honestly didn't know if she spoke the truth. Her word meant so little that he doubted a promise that should have been absolutely trustworthy.

That's why I must have left, she thought. *No other secret reason. I was just that selfish, just that horrible to him.* If he couldn't believe she, his wife, loved him, what other reason could there be?

"Cade, look." She twisted off her wedding band and showed him the tattooed *5:5*. "It took me a while to figure out what it meant. I had to read the fifth verse of the fifth chapter of every book of the Bible."

"Why didn't you ask? I would have told you it was from Luke."

"Luke? No, it's from Matthew. 'Blessed are the meek for they shall inherit the earth.'"

"*No*," he insisted. "It's from Luke. It's my favorite verse."

His favorite verse? She had tattooed his favorite Bible verse on her finger *after* she left him? Maybe he had been right about the lark on her wrist. Maybe she was always trying to fly back home, after all.

He took her ring and slid it back onto her finger, running his thumb gently around the band. "Peter had met Jesus for the first time after a long night of fishing failures. He was tired and aggravated, but Jesus told him to try again. In five-five, Peter says, 'Master, we have worked hard all night and have caught nothing, but at your command, I will lower the nets.'"

"And the nets were full to tearing," Alice finished.

"Exactly. 'I will lower the nets' became a prayer I carried. Whenever life became especially difficult, and God didn't seem to ever answer me, those words kept me going. Peter didn't do everything right. But on day one, he understood that Jesus had an answer he couldn't find anywhere else. Peter just had to trust Him and lower the nets."

She pressed a hand to his cheek, his beard coarse against her palm. "Cade." His eyes shifted back to hers. "I love you. Whatever else I may have told you, that's the one thing that was always true."

"You really want to stay?"

"I do." Her lips met his, his arms wrapped hers, and there, bathed in the glow of a solar storm, everything at last was silence.

22

The lights of the aurora danced across the sky above as Cade held Alice Ann in the crook of his arm, both of them in a state of half-dress with only the smooth moss for a bed and his jacket for an inadequate blanket. Her fingers traced circles across his bare stomach, and he felt her lips curve into a smile against his shoulder while all he could do was stare at the exploding sky in a rising state of panic.

We're married. I love her. I'm allowed to make love to her. Then why did he feel like what they had done was wrong?

"That certainly was something, wasn't it?" she said. "I don't remember it ever being like that. Time must indeed make hearts grow fonder."

"It must indeed." He rubbed a hand over his face then hooked it behind his neck to work out the tension quickly forming.

She'd said she loved him. Always had. Wanted to stay. But did she? Or was it another lie? She had lied to him before.

What if this moment of intimacy had created another child? Would that be enough to keep her here? It hadn't before. But would he want her to stay if she didn't really want it?

He needed to halt this stream of whys and why nots and what ifs and maybes before he had one of his episodes and ended up in a quivering lump of raw emotions on the rainforest floor. Alice didn't need to see him like that, not when she was declaring her desire to be with him. He couldn't fall back to that place of cowardice and indecision right when everything was right where he wanted it. He had to remind her why he had been a worthy husband in the first place.

Then it struck him. Why everything felt so wrong. Unlike him, his wife didn't remember their wedding. She didn't even remember the day he had proposed. But she did remember all the times they had been intimate without commitment, including the time that had created Julep.

He had made peace with his past sins, confessed them, and been absolved. Had Alice Ann? He honestly didn't know. Was it a sin to sleep with your spouse if she couldn't remember marrying you?

His chest felt like a stack of spruce logs sat atop it, growing heavier every minute. His heartbeat started to tick up to that dangerous point he knew it would take forever to come back from. One quick breath, then another, then another. He couldn't lose himself in that place right now. Too much was at stake. He had Julep to consider and his brothers. The goal at hand was to find the source. He could not fall apart.

Alice Ann immediately noticed. Of course she did. One couldn't be hip to hip with someone without noticing something like that.

Her hand stilled on his stomach. "Cade? Are you all right?"

"Just thirsty." Easing away—while wanting to bolt instead—he stood, tucked the jacket in around her, and walked down to the riverbank. Pink and emerald danced above, casting light ripples within the water, and reflecting the haggard appearance of a twenty-seven-year-old man whom he could have sworn was actually forty-five.

Dipping his hands in the cool water, he lifted a handful and slurped it down, then cupped another and poured it over his head. He slapped his wet cheeks in frustration. *Lord, show me what to do next. What do I say? How do I lower the nets?*

Alice knelt beside him on the riverbank, dressed only in her chemise, having left his jacket behind near the lanterns. She slipped her fingers into the water, dipping her arms up to her elbows. "Want to go for a swim?" she asked. She looked over her shoulder with a smile, and her burnished curls fell to the side, revealing her bare upper back. His jaw dropped at the sight, but this time, not from attraction.

Jagged black lines crisscrossed her back, peeking up above her neckline and semi-visible beneath the thin cotton of her chemise. Caught up in their earlier moment of intimacy, he hadn't paid attention to anything but the feel of her in his arms. Now, he recognized those marks as being similar to his own lashed scars and wondered how she had earned them.

Tentatively, he reached out, his fingers barely grazing her skin, his throat more parched than before. Confusing his interest for desire, she closed her eyes and sighed, angling her neck to allow him better access. He eased her chemise away from her back and confusion only mounted. Unlike the scar tissue from his own lashings, her scars were smooth, tattooed rather than whipped into existence. Exactly like the lark on her wrist or the Bible verse on her finger.

"Alice, what are these?"

She whirled and, caught off balance, nearly tumbled into the water. He gripped her wrists to steady her then quickly let go. Her eyes widened. "What are what?"

"On your back. There are tattoos, lines resembling lashing scars, but clearly not. So many, covering you waist to shoulder blade."

She cricked her neck to try to see her back and lightly trailed her fingers over the unmarked edge of her shoulder, the only portion she could see. "What do they look like?"

"Like my scars, only in black ink rather than pink or white as mine are. And of which I've received a second round since you left. I took a lashing to protect Garrett when we were enslaved." That made it sound more heroic than it was. Really, he had taken a punishment that Garrett earned, but considering it had been earned trying to steal back Alice Ann's farewell letter, Cade mostly blamed himself. Shortly after, the letter had been burned by the ship's captain, but that didn't mean Cade hadn't memorized every word.

I'm meant for the sea... she had written. And to the sea she had tried to go.

He turned his bare back to her and heard her slight intake of breath in response. The scars didn't appear enormously different than before, there were simply more of them. He felt her fingers trace each line, although with reduced sensation due to the hardened tissue beneath. When receiving them, he had passed out only to awaken and be thrashed some more. The wounds had stung and bled and he had been forced to shovel coal into *Arletta*'s furnaces while praying infection wouldn't take his life before he made it home. If not for Garrett, Josiah, and Melvin, he never would have.

"I know well where *my* scars came from," he told her. "That doesn't explain yours."

Her hands stilled then. Her gasp mixed with a hint of a sob she clearly tried to stifle.

"Alice?" She remained silent. "Alice, what is it?"

Then her touch was gone and she was hurrying back to their clothes, yanking them on as quickly as she could.

He chased after her, grabbed her shoulders, and swung her around. She stood in her chemise and unbuttoned dress, one shoulder drooped, her hands clenched against her stomach. Her eyes reflected distress he had only seen for one reason before.

"Did you have another memory?"

She nodded.

"What did you see?"

"Me. After I failed to go to sea, failed to find a proper job...just failed...I knew I couldn't return to Larksong. There was no one I could turn to. I deserved everything I got, and I deserved to be alone. You told me once that those lashes were what destroyed your courage and destroyed your life. But I destroyed my own life. The least I deserved was what you already had. I bartered for the tattoos, so that your scars would also be mine."

Her eyes shone with tears, their light slowly dimming as the solar storm began to fade, replaced by darkness. Not even the lanterns were enough to restore their glow. "What did I do before that, Cade? What did my letter say? And why would you ever welcome me back? You should have taken the compass and left me behind, exactly as you'd intended." Her tears fell then, and he wrapped her in his arms, holding her close while she silently wept against him.

Alice Ann had never cried with him before. She was too strong and impenetrable. She had cursed, spit fire, and shot pistols in his presence, but never let down her emotional walls. Never would he have imagined she might miss him so much she would trace scars upon the body he loved so dearly.

The lark, the verse, the lines upon her back...every spot of ink told of a sorrowful woman, one longing for love, for hope, for home. For him.

"Tell me what else I did," she moaned. "I can't remember."

Gently, he tilted her chin upward and pressed a kiss to all her tears. "It doesn't matter what you did, Alice Ann. You are my wife and I forgive you."

23

SEPTEMBER 2, 1859 — THE NEXT DAY
THOMPSON'S ISLAND, WASHINGTON TERRITORY

When Cade was five, being instructed to dig out a shipwreck would have had him snatching up a shovel and shouting, "Where is it? Let's go!" The reality of digging out a shipwreck as an exhausted and worry-laden adult, however, was not nearly as glamorous. After four hours of breaking up rock, stomping on fossilized wood, and flinging heaps of mud down the hillside, sweat rolled down his neck and back and his clothes stuck to every inch of him. He had discarded his jacket and rolled his sleeves long ago, the same as Daniel and Tobias, but he would really love to abandon propriety and discard his shirt as well. Tleyuk had and he envied the altered rules available to youth. Then again, perhaps he shouldn't complain too much. Alice Ann worked right alongside him, attacking her piece of the hill with a blunt hoe, while restraining both her dress and summer petticoat. She even wore stockings and boots. A wise decision given the landscape, but unusual for her.

Sweat glistened on her brow and in her hair where it lay slick against her scalp. When she glanced up at him, her cheeks were rosy from exertion. "Cripes, how deep is she? I would have thought we would have hit something by now."

"Who's to say how much mud that wave layered atop her. Could be a while yet." He leaned on the handle of his shovel and glanced at the sky, the sun directly overhead. "It almost makes me wish to be back in the rice paddies again."

"Hold your tongue," Tobias admonished. "Those paddies were twice as hot with four times the pests to bite us. I don't miss Carolina summers at all."

"A fair point," Cade admitted. Those mosquitos had sometimes carried yellow fever and malaria and often left welts as large and red as tomatoes on their skin. Now that he thought on it, today's task wasn't all that terrible.

He turned to his wife. "Alice, you can take a break with Anwillik and the children. Cool off in the water." For most of the morning, Anwillik, Julep, and Philip had collected the excavated debris and separated it by type into piles along the beach. After a few hours, however, the children had grown weary, and the native woman had suggested they rest on the blankets for a morning nap. Of course, both children insisted that only babies needed naps and ran down to splash in the water. That was where they had stayed, chasing fish and collecting polished stones.

Alice Ann's nose wrinkled. "I'm not going to be accused of not pulling my weight. I'll keep on until Mei and Linus bring us dinner."

So, on they dug and dug and dug, ever wondering when the *Oblique* would make an appearance, then wondering if she ever would. Over one hundred and fifty years had passed since her sinking. Perhaps, Thompson couldn't recall the exact location as he thought. After all, he had been inside the ship when she was covered. It's possible the wave had washed them farther down shore than he believed.

Thompson and Mei brought the mid-day meal right on time, rowing across from their island in their red-cedar canoe. The workers all washed their necks, faces, and hands in the waves before saying grace and situating themselves on wide quilts spread across the sand. There was cold smoked goose, crusty bread, and hearty bowls of baked and sliced potato soup, the same taters dug from the garden yesterday. Everything appeared delicious—and tasted it, too—but Cade was simply glad to rest his aching limbs. Alice sat beside him, devouring her meal, crumbs falling all about her skirt. When she finished, she wiped her mouth and leaned against his shoulder with a sigh.

"This is nice," she murmured, eyes closed. "I could sleep right here."

"We still have a ship to uncover."

"Hang the ship. We don't need to find the source. You think I'm fine without it."

"I do, but what if I'm wrong?"

"There are many what ifs in life. We can't let fear drive us. Especially after last night."

"What happened last night?" Tobias asked, one brow crooked with obvious suspicion. His lip curled into a knowing smile.

Cade and Alice glanced at one another, remembering full well what had happened last night, and he couldn't stop himself, he started laughing. Then so did she. They laughed together, full on belly caws, she wiping tears from her eyes with his disgusting shirt and he moving his arm to wrap around her grimy dress. They were both gross, and he was so happy. She loved him, and she was staying with him. Last night, he had finally found the strength to truly forgive her and let everything go. He thought. He hoped. He did.

He *did*.

"I paid my wife some compliments," he told Tobias. "Nothing you need to worry about."

"Except I'm the one you asked to help woo her, which makes it my business."

Alice pinched Cade's leg, still wiping away tears. "You asked him for wooing advice?"

Cade shrugged. "I had to ask someone. You're a difficult woman to appease."

"What's wooing?" asked Julep.

He felt his neck redden. *Oh, Lord, help me through this.* "It means you're too curious for your own good, and curiosity killed the cat, so run along and play. Philip, you, too."

Julep didn't budge. "Why'd the cats all die when they're curious? What about the rabbits or the deer? Why didn't it kill them? 'Sides, I'm not a cat, I'm a little girl."

Alice Ann snorted, releasing another burst of laughter that quickly found them all in stitches. "Julep," she said once they'd recovered, "will you and Philip please collect all the driftwood along the shore? We can make a fire to keep warm once the sun begins to set."

"Oh, boy, fire!" Philip cried and scurried off. The change in attitude was enough to distract Julep into chasing after him.

"Always within our sight!" Alice shouted.

"Yes, Mama!"

"Thank you! Mei, may I have one more scoop, please?" Alice held her bowl out to Mei while not realizing that Cade was staring and trying to keep his jaw off the ground. While *everyone* was apparently trying to.

Once Alice's bowl was filled, Tobias offered her the bread basket and released a low whistle. "What on God's green earth happened to you out in the woods last night?"

"Excuse me, what?" she asked in between bites.

"You're acting like a regular person, all politeness and mothering. It's unnerving. Did Cade say you have a neck like the tower of David?"

Alice almost choked on her potatoes. She grabbed for her tin cup, gulping water. Cade rubbed her back as she coughed. "Excuse me, but *what*? Why would I ever say that?"

"It worked for Solomon. How about cheeks like pomegranate halves? I know that one always gets Sarah all aflutter. No, no, wait, I know what it was. You definitely complimented her hair. Said it looked like a flock of goats?"

"If I said that, I wouldn't have made any headway."

Tobias wiggled his eyebrows. "So, you did then? Make headway?"

"Ugh." Cade slapped his forehead, while his brother grinned like a fool and Daniel rolled his eyes. Alice, having finally recovered from the soup trying to choke her, asked for an explanation. "Back in Charleston, Tobias memorized the Song of Songs to woo women. Apparently, it also works to embarrass brothers."

Daniel stood then and, handing his bowl back to Mei, grabbed his shovel. "Sounds like you both have too much time on your hands. Idle hands make for the devil's work, so let us do something better with them." He offered Anwillik a hand up, but she politely waved him away and began collecting dishes into a neat stack. The women would wash them in the bay then rinse them from the well when they returned to Thompson's Island later that evening.

Cade and Alice both handed her their dishes, then he passed Alice Ann her hoe and reclaimed his dented shovel. The tool's mar must have happened while bashing apart one of the many rocks on the hillside.

As they trudged back up the hill, Alice whispered, "Didn't you memorize any of that book? You didn't want to woo women, too?"

"Never figured there'd be anyone for me to woo."

She pressed a quick peck to his lips. "Well, now there is."

He grabbed her around the waist, their tools clanking together as he kissed her a second longer. "Yes," he smiled. "Now there is."

Another hour passed before Cade's shovel knocked against wood that didn't sound like crumbled branches. It barely dented when the shovel struck it. Carefully, he chipped the packed earth away until he could make out the separate lines of a ship's decking. Giddy with excitement, he excavated until he discovered a hatch. Its metal ring had been rusted away, but the distinct outline of a door remained.

"I found her!" he shouted. "Help me get her open!" In a frenzy, Alice Ann, Tobias, and Daniel hurried over. Between the four of them, they managed to break through the wood and smash the pieces inward. The hatch's remains fell into the opening, revealing a rickety ladder down into a dark hold.

"We're in!" Daniel called back to the others. "Linus, Mei! Come and see."

Thompson and Mei glanced at each other then back up the hill, their expressions apprehensive as they climbed it hand in hand. For Thompson, this moment must have reopened memories long retired and for Mei, likely brought to stark clarity all her husband had endured before she came along. Without the wreck of the *Oblique*, she would have no husband, forever trapped on Strawberry Island; but without the wreck of the *Oblique*, all of Thompson's crewmates would have lived. Likely not as long as he had—without the crash, none of them would have been Gifted—but a good many sailors would have returned home to their families.

Without the *Oblique*, life would be different for them all.

Julep and Philip both cheered, dropping all the driftwood in their arms to trip across the rocky ground. "Maybe there's treasure!" Julep cried. "Come on, Phil, let's go see."

"Not so fast." Tobias grabbed both their collars, holding them back to cries of protest. "We need to be careful the entire ship doesn't collapse around us. You children must remain out here until we know if it's stable. That includes you, Tleyuk."

The older boy frowned at him, but didn't argue. Unlike Philip, who continued to complain until his father threatened him with a solid spanking. Then he stomped down to the water and plopped himself in the sand to pout.

"We are still allowed to go to the source with you, though?" Tleyuk asked. "I wish to go."

Clearly, despite all her talk of trusting her son's adventurous spirit, Anwillik did not expect that response. She paled and offered a flustered, "Tleyuk, you will not stay?" followed by a few words in the Chinook Jargon.

His eyes lowered. "I am sorry, Mama, but it was you who said Quea'Quim would have wished it. I want to go, not only for him, but for myself. To prove I can."

Her bracelet spun, shells and beads all clacking together in a racket. Then she released it and laid a hand on her son's shoulder. They stood at nearly the same height, he soon to be the one who looked down on her. "You are right. If I expect you to be a man, I cannot be sorrowed when you choose to be one. I am proud of you, Tleyuk."

"Thank you, Mama."

She smiled. "For now, I will cherish what time we have. I will stay with you and the children while the men make certain all is safe. Mei, Alice Ann, you will join us?"

Alice visibly balked. Being told to stay behind with the womenfolk wasn't in her nature, not when something more perilous and exciting was available. She folded her arms and opened her mouth in a huff.

But then something peculiar happened. She closed it again and nodded. Laying her hoe upon the hillside, she took Julep's hand, then Philip's. "Be careful, won't you?" she said to Cade.

"Of course." He watched as she and Anwillik ushered the children back to the campfire, collecting their discarded driftwood along the way. Together, they placed it into the fire, sparks popping through the air. Mei gave her husband a kiss and quietly followed.

Tobias leaned in close to Cade. "Seriously, whatever you did to her, keep doing it."

Cade again pictured the two of them together last night under the shining auroras, the feel of her in his arms, and the realization of all she meant to him. "Trust me," he told Tobias. "I thoroughly intend to.

"Will you be able to show us the way to the cavern?" Tobias asked Thompson. The man stared into the darkened opening as though it were the entrance to his own grave. "Otherwise, we can find it on our own."

The older man shook his head. "No, it is time I encountered these ghosts again. Light the lanterns and I will guide you."

The group remained silent as they explored the *Oblique*'s abandoned rooms, first her top deck then her lower. At times it was a struggle to navigate with the ship halfway on her side, requiring more force than usual to shove crates aside and open doors. Nothing stood out as particularly noteworthy from the scattered belongings. One wall had a series of hash marks, counting the time spent trapped aboard; however, no special designs like that of the compass.

Then Thompson introduced them to the crew—twelve skeletons in worn garments laid out in what appeared to have once been the crew's quarters. Each one's hands folded upon their middles, their empty eyes focused on the ceiling, smiles frozen in place. A rectangular piece of wood lay above each sailor's skull carved with a name and a date—gravestones of the fallen. Across the room between two mangled hammocks, a splintered hole had been broken through the hull, large enough for a grown man to climb into the darkness beyond. That had to be the way into the cavern, and ultimately the sailors' way to freedom.

"They were so close," Tobias said. "The way out was only feet away.

If only they'd broken through that wall sooner."

"We didn't know we could." Thompson remained frozen beyond the doorway, its wooden beams framing him at an angle. He gripped either side and stumbled through, Daniel managing to grip his arm before he fell. "Thank you, son." Daniel nodded and moved aside so Thompson could shuffle over to the feet of his crewmates. Sorrow etched his expression, an uncertainty within despair. Horror over his fellow sailors' current physical state blended with guilt over his own survival.

"As I explained earlier, we believed we were trapped in here. We prayed someone would search for us while knowing no one would. The deck hatches were sealed by the mud and all the portholes were covered. If not for Jint's descent into lunacy with an ax, we would have never known otherwise."

Jint must have been the one who broke through the wall and found the cavern. "Did he survive?" Cade asked.

"No. He tried to climb a wall in the cavern via an impassable trail. Fell on the rocks below."

What a terrible fate. To find hope at last only to lose it. His death reminded Cade of devious Ashley Sterling's mysterious disappearance, though they were nearly certain he had thrown himself into a chasm beneath his own abandoned mine. Neither sounded like a pleasant way to die.

"The plaques were Lucero's idea," Thompson continued. He knelt before a body, third from the right end of the final row. The skeleton wore a tattered white shirt and navy trousers, but no boots or belt, the same as all the other men. Thompson rested his fingers over the skeleton's hand and bowed his head. "This was him, Lucero, our captain."

"What happened to their shoes?" Daniel asked.

"We ate the leather. Other than lanterns, we couldn't risk a fire, so we chewed it raw. Toughest, most vile thing I'd ever eaten." A shadow passed over his features, and he shook his head as though to clear it. "It had been Lucero's decision to continue sailing north, to find the Atlantic passage and earn us all fame. He knew he didn't deserve to make it home after he lost half the crew. Always planned to stay behind. Refused to eat if it meant someone else couldn't. He was a good one, Lucero. I was there when we told his wife."

A somber silence descended belowdecks with each living soul no doubt considering his own mortality. These men had begun life no different from themselves, each chasing dreams and planning for the future.

Cade had once believed it would be better to never know what had happened to Alice Ann. To let her fade into the past and move on with his life. Now he knew that he would have never been satisfied taking that path. These men, too, had families who always wondered about them. They had received news of their deaths, but never had the chance to face it, to find the closure that comes from a funeral with a casket and a final viewing of the one they loved. Cade had that with his sisters and his father. Even though his mother's funeral hadn't been in a church, viewing her body laid out on the dining table had still helped him make sense of it.

"We need to send their belongings home to their families," he said.

"Their families are long dead," replied Thompson.

"Those who personally knew them, yes, but there could be descendants who will cherish these items. It could close the door on questions they've had for decades."

"I'll do it," Daniel said. "While you're searching for the source, Anwillik and I will gather and separate what's left. We'll package everything into one of *Gratia*'s crates and can deliver it to Seattle's port on the way home. I have connections in Charleston who will know how to find their families."

"Perfect." Cade grinned. For once, everything was falling into place. "Now, we just need to prepare our supplies."

"And you'll need this." Thompson handed him a folded sheet of makeshift paper. It looked like it had been mushed from grass and wood fibers. Dark charcoal lines created a map through the caverns with landmarks such as *big hole, river, ice cave, hot spring,* and *source.* "I drew this last night when I couldn't sleep. Back then, the path was straightforward. Always veer right. There are few diversions from the trail, although that was many years ago, so there could be more now. Take plenty of candles for your lanterns, food, and water.

The underground is both warm and cold at different spots, but we have a few items you can borrow. Blankets and hats and gloves."

"We have several of those on our ship. Also coats. We didn't know where this trip would take us and wanted to be prepared."

"Wise. It's possible you may find the source after all." He clapped Cade on the shoulder, his dark eyes staring deep into the younger man's. "And when you do, I pray you recognize it."

"Thank you, Linus. Truly. I know this must be difficult for you to relive."

"It is." Then the older man turned and guided them back out of the ship into the daylight and the rumble of a rain shower on the horizon. There was a feeling to the earth that counteracted Cade's usual inclinations, but he chose to dismiss it when Alice Ann ran over to him, her expression aglow.

"Did you find the entrance?"

"We did. Tomorrow, we set out. Within a few days, we'll have found the source and be on our way home."

She smiled. "Home sounds nice."

"It certainly does." Tugging her close, he kissed her long and slow, full of the promise of a future that, for the first time, he was starting to envision.

24

SEPTEMBER 3, 1859 — THE NEXT DAY
THOMPSON'S ISLAND, WASHINGTON TERRITORY

B roken and rotted boards crunched underfoot as Alice Ann
followed Cade through the ship's hull into the darkness of the
cavern beyond. Julep and Philip trotted along behind them,
whispering among themselves, their voices still carrying in the rocky
space and echoing back around them. Tobias and Tleyuk brought up
the rear of the group, both carrying deer hide rucksacks on their
backs, similar to the ones Alice Ann and Cade carried over their
winter coats. The adults also held tin lanterns, their flames sending
firelight over the walls like a thousand flittering fireflies.

The air felt warmer than she had imagined, moist like the
rainforest on the surface above, and before too many steps, caused
her heavy coat to cling to her. She wished she could shed the garment,
but odds were that the temperature would grow colder as they
traveled, especially when they reached the ice cavern Thompson had
mentioned. That meant she would need to carry her coat, and she
couldn't afford to not have her hands free for navigation. There were
plenty of rocks to climb over and skirt around, tight spaces to squeeze
through, and cave streams to lift her hem above to keep from being
soaked. Despite her intense disdain for shoes and stockings, she
would admit that Cade's suggestion to wear boots had been valid.

She watched as her husband easily leapt a three-foot gap, then
reached out and assisted both Julep and Philip across after him. He

held his hand out for Alice Ann and said seriously, "This isn't because I don't think you can make it. I just want you to know I'm here if you need me."

"I know." Gripping his fingers, she accepted his invitation and easily hopped across. She skittered to a halt against him, his chest pressed close to hers, his breath warm upon her face. The dim light carved deep lines through his features, but it could not erase the comfort she found staring back at her.

"It doesn't matter what you did, Alice Ann. You are my wife and I forgive you." He had said those words mere days ago, words that meant everything to her. To him, she still held worth, even after all she had done. She was starting to feel again, to believe that a home and a family might be waiting back in Larksong. After sharing their love under a blanket of stars, how could she not allow herself to feel *something*?

Her sister was happy being married. So were Sarah, Martha, Marie, and Mei, along with so many other women. Couldn't she be too if she tried? She loved Cade. On that matter, she had never lied. She had always loved him in her own way, even when she didn't know what that meant, or how to tell him. Even when she had been too stubborn to show him exactly how she felt.

Which was why she couldn't understand what had happened to once cause such an impenetrable rift between them. Cade adored her, Julep had quickly accepted her, and Coraline had helped her without question. If her desire for new horizons had been so strong, couldn't she have expressed that to Cade? Wouldn't he have understood that she'd needed to escape Larksong, at least for a little while? They had regularly traveled to Astoria for their fishing business, although that had clearly not been enough for her other self. But what about Julep? She was precious and, except for her tendency to eavesdrop, well behaved. How would Alice Ann have ever believed her to be a thorn rather than a flower? It didn't make sense.

"You're overthinking it," Cade whispered against her ear. The rest of their party had crossed the gap and were now hiking away, Tobias leading their navigation with map in hand. Cade must have handed it off to him as they'd passed.

He lightly kissed her temple. "Overthinking is what landed us in this mess to begin with. We're both too intelligent for our own good. It causes us to question."

"I don't want to question. I feel like I probably spent most of my forgotten years doing exactly that."

"You did. I did, too."

"What a pair we make."

"Indeed." A question appeared deep in his gaze, the flickering light revealing both doubt and longing. "Do you really believe that this time—"

"Don't overthink it, Cade." She pressed closer, only their winter coats keeping them apart as she kissed him. His hands slid around her waist to lace beneath her rucksack, his lips keeping perfect time with every move she asked of them. This was where she wanted to be. Right here in his arms, whether that led them into a cave or a ship or into the monotony of a log cabin burning pies and cooking lousy fried chicken for supper. Her other self had been wise to erase her memories. Now she could begin again, without all those mistakes crowding for room.

"Hey, you two!" Tobias called.

"Mama, Papa, what're you doing?" Julep echoed.

With much effort, they pulled themselves apart, both giggling like fresh-faced newlyweds as they lifted their lanterns and hand in hand rejoined the group. Tobias smirked at Alice. "Cade told you your hair looked like a goat again, didn't he?"

She laughed. "Yes. I simply couldn't resist."

He looked between them and smiled; his tone turned serious. "I'm happy for you."

"We're happy, too." And she meant it.

Julep ran up, her curls bouncing under her hood as she gripped Alice Ann's hand. "I'll walk between you and Papa so you don't get lost again."

"Oh, we weren't lost—"

"Just let her think we were lost," Cade hissed. "I don't want to explain the birds and the bees while in a cave."

"Ah, yes, right you are. I have a lot to learn about parenting."

"Admitting I'm correct is the first step, and you're allowed to do that as often as you like." She took a swipe at him but he danced out of her reach, tossing her a cheeky grin as he marched off down the trail again. Alice Ann couldn't help but smile. Since they'd found their way back to one another, Cade had seemed lighter, more carefree, as though a boulder had been lifted from his shoulders and tossed away. She loved this side of him and wondered why she had never noticed it in all their years before. Had it never been there or was she simply not paying attention?

Before too long, a slight turquoise river appeared to their right, growing wider as they walked, exactly as Thompson had indicated. Even so, the cavern became blacker than a moonless night; it felt even more so than the darkness they had traversed on the first leg of their path. Unable to see more than a few feet, it became easier to stumble and overlook low stalactites lying in wait for one of them to bump their skulls. Lest they also misstep into a crevasse, they kept close together, no more than a few steps behind the person in front of them, always following the river's edge.

At one point, Tobias's lantern fizzled out and Philip shrieked, momentarily unable to locate his father in the darkness. Cade, however, was already digging through his pack for another candle and relit the lantern once again. Even so, Philip wouldn't let go of his father after that. He clung to Tobias's hand as they maneuvered between a series of stalactites and stalagmites, some nearly touching in the center. Their smooth watery sides slipped under their fingers as they attempted to use them for support.

"What if we run out of candles?" Philip asked.

"We won't," Tobias assured him.

"But what if we do? What if we get lost and can't find our way out? Will we starve or will we have to cook each other like cows?"

Cade and Alice Ann both halted and turned to stare at the child. "Where are you hearing such tales?" Cade asked.

"Ain't heard. I have a 'magination."

"Well, imagine a little less, son, please. You're scaring me." Tobias gripped Philip's shoulder and turned him back on track. "We won't run out of candles and we won't starve to death. Mr. Thompson said his crewmates made it out of the cave in only a couple days. There's no reason we won't be able to do the same."

Another hour passed, mostly in silence, save for consulting the map and offering direction. Alice Ann joined in the group's cheers when the darkness eventually ended in a narrow hole with dim daylight on the opposite side. After chipping away some extra calcite, they squeezed through into the largest cavern she had ever seen. There was a near collective gasp as they all stared at its immensity.

Stunning was hardly an apt descriptor for this place of beauty. Enchanted, perhaps? Unlike anything she had ever seen or could imagine ever experiencing again. A forest of flora spread out before them, plenty for *Oblique*'s sailors to have eaten after escaping the ship. Tropical Lady Fern, cascading ivory Bear's Head mushrooms, and moss—so much moss! A carpet of vibrant green slipped beneath her boots as she walked toward daylight's source. Hundreds of feet above, a massive sinkhole opened to the grey sky, its perimeter surrounded by rainforest and draping Spanish moss.

The cavern walls rounded up to the opening where a waterfall cascaded down from one side, its water crashing against the rocks below. It spilled away into several small underground streams and the main river which they had been following. The river curved through the cathedral cavern and off to the right into the darkness beyond.

Perhaps the most incredible aspect, however, was what lay within the water and on the smooth grey rocks surrounding it. An effervescent blue glow emanated across everything, its light rippling beneath the surface. Alice Ann recalled a similar phenomenon sometimes appearing in Larksong's shallows on warmer nights. Cade had said the natives believed it was the spirits of the water showing their true form; however, he believed it was simply another beautiful way for God to show himself. All Alice Ann knew was that it wasn't something she had read about in any of her books, nor did the Larks have a Gift for identifying its true nature. It must not be needed in any medicine, otherwise Jamison would surely have known.

She imagined *Oblique*'s crew standing in this same space, cold spray against their faces, oblivious of the surrounding beauty as they stared up at the open sky above them. They would have longed to escape, yet knew there was no way to reach it. Probably arguing amongst themselves about what to do, where to go.

"There must be a way to climb it," one would say followed by the rebuttal of, *"But how?"* The walls were slick and without sufficient footholds. Even if they made it to the top, the ceiling must be crossed to reach the outside. How could they climb across a ceiling? No one was that Gifted nor had those men even received their Gifts by that point. Perhaps this was where Jint had fallen to his end.

Having to continue on through the cavern, wondering if they had left their one chance for survival behind, must have caused such despair. So many of their crew had already died. Had they escaped from the ship only to die beneath a mile of stone?

The Larks' discovery party always had the option of turning around and crawling back out through the ship. Those on the *Oblique*'s original crew had had no such option. She shuddered at the thought of wandering the passageways until their last candle flickered out.

"Are you warm enough?" Cade asked.

"I'm a little chilly." She didn't want to admit that she had been overthinking again, exactly as she had told him not to. It was sound advice and she didn't want to dismiss it so quickly.

"Let's stop here for dinner before carrying on," he called to the group. "Downriver is the ice cave then the hot spring. The nearby lava flows should leave it warmer than fire-heated bathwater. We can stop to soak our feet."

"Yippee!" Julep and Philip shouted together, their excitement echoing off the rocky walls. They both proceeded to call different words into the air, laughing as each one bounced back.

"Let's try animal calls," Tleyuk suggested. "Hold your hands like this then blow through them and it sounds like an eagle." He showed them the correct way to grip their hands then blew, the result a screech almost like an eagle cry. Delighted, Julep and Philip clapped their hands together and tried to do the same. Philip managed to succeed almost immediately, but Julep's attempt resulted in flat air.

"I'll never get it," she pouted.

"Sure, you will. Try it again like this." Tleyuk took her hands in his, repositioning them so she could try again. The result was much the same. "You'll get it. Let's eat and then we'll keep trying."

"Just one more time now?" she asked.

Tleyuk looked to Cade who nodded. The boy turned back to Julep. "Yes, one more time."

"He's a good friend to her," Alice Ann said quietly to Cade as they unpacked their meal of venison jerky, raw green beans, and boiled potatoes. They sat on two dry rocks away from the waterfall, Tobias beside them.

Cade ripped off a piece of jerky, chewing thoughtfully as he watched his daughter play. "He is. Sometimes, I don't wonder if one day, he'll steal her away from me."

"Would it be so bad if he did?" Tobias asked. He tore off a few pieces of venison for Philip and let him run back to his cousin. "Tleyuk's growing into a fine young man."

"He is. From what I've seen, I couldn't ask for better for her. But it's still frightening to think about letting her go."

Alice snapped the ends off a green bean and tossed them aside. "She's not yet six. There's plenty of time for wedding her off."

Cade continued to watch Julep as Tleyuk held her hands in place with his own. She blew through them, releasing a screech. "Papa!" she cried. Her face lit up as she ran to Cade and repositioned her fingers. Tleyuk stood behind her, appearing pleased as punch. "Listen, Papa! I can do it now." She demonstrated with another long eagle cry and the cavern gave a resounding echo. "Tleyuk showed me how."

"That's wonderful, my jewel," Cade said. "Now, let's sit and eat our dinner so we can continue on the adventure." Once they were all settled around on the rocks and munching their meals, Alice Ann considered what Cade had said about having to let Julep go. He still stared at her like today might be that day and he wanted to hold her so tight she could never break free. A glance down showed his fingers twitching against his thigh, a movement Alice Ann now understood was meant to conceal their anxious shaking.

She reached out and, taking his hand, laced their fingers together. He observed her with a sigh. "Time passes quickly, Alice."

"Then we make the best with the time we have."

Alice Ann froze as her words ignited a memory, rushing in to fill another empty part of her mind. She saw herself in a dress the color of plums, bare toes in the surf as she watched a merchant schooner sail by Larksong. She had longed to be a part of its journey and was thinking she might dive into the waves, when Cade met her on shore.

They had stood side-by-side, staring out across the water. "Tomorrow, we leave for Jamison and Coraline's wedding," he had said. "With the priest there and all, I think we should get married, too."

Her hand had immediately shifted to her stomach where a tiny babe, their son or daughter, was growing. When a couple made a baby, they got married. That's what they did.

"I know it isn't ideal," Cade had continued, "but I think we'll do the best with what we have. We have to. For the baby." He knelt and took her limp hand in his trembling one. "I love you, Alice. Will you marry me?"

Her gaze had shifted to the open ocean, to the sinking sun. She raised a hand to shield her eyes and searched for the ship. Like all the others, it had left without her.

Someday, I'll be out there, she had thought. *Someday, all my dreams will come true. Until then, I'll make the best of what I have.*

Then, she had turned back to her fiancé and nodded. "Sure, Cade. If that's what you want, I'll marry you."

25

"Alice, Alice, wake up! We don't have much time."

Alice Ann jolted awake. She had been resting against her rucksack, her head on Cade's knee, hands folded beneath her cheek as she slept. Dinner was over and packed away; the children now tossed pebbles in the waterfall and ran about playing explorer. Tobias rested against his own pack, his hands clasped behind his head, eyes closed and oblivious to the world. Cade's focus, rather, bored into her with urgency.

"Get up," he said again. "We have to leave right now." She sat up and he sprang to his feet, shaking his brother's arm to usher him awake. "Tobias!"

Tobias startled, his voice groggy as he tried to focus. "What's wrong?"

"We all fell asleep and the volcano is erupting."

"The *what*?" Tobias's eyes shot wide open. As though in answer, a rumbling sounded somewhere beyond the cavern walls, the rocks beneath their feet shifting more than slightly.

Even the children ceased their play. Save for the waterfall's splatter, silence filled the cavern as they stared at one other, uncertain what to do. Then everyone spoke at once.

"Papa, what was that?" Philip asked, then Alice Ann, "There's a volcano erupting over us?"

"Only a small one," Cade backpedaled. "Nothing major up top, but there will be lava flows underground."

"Where we are?" said Tobias.

Cade swallowed hard. "Yeah."

"And you didn't know this was coming?" his brother gaped. "I thought you could predict the weather!"

"I should have, but I thought it was nothing. There's always volcanic activity under Washington. I feel it all the time and nothing ever happens, so I've learned to ignore it. But this time is different. Remember when we were along the Platte River and we encountered that tornado?"

"Yes."

"And I had an emotional episode, so you thought I was overreacting and ignored my warnings?"

"Is this time like that?" Tobias asked.

"I think so."

"Hell's hollyhock, we need to get out of here. Children, over here, now!" Tobias slung his rucksack across his shoulders and grabbed his lantern, digging for a new candle and flint to light it. Cade and Alice Ann scrambled to do the same with their lanterns, both managing to get them lit as Julep and Tleyuk rushed over. Philip held the lantern for his father as Tobias was finally able to strike spark to wick and latch the tin door.

The earth rattled beneath them again, the force knocking the children to the ground and tumbling Alice Ann against Cade. Everything shook—it seemed even the waterfall quivered—and the group threw their arms overhead for protection as pebbles and dirt dislodged from the ceiling. Not more than ten feet from where Tobias stood, a substantial piece of stalactite fell, its pointed end slamming into the ground and cracking clear down its center.

"Head for the river," Cade ordered. "Stay against the wall and keep moving."

They ran for the trail Thompson had indicated, Cade and Alice Ann in the lead, followed by Julep and Tleyuk, and finally Tobias with Philip clutched tightly to his hand. It wasn't more than thirty feet, however, that the path narrowed to less than a yard wide, forcing them to move single file. All the while, the earth continued to shift, making an already slick progression even more precarious. Alice Ann tried to keep a hand on the wall for support, but it was nearly impossible. The water-washed rock was slick as ice and the uneven ground constantly threatened to upend her.

"Stay close," she called back to Julep."

"I'm close to Tleyuk," Julep assured her. "He's right behind you."

Alice Ann turned to see, to ask that the native boy switch places with her daughter, when the volcano quaked so terribly that it felt as though the earth would surely crack in two. The force knocked Alice into Cade's back, who dropped to his knees and barely wrapped his arms around a nearby stalagmite to stop himself from sliding into the river. Alice landed beside him, clinging to his arm as the world shifted and swayed. She kicked out her boot to secure her lantern, pinning it against the wall while its flame fluttered and threatened to plunge them into darkness.

Something splashed into the river, another piece of the ceiling no doubt, another piece which had nearly been their end. But then Tleyuk screamed and she knew that what had fallen was no rock at all.

Cade and Alice Ann both turned to where the boy stood, frantically peering into the dark river. He glanced at them for barely a second, shouted, "It's Julep," then disappeared beneath the churning swells.

Cade leapt to his feet, lantern in hand, and attempted to run, while actually sliding, toward the river. He could not lose his daughter again. Sterling had almost stolen her from him and whatever else may happen in this life—whether Alice stayed with him or not—he could not lose Julep.

As he held his lantern out over the river, he caught sight of Tleyuk, his arm firmly around Julep as they bobbed together in the water. She looked up at Cade with a grin that stopped his heart with relief. "I'm all right, Papa," she called. "Took a little tumble."

Alice Ann gripped his arm, her nails digging in even through his coat sleeve. "Thank God," she whispered.

"Yes," he agreed. *Thank you, God.*

At last, the ground ceased its shaking, and the water stilled;

however, the uneasiness inside him didn't lessen. Usually, the physical effects of his Gift would clear once the danger had ended, but this time they didn't. His stomach flipped; his heart pounded. It was as though his anxiety and his Gift were playing in tandem, and he couldn't distinguish one from the other.

From down the trail, a sharp splintering crackled through the cavern. "What was that?" Tobias asked him, while Philip cried fat crocodile tears against his father's stomach.

Cade held his lantern higher, pacing a few steps as he observed a rounded passage that jutted off from the one they were on. From within the darkness emerged a soft orange glow, barely apparent at first then growing brighter.

Alice's grip tightened on his arm. "Is that a lantern? Is someone else coming?"

Amber lit the tunnel in a solid wash, rather than the flickering that a lantern flame should produce. Soon it appeared as the radiance of sunset, that perfect golden hour where no artificial lights are needed. But the hour was too early for sunset and by his estimates, they were still rather far underground. No hand lantern or torch could provide that type of illumination. Nor the amount of heat quickly filling the cavern.

Lord in heaven, help us. He knew exactly what that was.

"Julep, Tleyuk!" he shrieked. "Out of the water!"

Hand in hand, they paddled toward the side as another tremor struck, sloshing the water and causing them to lose their bearings again. They clung to one another as molten amber lava rounded a bend in the adjacent tunnel and rolled down the tube toward them. Another hundred feet and it would slide into the water, its heat boiling anything within, including the children.

Cade and Tobias stared at each other in horror, both realizing the situation's gravity at the same time. "Everyone, cover your ears," his brother shouted. Then he yanked his revolver from its holster and aimed it at the ceiling.

"What are you doing?" Cade grabbed for his arm, but doubled over at the revolver's thunderous discharge, his hands plastered to his ringing ears. His mind swirled and all sound seemed rather far away.

He winced as Tobias fired again, once more at the same target. This time it struck its mark. The rock cracked, crumbling into pieces and splashing into the water below. The boulders now blocked the lava tube, keeping danger at bay for the moment.

Before Cade could breathe again, however, Alice Ann ran past him, dumping her rucksack on the path and screaming Julep's name. He heard the shrill, yet still muffled, call that followed—Julep's sweet voice—swallowed up by rushing water as she and Telyuk were dragged downriver from them. The cave in had stopped the lava, but it had also redirected a current ready to whisk the children away into uncharted darkness.

Cade raced past his wife, shoving her behind him in his desperation to save their daughter. He shed his pack and dove into the restless water, silt and stone and unexpected cobalt luminescence all swirling into an ethereal fog. Like a strange dream rather than this, his terrifying reality. Lungs burning, coat dragging him down, he swam after the children, his hand stretched outward until his ligaments threatened to snap.

"Papa!" Julep's tiny fingers reached for him, her eyes full of fear right before they disappeared into darkness. One final scream emerged as the current tore her away from Tleyuk and sucked her through a gap in the rocks, one too narrow for a grown man but the perfect size for a five-year-old girl.

Cade heard Alice Ann wail from the path behind him but it barely registered. He locked eyes with Tleyuk who hesitated but a moment, as though to say, *"Tell my mother I love her,"* then squeezed himself through the hole after Julep.

"No!" Cade smashed against the wall after him, the wind knocked out of his chest with the force. He tried to squeeze through the hole to follow them any which way he could, but nothing worked. He was simply too big. If he had managed to enter, he would never make it out the other side, wherever the other side might be.

If there was another side.

"Tobias," he screamed. "Shoot this wall!"

Without question, another shot exploded through the cavern, the bullet striking the rock exactly where it should, but only scattered shards into the water.

"Again!" Another shot fired and another failure.

"Again!" On and on they went until one time, Cade ordered a shot and no reply came at all. His ears were ringing, his brain addled, his eyes practically unseeing for the pressure built within his skull.

"Tobias, I said, again."

His brother's voice was quiet, yet echoed in the space. "I'm out of rounds."

"Don't you have more in your rucksack?"

"Yes, but, Cade, those shots barely made a dent. We would need something much stronger—"

Cade slapped his hand on the water, droplets flying. "Then we come back with dynamite! We don't give up."

"We don't have any on the ship. It would take at least a day to reach the nearest mine and at least a day back. By then..."

Cade heard what he was saying. By then it would be too late.

It was already too late.

"Julep..." He banged his fist against the rock while tears flooded his eyes and stained his cheeks and chin and ears. He slammed his palms against the stone, the heat at his neck in opposition with the ever-increasing chill of the water against his torso and legs. If he stayed here, would he freeze to death? Would Julep and Tleyuk freeze or drown first? Or would they encounter another lava tube and...either way, his little girl—his *only* child—would die horrifically. He had done this. Him and his desire to find the source.

Screams tore from his throat. Inhuman cries that felt as though they weren't even part of him anymore. He wasn't here. This was someone else in the water watching his life disappear into a rock wall. Not him. It couldn't be him.

Suddenly, Alice was there in the water with him. Without a word, she sank down to her chin and tried to fit through. She managed to squeeze in farther than Cade had, but not far enough. She resurfaced, her hair stuck to her shoulders and teeth chattering. "I can't," she gasped. "I won't fit. There's nothing I can do. I—"

Her eyes fell empty then, staring blankly at the wall, her lips slightly parted. Another memory had taken control of her present moment, for which he would have normally been grateful, but not right now. He had lost Julep. He needed his wife.

Wrapping an arm around her waist, he gripped the wall and slowly dragged them back to shore. Tobias reached in and helped lift them both out of the water, retrieving blankets from their packs and bundling them up. To Cade's surprise, his eyes were dry. He moved methodically from one task to the next: the blankets, then chewing a bit of jerky, then a drink from the canteen. He relit the lantern that had been knocked over in his haste. Philip huddled against the wall where eventually his weeping quieted to sleep-induced thumb-suckles.

"Cade?" Tobias said.

Cade ripped off another piece of jerky, chewing it while he watched his wife lost in thought. He wondered what part of their life had returned to her. He wondered if it was important or if he'd even care.

Tobias lowered himself to one knee on the ground beside him, one hand resting on Cade's shoulder. His brother appeared haunted. That made sense. He imagined it would be fairly traumatizing to see your niece and your friend's son sucked into a dark, watery grave.

There won't be any bodies, he thought. They didn't even have a priest back in Larksong, so no traditional funeral either. The family would pray for them, of course. You had to pray for their souls, help them out of purgatory and all that. But they were just children; how much absolution could they possibly require?

"Cade," Tobias said again. What could he hope to say that would make this better?

"I'm all right," Cade told him.

"No, you're not."

"No, you're right. I'm not. But what does it matter anyhow? I never have been."

Alice Ann gasped. She jerked upright, the blanket falling away as her fingers snatched Cade's soaked coat sleeve in an iron grip. "I...." Her voice choked, and she swallowed hard. Cade noticed that look in her eyes as one he had never understood all those years ago, but now could recognize for what it was. She was considering if she should lie to him.

199

He was weary of these games. Weary of life. Just so, so weary.

"Tell me, Alice. Honestly, how much worse could things be?"

"So much worse. Oh, Cade, I'm so sorry. I remember the real reason I left."

26

After a childbirth that was quick but, in her mind, not easy, Alice Ann collapsed back in bed, exhausted from the ordeal of forcing a person out into the world. Nothing about that had been enjoyable. No other pain would ever be comparable. Only one word sprang to mind when she saw Cade hold up their freshly birthed child, covered in blood and fluid, and that was *repulsive*.

Yes, repulsive. It sounded an awful way to describe a baby but could anyone truly blame her? The entire process of childbirth was vile and disgusting. How her mother had willingly suffered it three times—how some women did so over ten times—would remain a mystery she refused to solve. One was plenty for her.

Using the corner of a washrag, Cade gently wiped clean their daughter's face, while tears streamed down his own. His smile could have warmed the room; never had she witnessed such genuine happiness in his expression. Certainly not extended toward her, in any case. It made sense. The baby had his dark hair. She had read that animal babies tended to favor their fathers, so the fathers wouldn't grow jealous and kill them out of spite.

As if Cade could harm anyone. He was the most passive coward she had ever known.

He wrapped the child in a blanket and carried her back to the bed. Holding her in the crook of his arm nearest Alice Ann, he maneuvered onto the mattress beside her and leaned back into the pillows. The baby's eyes were closed, her lips puckered in a small "o" as she mewled like a helpless kitten. A rather annoying sound, although up close and cleaned up, she was slightly sweet-looking.

Alice ran a finger over the infant's downy scalp, her fine hair like baby bird feathers. Her head turned at the touch, and she released a sharp cry as her lips foraged helplessly.

"I think she's hungry," Cade said. "Would you like to try to feed her?"

Feed her? Oh. Yes. That was to be expected. Even now, Alice Ann could feel a strange tingling sensation beneath the edge of her breasts, working its way toward the center. Uncomfortable and unwelcome to be sure. But she supposed there was no other way around it. The child needed to eat and no one else could feed her. Even though Sarah had recently birthed Philip, she doubted her sister-in-law would agree to being a wet nurse.

Alice Ann held out her arms and allowed Cade to lovingly deposit the baby into them. Then he scrunched the quilt under her elbow like a pillow and helped adjust her chemise so their daughter could lay comfortably upon Alice Ann's chest. The baby dove into her first meal as a child dives into a candy bin at the general store, eagerly feasting while taking no heed to her mother telling her to take it easy.

Even so, despite the discomfort, there was a strange intimacy to it, a bond that Alice Ann didn't know how to deal with. She wasn't prepared to care about this baby, hadn't thought she would, or would want to. Yet, Cade sat beside her, his arm wrapped around both his girls, his lips caressing Alice Ann's temple while he told her how happy he was. He was such a weakling, but he also loved her, and for the first time, she thought maybe they could create a family after all. It was difficult to believe such a beautiful child came from two deeply wounded people, but here lay the proof in her arms, perfect and lovely as the shore at sunrise.

"What should we call her?" he asked.

She stared down at that angelic face. The baby's hunger now satiated and her tomato cheeks rosy from exertion, Alice Ann knew exactly what to name her. "Julep."

Cade's face screwed up. "Like the medicine or the liquor?"

"Neither. She's lovely as a jewel and her cheeks as bright as a tulip in spring. Therefore, Julep."

"Ah. I like it." He relaxed back beside her, easing his arm away so he could lay his head against her shoulder. He ran a palm over Julep's hair and she wiggled in her sleep. "Can her middle name be Geraldine?"

"Isn't that a little old-fashioned?"

"It was my mother's name."

"Exactly. She was born in, when, around 1815? 1820? It's 1859 now, Cade. Julep needs a more modern name. How about Dina? It keeps the last syllable of Geraldine." A knock sounded at the door just then and Coraline entered, effectively ending the discussion. As usual, Alice Ann had won and Julep Dina was so named.

Cade ran to greet Coraline and grabbed her arm, dragging her to the bed. "Meet Julep!" he cried. Fresh tears lined salt rivulets down his cheeks. "We have a daughter."

Cora sank onto the bed. "What did you say?"

"A girl!" he repeated. "The Larks finally have a girl and she's ours."

One by one, their other family members came to visit, each of them overjoyed at the news. Even Tobias and Sarah, who had recently lost their daughter, Mary Grace, feigned excitement for Cade's sake. Jamison said a prayer over the baby and their new family for blessings and peace.

Once everyone had departed, Alice Ann shooed Cade away, too, insisting that she needed to rest and could tend to herself and Julep while he tended to the chores. Brow furrowed, he kissed her, then the baby, and tucked them both in, promising to be back soon.

What felt like minutes later, Alice Ann jolted awake, her heart pounding as Julep wailed in her arms. The baby cried and cried. And, blast that tiny thing, she cried some more. Where was Cade? Where was anyone? Coraline and Jamison owned the other half of the lodge from theirs, right on the other side of the wall. But maybe they were out with Cade tending to the chores. Had they truly left her all alone? Were they trying to teach her a lesson for being grumpy during the pains of childbirth? How could they leave her with this baby she had no idea how to care for? How selfish could they be?

She tried everything she could think of to calm Julep but nothing worked. The baby didn't seem hungry and didn't want to be bounced or soothed with a rub to the back. When Alice Ann tried to ease from bed to change Julep's diaper, she nearly collapsed to the floor. She caught the edge of the mattress and sank back barely in time. From her waist down, every muscle screamed with torture. A sharp pain ripped through her legs and she leaned back against the pillows, panting. Both arms clutched Julep to her chest, and she scrunched her eyes closed, willing the bothersome creature to be quiet.

That was when an even worse agony emerged. Pain exploded through Alice Ann's brain as voices crowded for purchase within her mind, forcing memories, one after another until they drowned out even Julep's cries.

Her father reprimanding her. "You must do this for Coraline. Think if it were you who had gone blind."

"It's always about Cora. What about my dreams? I would rather gouge my own eyes out than go to this godforsaken land you're sending me."

Her sister belittling her. "You are a lady, Alice Ann Owens, and you need to start acting like one."

"Maybe I'll leave this horrible place, get on a ship and sail away from here. Then you wouldn't need to worry about me anymore!"

Tobias trying to command her. "Stop passing edicts like we're part of your claim," she had screamed at him. "I don't take orders from anyone."

"You're married now, Alice Ann. You had better get used to taking orders."

Finally, Cade crying to her like a baby in the pouring rain. "I don't want to lose you, Alice."

"Then you should have taken my side. I'm sorry I ever laid eyes on you, Cade Lark!"

One after another, memories rammed against her skull in bright flashes, tumbling over one another to make room. Things she hadn't forgotten, but had never bothered to dwell over either, now brought to the forefront. The tiniest details she could recall with perfect clarity. What color dress she wore, how she took her breakfast that morning, every word she'd said and how she'd said it and who she'd said it to. How they responded. Doors slammed. Boots pounded in anger and frustration.

They had been horrible to her. She had been horrible to them.

Everyone had tried to steal her dreams. They *had* stolen her dreams. Her father and mother for demanding that she come to this wilderness with Coraline. Coraline with her infuriating eye disease that meant Alice Ann would always have to care for her. The Lark brothers for mocking her fishing business. Cade for refusing to leave this awful town and travel on their own adventures. They were married. Didn't that mean they were supposed to claim their own life, make their own way? Not cling to the one their siblings had set aside for them. *A man leaves his family and cleaves to his wife*—the Bible said it and Father Lionnet had preached it at their wedding. Instead, Cade bowed to everyone else and denied her all she wanted. Rather than granting her adventure on the sea, he had given her a baby to care for. This child sealed her fate and ensured she would never have the life she was meant for.

Loosening her grip, she let the wailing infant slide down her chest and tumble sideways onto the bed. Julep's face burrowed into the quilt, her cries muffled by the straw-stuffed mattress. Her little arms flailed out to the sides, fingers grasping for survival.

I could let it die, Alice Ann thought. No one would question an infant's death; it happened so often, it was as natural as spring water over rocks.

Julep wasn't yet baptized. If she died now, would she go to hell? Sarah and Tobias's daughter, Mary Grace, had been stillborn, not prayed over until it was too late. They believed her to be in heaven, so why not Julep? Even with as lukewarm as Alice Ann's relationship was with God, she couldn't believe He would condemn a baby.

Although, He might condemn her.

Another memory invaded of herself in green and gold calico, her fingers entwined with Cade's and his warm smile only for her as they exchanged marriage vows. Jamison and Coraline stood near them, her sister appearing more stunned than a blushing bride should. Not as stunned as she would be when she learned that Alice Ann was already with child. Nearly four months along in fact. How disappointed Cora would be, how ashamed. It wasn't anything Alice Ann hadn't expected. Her sister was always disappointed in her for something.

At least Alice would experience something Cora never would. Once Cora went blind, she probably wouldn't have any children. Why would Jamison even want to touch her after that? Alice Ann saw what caring for their father's blindness had done to their mother. Octavia Owens had worked her fingers to the bone to keep enough income. They'd lost their city townhouse, the fishing boat, everything of value. Jamison would experience it, too, and then he would loathe Cora. Alice Ann would be the one with the successful fishing business, the doting husband, and the bouncing baby. Cora might be disappointed in her, but she would also be jealous.

Alice Ann gasped as the memory faded and she found herself back in bed with a writhing infant. The feelings that had returned, those of her wedding, didn't feel like the happiness of a bride. They were painful, desperate, angry, and vengeful. She hadn't married Cade because she loved him, although she thought she did. She hadn't married him because he was the best option, because he certainly wasn't. He wouldn't lead their family and she didn't want him to. For her whole life, she had controlled her future, until her parents and Cora had set her on a different course. At least marrying Cade would trump her sister's happiness.

Julep still squirmed upon the quilt, her face against the fabric and struggling for air. In that moment, Alice Ann desired to let it die. Her life would be better off without it. Being a mother was too much struggle, and she wasn't cut from the mothering cloth. Odds were, she would grow frustrated and kill it later anyhow. Whether accidentally or purposefully. Wouldn't it be better for everyone if she ended it today?

But, she reasoned, if she did, Cade would become petrified of losing her, too, and seal her fate in this wretched town. She needed to keep their daughter alive long enough to either convince him to sail away with her or for Cade to become competent enough to keep Julep alive instead.

And so, Alice Ann lifted that flailing little girl from the mattress and held her gasping against her chest. She fought through the pain to change Julep's diaper, then fed her, and rocked her until her cries finally turned to whimpers. Then, beyond exhausted and equally tearful, she laid the baby down to sleep. When Cade finally returned, sweat-soaked and drained from hauling in fish at the shore, she ordered him to take Julep and go somewhere else.

"What's the matter?" he asked. "You seemed happy when I left."

"That's exactly the matter. You left me alone with a screaming child. I hate this role. I'm not a fit mother."

"Yes, you are. You're a perfect mother." But when he said it, his smile was directed at the infant in his arms, rather than her. "Isn't she, my sweet jewel?" he cooed at the child. "You have a wonderful mama."

In that singular moment, Alice Ann believed she would never hate anyone as much as she hated that child.

27

Fury such as Cade had never known burned through him as Alice Ann finished her story. An episode worse than any bout of anxiety he had ever faced coursed through his blood and bones to every tip of his being. He was soaked in cold cave water, yet felt as though every hair was on fire across every inch of his skin.

Alice Ann had wanted to kill their daughter.

His *wife* had wanted to kill their daughter.

He wished he had left her in the Ghost Forest. He wished he hadn't even met her. All she had done was ruin his life and Julep's.

"You probably wanted this," he spat. "You're probably glad it happened. Now she's gone and you don't have to be a mother anymore."

An expression he could only describe as tortured passed over Alice Ann's face. *Good*, he thought. *She should. It's the same way I've felt for the last six years.*

"You don't know she's dead," she said softly. "We could look for her."

"How? Didn't you hear Tobias? We can't get through to her this way and we have no idea how to find the other exit. It probably doesn't even have another exit. What's worse is, not only did I lose her, but I lost Tleyuk, too. I have to tell Anwillik that my fool's quest killed her only child. My fool's quest to save *you*."

208

"Cade!" Tobias growled.

Cade ignored him. "We should keep moving. After all, we have a source to find. Might as well accomplish what we came for." He picked up his rucksack and his lantern, but made it no more than a few paces before Tobias gripped his arm and whipped him around.

"The source isn't important, Cade. Talk to your wife."

"Is she my wife? Maybe for today but now she knows why she left. It's only a matter of time before she does it again."

"That isn't fair," Alice cried. "I told you things were different this time. I want to be here. I want to stay with you."

"Probably because you can't remember everything yet. When you do, you'll remember this isn't what you want. You made it very clear in your letter and now from your memories."

"That wasn't me. *This* me. Who I am right now. I don't want any of that."

"You know what was worse than finding you gone in a letter?" he continued as though she hadn't spoken. "What came after that. You hadn't even told me you were serious about leaving. You always threatened it, but no one believed you'd actually do it. Then you did, and when you did, you didn't just leave me. You *destroyed* me, Alice. Having you back now, with this false hope, this possibility that maybe things could have been different, it's destroying me all over again. So, when we get out of here, whether we find the source or not, you can go back to the Ghost Forest or wherever you'd like. I'll pay your way exactly as I promised. I'd rather be alone than be with you."

"You don't mean that," she whispered and the sound almost did him in. He didn't honestly mean it, but he wanted to. He couldn't go on living life like this. He couldn't cower from what was right in front of him.

His heart pounded and his hands were sweaty and he wanted to puke, but he had to accept what was. He wanted to run into the darkness of the cavern, break his lantern, and let his feet take him somewhere he couldn't even find himself. That wasn't how life worked, though. You either dealt with the pain or you died and there was no sense in dying when the Lord hadn't called you yet.

Julep *was* dead though. His daughter was dead, and his wife had wanted to kill her. She had thought about it more than once.

Alice gripped his sleeve, and he shook her away. She grabbed it again, and he shoved her back. "Cade, please."

"Alice, no."

She threw herself at him then, arms wrapped tight around his middle, head tucked beneath his chin, her tears smothered within his coat while their wet clothes chilled them both. He didn't want her there, tempting him. While she gripped him in desperation, he stood still as stone, all the while longing to cling to his wife.

He didn't have a wife. That was done now. Gone the second Julep had disappeared through the rock and Alice had told him the truth. This was a conversation they had needed for years. What better time to hash it all out than on the grave of the daughter she'd never wanted.

"Cade, please, just listen. My mind wasn't right, you have to understand how fragile it was. I couldn't handle the thoughts, the memories, that forced their way into my brain. I thought if I focused on my dreams, then maybe I would be content. But I wasn't. I still wanted to slay sea monsters and fight pirates, but what I didn't realize was that I didn't want to do it alone. I wanted you and Julep there more than I wanted the adventure. You were tender and loving to me, things I couldn't see beyond my irritations. It took leaving to realize how I truly loved you. Think of my tattoos. Isn't that proof enough that things changed?"

He sighed. "Then why didn't you come back?"

"I don't think I could. I didn't deserve your selfless love when mine has been so selfish. And I finally think I know why I erased my memories. How could I face your family or mine—how could I face Julep—when I couldn't even confront myself?" Her eyes rose to his, pegging him with irises barely visible in the lantern light. "I wasn't right, Cade. Just like you aren't right. You're the only one who really understands."

He looked away. "I'm fine."

"You're not. I've seen it. I remember now how I used to feel it, too, out there all alone in the Ghost Forest. Imagine all the books I've read, all the knowledge I remember. All the things I know that can go wrong. The people I could lose and every way I could lose them. And now, Julep—" A sob escaped. "The fear paralyzes me as I know it paralyzes you."

His chest felt like it was about to explode. He didn't know what to do! He didn't know what to do! But he had to do something, say something, for he couldn't keep this storm inside himself and hope to survive.

So, he did something, he said something. Something he shouldn't have, but in that second, he couldn't stop himself. He was falling down a well, but the sky was high above and the walls were slick and there was nothing to grasp. When he hit the water, he was going to drown and, God forgive him, he didn't want to die this way.

"Fear didn't paralyze you, Alice. Only a monster would do the things you've done."

"Cade!" Tobias seized his brother by his coat and swung him away from Alice Ann. The unexpected force sent Cade stumbling, and he landed on his behind, scowling up at his older brother's finger, now jabbed in his face. "You are out of line. Don't you see what's happening here?"

He leapt up and pushed his brother away. "Don't you?"

"I do. Clearer than you right now. You're out of your mind, saying things you would never mean."

Angry tears swelled. "Of course, I'm out of my mind, Tobias. My daughter is dead."

His brother's expression eased. "I know. Mine is, too, and I didn't handle Mary Grace's death any better. If you recall—and I know you do—I yelled and cried and cursed things. I blamed Jamison; I blamed Sarah; and I blamed myself most especially. I hurled accusations I can never steal back." He glanced down at his son, somehow still mercifully asleep despite the furious echoes all around him. "Philip still cries from missing his twin. He doesn't understand that's why, but he'll say he's lonely and cries a lot. We hold him and eventually he livens up but you can tell that our comfort only runs so deep. He wants his sister, and there's absolutely nothing I can do to fix that. Ever."

Tobias leaned in, his voice full of compassion. "We all make

211

mistakes, Cade. You're not alone in that. But don't let this be one you can never fix." He pointedly nodded at Alice Ann who stood with hands clenched upon her middle, eyes downcast, and tears streaming.

God, what am I doing? Cade thought. *What have I done?*

He was the head of their family. Yes, Alice Ann had done terrible things, but he had done some, too. She had apologized, tried to ask him to understand. He needed to forgive as much as he needed forgiveness, to lead them into whatever future God had planned for them now that it was just the two of them. They had been married in a church in front of God and with all the saints and angels gathered around. That wasn't something he had ever taken lightly before. He had prayed for Alice to come home; he had prayed for her to stay, and God had given him exactly what he wanted.

Then grief had drowned his good intentions and the devil had stolen his sense and...and...he had no excuses. He had chosen to act this way. Rather than grieve with her, he had grieved at her, wielded his distress and insecurities like a weapon to wound her as deeply as she had wounded him all those years ago.

"Alice, please forgive me."

She continued to sob, her shoulders heavy with a defeat he had never witnessed before. Pushing himself to his feet, he reached for her, but she turned away. Her words clipped through her tears. "You don't need to apologize. You were right. I wanted to kill our child." She spun around, starting to run, but slammed straight into Tobias on the narrow path.

He wrapped her in his arms, exactly as Cade should have done the moment she'd told him her story. "Alice, you did not want this."

"A part of me, in my past, wanted it though, and I got what I wanted. No one should ever forgive me."

"But you don't want that now."

"It doesn't matter. Julep's still dead, isn't she?"

He paused.

"Isn't she?"

"Yes."

"Then it's the same as if I'd killed her. If I hadn't left, if I'd just...Cade shouldn't love me. No one should. I might deserve forgiveness, but I don't deserve love."

She broke away from him then and, snatching up a lantern, fled down Thompson's path.

Alice Ann stumbled through the cavern, more glittering stars of luminescence twinkling off the calcified rocks and shallow pools alike. She tripped and fell and rolled down a slight slope, landing in darkness where she began to bawl. Dreadful wails echoed through the dark chamber, exactly like the monster she knew she was.

His wife's cries echoed back to Cade through the cavern, hollow and soulful, as though her sobs were a choir's lamentations reaching to the cathedral's heights. A song he had never wanted to play, nor one he wished to hear.

Lower the nets, my son. Trust.

Julep was gone, but his wife was here. Tobias and Sarah had lost a child and together persevered. Over five years later, they were stronger than ever before.

Forgive me, Lord. Even with this ache in my soul, show me how to love my wife.

Then he crossed himself, took his lantern, and went to her.

28

Eventually, Alice Ann's sobs turned to silent weeping. She lay in the blackened cavern, curled into herself amid the flickering lantern light. Eyes squeezed closed so tightly that a kaleidoscope of colors swam within her vision.

Humble and meek. Why couldn't she have been humble and meek from the very beginning? Then everything would have been fine. Back then, Cade may have been a coward, afraid of life, but he had been kind and gentle and all the things she never was. Never could be. Why hadn't God killed her along the westward trail or while fishing or in childbirth or alone in the Ghost Forest? He'd so many opportunities to protect the world from her—to protect Cade and Julep especially—so, why hadn't He?

Now her daughter was dead and she'd hardly had a chance to know her. She had spent most of Julep's first two years resenting her, fighting off feelings of wanting her dead or perhaps abandoning her in the woods. She knew she hadn't really wanted that, but she also couldn't explain where those thoughts had come from or where they'd disappeared to. She hadn't felt that way while in the Ghost Forest. If anything, she had missed her daughter terribly and regretted the years she had given up. But she hadn't returned because she'd known she didn't deserve to. How Cade had reacted was exactly how she'd believed he would.

He loved her, yet he resented her. He forgave her, yet his heart was full of pain. He ordered her to go, yet wanted her to stay. Now she understood why all of Larksong mistrusted her and kept their distance. No one wanted her, nor should they. Not after all the awful things she had done in life.

Give Me your pain.

The words called like a command. She heard them clear as day, yet no echo resounded. It was more a thought, a feeling, than an actual sound. Words in her head, only for her. From a Voice she hadn't bothered to listen to for most of her life, not since she was a little girl on her Papa's knee. Before her world tipped upside down and she along with it.

Open your eyes.

Slowly, she raised her lids and gasped. Her fingers flew to her lips as the cavern lit up like glittering diamonds, white ice crystals inexplicably all around and beautiful. They dripped from the ceiling and clung to the walls, some jagged like knives, others smooth pillars rising from the floor. Tiny blue-grey gems covered the floor upon which she sat, allowing her to dig her fingers into them like sand upon the shore. Despite lava flowing through the adjoining cavern, they remained bitterly cold. How was this possible? She had discovered Thompson's ice cave, but what was causing it to glow?

Lower the nets, Alice Ann.

What a difficult thing He asked. Trust wasn't something that had ever come easily to her.

But she had tried everything else and nothing had worked. Most of her life, she had been unhappy, certainly unholy, and all alone, even when surrounded by people. Rarely, had she allowed herself to truly believe someone loved her or to love anyone fully. It was simply too hard. People hurt each other, disappointed one another, sent you off into the wilderness "for your own good."

"It's too hard, Lord. I can't do it. It's too hard."

Not for me.

"I'm not you."

You don't have to be. That's why I'm here. Give up the weight. Cast it over the side. Let me bear the load and then see the catch I will return to you.

Could she though? Could she trust God enough to let Him handle what she hadn't been able to? Trust him with her doubts, her fears, even her marriage and the overwhelming grief that was to come? It would be easier to face it alone.

My yoke is easy and My burden is light. Take My yoke upon you and find rest.

She could do this. Who knew what would happen once she stepped out of this cave, but at least she would know she didn't face it alone.

Her eyes slid closed, and she exhaled a final breath, all her need cast to the One who asked for it. "Ok, Lord. I'm trusting you. At your command, I will lower the nets."

This time there were no audible words, although a simple peace filled her heart.

"Alice?"

She opened her eyes at Cade's quiet call and found herself back in darkness. She could feel the cold ice beneath her hand, but it no longer glowed. Cade's lantern scattered firelight across the grey ice, all its glorious sheen gone. Had she imagined it? No, she had no doubt that everything she'd seen—and heard—had been real.

Cade watched her as though afraid to approach. It was the same as from all their early years together, him always slow to speak his mind or upset her. A struggle for power where only one side fought. Right now, she wanted nothing more than to be comforted by him and to comfort him. For them to comfort each other. To be bonded in a way that no power on earth could break.

"Cade—" That was all she could manage. Her voice broke and she broke again with it. She opened her arms, and he went to her. Slipping across the ice, he fell at her knees.

"Alice, forgive me. Please, forgive me. Those things I said, I never should have. I love you. I want you with me. I've always wanted you with me."

"I know. I'm sorry I didn't love you as you deserved before. But I do now. Please believe me."

Gently, he cupped her cheeks in his hands, her tears falling upon his thumbs. "I do." Then he kissed her softly, sweetly, the type of kiss she wasn't sure they had ever shared. Their first kiss had been the fumbling awkwardness of youthful adolescence. Most after that, either heated with dishonest passion or to placate her erratic moods. Only their night together during the solar storm had come close, but even that did not contain the devotion they now shared. This should have been their first kiss, their wedding kiss, the one that promised life together despite all its trials.

It was only the two of them now. Their family of three had been reduced to a tintype and memories that she prayed would never fade. Somehow, they would have to move forward together until the day when they saw their daughter again in heaven.

"Let's sing something," he whispered.

"I'm not a singer and as I recall, neither are you."

"I'm not. But Martha's singing helped her and Julep survive the circus, so maybe it can help us survive this."

"But Julep...she's—"

"I know." He swallowed hard and for a moment, appeared as though everything hinged on her answer to this request. She had spent most of their marriage denying him. Perhaps there was more than one person she needed to trust with control of the proverbial nets.

"All right, Cade. Let's sing."

Shifting his back against the cavern wall, he pulled her onto his lap and held her close. She rested her cheek against his chest and closed her eyes, listening to the sharp staccato rhythm of his heart. A heart so full of love and beauty that she had never appreciated before with a generosity she had always taken for weakness. She loved that heart. She wanted it to hold hers forever.

Softly, Cade began to sing a church hymn she hadn't thought on since her childhood. His low tones whispered through the cavern, their echoes blending in beautiful harmony.

In all I am, all I can do, I fail your goodness once again
Incomplete, full of nothing, Full of sorrow, pride and pain
Full of anger, full of longing, Full of question, full of stain.

I'm trying to find the reason to the landslide in my soul.
Trying to listen closely, To let You be in control.
When will I know the answer, To all in life left incomplete?
What for this hollow feeling that still looms inside of me?

When she joined in, her soprano wasn't the most melodious and wasn't always on pitch, but with every word, she felt Cade's heart rate descend.

All I am, all I can be, all I'll ever want
Lies right here, held inside, the pool that fills me up.
Yet the waters that I swim in are hard to see from land
When I can't let go of my shore, when I'm afraid of jumping in.

But I know I'll see the glory of the joy that fills my soul,
The Precious Blood that calls me in until I know I must let go.
Let it flow down and consume me, let me truly breathe it in.
Let Your love come and surround me, until I give up and give in.

As the final notes echoed away, they found themselves in silence once again, alone yet not alone. At peace, yet dreading what must come next. Walking back to Tobias and Philip, continuing to the source, then returning home without two of their loved ones. How she was going to miss her daughter's smile, that simple laugh, the way Julep had so readily accepted her.

Tears filled her eyes once again, and she buried her face in Cade's damp coat. She could almost hear Julep's tender calls of "Mama" filling the cavern which made her cry all the harder.

"Alice Ann, be quiet."

"That's not very kind—"

"Shh." In a swift motion, Cade pulled her to her feet and grabbed the lantern, swinging it back and forth across the ice. Two additional tunnels exited the space, separate from the way they had entered.

"What?" she whispered. "What is it?"

"I thought I heard...Hello! Is someone there? Tobias?"

"Didn't you leave him and Philip back—"

"I did, but I thought..." Gripping her hand, he dragged her up to the first tunnel. "Hello! Julep?"

Was he deluded? She wished it could be true as much as he did, but that was impos—

"Papa! Mama!"

218

Cade looked at her. "You heard that, right?"

"Unless we're simultaneously hallucinating."

"Let's hope not." Together, they sprinted down the tunnel, vaulting over rocks and squeezing through tight spots as quickly as they were able. Cade pulled Alice along as much as she pulled him, all the while screaming Julep and Tleyuk's names and hearing the dual calls of "We're here! We're here!"

How was this possible? This wasn't possible.

But then their lanterns swung into a small space, its ceiling not more than five feet high, where a thin ledge ran alongside a river sourced from a three-foot hole in the rock. Large enough to expel the two children huddled on the ledge beside it. Battered, wet, and chilled, but alive.

Alive!

"Papa! Mama!"

Cade let go of Alice and scooped up their daughter, breaking down in a torrent of tears. He clutched her close, both of them shivering against one another. Suddenly, Alice Ann too felt the cold that must have been there all along but wasn't as noticeable before. As much as she longed to join the embrace of her family, she also knew how it felt to be alone. Without Anwillik there, Tleyuk needed someone, too.

Despite barely knowing the boy, she pulled him close and his arms immediately rounded her as though she were his own mother. "You found us," he said. "I told Julep you would. We heard you singing."

She placed her hands on his cold cheeks and peered into his misty brown eyes. "How is this possible? How did you survive?"

"I don't know. We just kept swimming."

"Tleyuk saved us," Julep told her. "When we fell out of the hole, it was dark and cold. I wanted to cry, but he said we just had to wait, like I did at the circus. That Papa would find me. If we walked too far, we might get lost."

"He's an intelligent boy," Alice Ann smiled while Cade continued to blubber and hold Julep tight. What struck her as strange was how his tears didn't bother her anymore. Once upon a time, she would have seen such emotion as weakness; now, she could appreciate it as beauty to behold. Everything appeared different now.

"Should we head back to Tobias and Philip?" she asked. "Gather our blankets and get out of this blasted cave?"

"Yes!" Julep cried, pulling away from her father. She squeezed Alice Ann in an enormous hug, yet quick enough that Alice barely had a chance to wrap her arms when the girl was gone again. *Children*, she thought. *Even after a near-tragedy, they're already flying away. Time really does move too quickly.*

Cade instructed each of the children to hold tight to a grown-up—he with Julep and Alice Ann with Tleyuk—then with lanterns raised, they reversed their steps back through the ice cavern.

"Praise God, you found them!" Tobias shouted as they emerged. He grabbed his brother by the shoulders. "How can this be? We thought they both—"

"I know." Cade shook his head, incredulous. He glanced at Julep who was now regaling Philip with her and Tleyuk's miraculous escape and adventurous rescue. "It's exactly as you said, Tobias, we have to praise God."

29

Eager to be rid of the cavern, they bypassed the previously much-anticipated hot springs and continued on toward the source until late afternoon. Chilled and exhausted, Cade breathed a sigh of relief when the passage started to climb upward, the air warming again as they neared the forest. Up ahead, a pinprick of light appeared, initially causing dread that another lava flow awaited, but this light glimmered with white warmth rather than the burnt orange of the volcano. With every step, it brightened until they could eventually navigate without the lanterns' assistance. Soon, they found themselves at the bottom of a steep mound of mossy rocks, foliage cascading down and around from a round hole above, the sun so radiant they could make out nothing else.

The last landmark on Thompson's map was marked, "The Light at the End of the Tunnel." That must be it. And beyond that, the source. What they had journeyed to and nearly lost their lives for.

Everything had led to this—years spent under their father's thumb, all the lashes and the abuse, their mother's death to keep the compass safe. Finally, they would learn what it was worth. They would have the opportunity to restore Tobias's Gift, remove Alice Ann's, and to offer Gifts to other townsfolk, too, if they so wanted. Perhaps, Cade should remove his Gift, also. While, in the end, he had found it to be a blessing, in many respects, it was also more than he wished to bear. There was something appealing about taking one day at a time as others did, with reliance in God alone and nothing else. He had Julep back and he had Alice; that was all he truly needed.

"Finally. We found it." Alice Ann looked to her husband, then to her brother-in-law, relief reflected in her eyes. "Are you ready?"

"Are you?" Tobias asked. "If this works, you won't have your Gift anymore. You won't remember everything all the time."

She gave a small smile. "It wouldn't be the worst thing to happen to me. What about you? What if this doesn't work? You still won't have your Gift."

Tobias glanced up at the light, expression thoughtful. He had mourned the departure of his Gift for so many years, had complained and even fallen into deep melancholy over his loss. Would he be able to accept the rest of his life, exactly how it was? He had a new baby on the way, a new life to cherish, and all the blessings that were to come from that.

"You'll always be a builder, a fixer, even without your Gift," Cade told him. "You helped build our family and helped restore mine. You should know that means more to me than every day you had your Gift combined."

"Thanks, Cade. That really means something." Tobias turned away from the light, his face cast back in shadow. He rubbed his right eye and blinked. Then he reached for Philip's hand and ushered his son into his side. "If it's God's will, then it will happen, and if not, then I pray we have the strength to accept it. We know that while He heals many, there are many more he chooses not to heal, and both outcomes are still for our good. We might not understand, but I believe we can still be content with what we've been given."

Truer words had never been spoken. True and yet difficult to live.

"Now that Jamison's the leader, maybe you should be the preacher," Cade told him. "You've sure developed the speech for it."

Tobias gave a half smile. "Maybe." He gestured to the light. "Onward and upward?"

One by one, they maneuvered up the final leg of their journey: Cade in the lead with Alice Ann at center and Tobias last, the children in between them. Before Cade knew it, he was pulling himself up and out of the cavern, refreshing air washing over him after the stagnation underground. He helped Julep up behind him, then Alice Ann, who turned back to help Tleyuk.

Even before Cade's vision adjusted from the darkness, he had assumed he should feel different. They had reached the source. Shouldn't he know if his Gift was gone or even if the opposite had occurred, leaving him with heightened abilities? There were no voices from heaven, no lightning storms, or angels singing. What he had taken for the light of a miraculous source appeared to be no more than radiant sunlight. Oddly, he felt exactly as he had.

Blinking, he shaded his eyes and, as the surrounding landscape came into focus, he couldn't believe what he saw.

Truly, absolutely, couldn't believe it.

The hillside sloped down to the shore, calm waters spanning out for about a mile. Amid the waters sat an island and upon the island, a red-cedar cabin with a fenced garden and a chicken coop and below that, offshore anchored a familiar fishing schooner.

They had ended their quest right back where they'd begun.

"Isn't that the *Gratia*?" Alice Ann asked, coming up beside him.

"I believe so."

"But how? Did we take a wrong turn?" She glanced over her shoulder, back into the hole from which Tobias had just lifted Philip through. The boy sat on the moss-covered earth, blinking away the light as the others had.

"Whadaya mean, we took a wrong turn?" he whined. "I don't wanna go back in the hole."

Cade didn't know how to answer. He was baffled himself. Thompson's instructions had seemed clear, but in all the commotion, perhaps they had gone the wrong way. He really *really* didn't want to go back into that cavern.

He offered his brother a hand to help shimmy through the opening and to his feet. Tobias shielded his eyes and quickly realized what the rest of them had. For a solid minute, they all stood in silence, staring at the surrounding landscape. They watched as a figure emerged from Thompson's cabin, too distant to indicate who, but by his sandy-haired appearance, undoubtedly Daniel. The man peered out across the water and Julep leapt up in excitement.

"Uncle Daniel!" She waved her arms overhead and jumped up and down. "Here we are, Uncle Daniel! We made it back!"

Daniel turned without acknowledgement and walked down to the dock where Thompson's canoe was moored. He stepped in and untied the line, then lifted the single paddle and angled the canoe toward the *Gratia*. He must be heading back aboard for additional supplies. Anwillik must still be in the house with Thompson and Mei. The chickens clucked in the yard, their squawks carrying clear across the bay.

Julep yanked Philip up from the ground, shaking him soundly. "Come on, Philip. Help me call for Uncle Daniel. He can bring the boat to get us."

"Good 'cause I'm tired of walking."

"Race you to the bottom!" Without asking permission, she took off down the hill, half tripping, half falling, her bum in the dirt more often than upright where it should be. Philip and Tleyuk immediately raced after her.

"Philip, stop!" Tobias shouted, but his son was past the point of caring, all concerns over wrong turns and cave holes forgotten. "That child..." he sighed. "Pray that I don't break my neck chasing after them. I'd like to hear Thompson's excuse for this wild goose chase." Then he tramped down the hill after his son.

Trying to keep up, Cade also attempted to keep his heart rate at a normal level. He had almost lost Julep in the cave—lost her for good— and with every stumble and every fall, he could picture losing her all over again. A lifetime of tragic endings flooded his head and his anxiety couldn't deal with all the possibilities.

His vision darkened as his stomach swooned. He felt himself being pulled under and wondered if life would always be like this. If, even after surrendering his life and placing it in God's hands, he would still have these feelings, still have these fears. He knew the Lord carried him, so why couldn't his body figure that out?

Then Alice Ann was taking his elbow and threading her arm through his. She held him up as they navigated down the hillside and every time he felt as though he would succumb, she encouraged him with a simple squeeze to his arm.

"I'm here," she whispered, low enough so only he could hear, although the children's racket through the underbrush was loud enough to drown all else.

She is *here*, he thought, and this time, he truly believed that she always would be, every day, every hour until death parted them. She was different. They both were. This journey, the ice cavern, and the source had seen to that.

But not as they'd first believed when they'd opened the compass on that stormy night. None of them had expected this outcome.

He reached out to snatch a tree trunk, bringing them up short. He held on tight to Alice as she skittered to a stop beside him, pebbles bouncing down the hill before her. One glance between them and he knew what she was about to say.

"So, there is no source? Or was the *Oblique* the source all along?"

"What if it's neither? Consider the story of the sea serpent in the storm, the one Anwillik told us. The earthquake shook everything, which caused the tidal wave and the mudslide, which trapped our ancestors underground. What if the storm was actually the source? We know that Gifts don't manifest immediately. It can take years for them to appear. What if the sailors didn't realize they had Gifts until they returned home, so, they attributed them to the ship itself?"

"That makes sense, but the storm raged up and down the coast. Shouldn't more of the natives be Gifted then?"

"We hid our Gifts for years. They could be, too. And, as we know from Daniel, not everyone receives one. A storm isn't something we could ever replicate. There is literally no way to recreate that moment."

Alice Ann turned her attention back to the children, watching as Julep reached the shore, continuing to call out to her uncle. Philip and Tleyuk tumbled out of the shrubs beside her, while Tobias, being now on the cusp of forty, carefully stepped his way along.

"Thompson must have known," she said thoughtfully. "Why would he have sent us here if he knew there was nothing to find?"

"It's possible you may find the source after all," Cade recalled Thompson saying. *"And when you do, I pray you recognize it."*

He released a slow chuckle. Perhaps there were some things you could only appreciate over one-hundred-and-seventy years. "Because he knew we wouldn't let it rest until we saw it for ourselves."

"He would have been right." She smiled. "I happen to like this new stubborn version of you who won't let things rest, even when you should."

"I still worry about everything. About you, especially, and Julep. I doubt that will ever change." He raised his hand to caress her cheek, her skin now warm from the sun rather than chilled from the cavern. Feeling more alive than ever before, yet how much longer would he have her to hold onto? "I so wanted to find the source for you."

She covered his hand with hers, then turned her head to press a kiss to his palm. "Cade, I could roll down this hill, break my neck, and die right now. Do you realize that?"

"I didn't, but thanks for giving me something else to worry over."

She shook her head. "I can't stop your worrying, but I want you to trust that my life isn't in your hands. I can't rid myself of this Gift. Maybe that means I'll be dead by next year. There's nothing we can do about that now. Can't we simply treasure what we have and pray we might be granted more of it?"

Tears welling, he nodded, his throat tight. Four years ago, Alice Ann would have sniffed at his crying and called him a milksop. Today, she silently wiped his tears away with a smile...and a few of her own.

Arm in arm, they descended the rest of the way to the shore. At last, Daniel had noticed the children's dancing and now stood in the canoe, hands waving overhead, the boat swaying precariously beneath him. Bending low for balance, he called toward the house. Within a minute, three additional figures had emerged, one man and two women. All three rushed toward the dock with one tan-skinned woman running much faster to see her son. Daniel brought the canoe about and back to the dock and Anwillik took his hand to step inside. She sat against the bow and peered out toward the group, waving with all her vigor.

Soon, she would be reunited with Tleyuk, unaware that such a reunion had almost never been. Cade and Tobias would be reunited with their brother and hear what had transpired during their brief time apart. Then, *Gratia* would sail home to bring all the Larks together once more, to finally be the family their mother had envisioned. The one they should have always had. Amidst the anxiety, the worries and loss, they would still sing their gratitude as a lark sings on the breeze.

Behind them, the mountain rumbled, threatening to strike again, but Cade knew it wouldn't be where they were. Storms would come again, of course, over and over. They would weather them through the grace of God, through love and unending forgiveness.

As he and Alice reached the others, he declared it to be a beautiful day. "One of the best since we've been in the northwest, if I had to wager."

Tobias glanced at the sky. "No storms?"

"Not today." Cade squeezed Julep's shoulder, just enough to stop her bouncing. "Should we head home to Larksong?"

She peered up at him in excitement. "Mama, too?"

He wrapped his arm around Alice Ann and smiled. "What do you say, wife? Ready for a little less adventure?"

"Hear, hear. As long as we're together, I think perfectly ordinary will suit me just fine."

EPILOGUE

SEPTEMBER 1870
LARKSONG, WASHINGTON TERRITORY

I t was hard to believe over ten years had passed since that day. Ten years and a war. The country fell apart and put itself back together and none of them were there to see it. Alice Ann's papa, mama, and Mercy escaped Charleston only weeks before Fort Sumter was taken in April of '61, heading for relative safety in Apple Creek, Missouri. Later they learned that the former Larksong Plantation had been requisitioned by Southern troops in '62, turned into a hospital, and subsequently burned to the ground by the North. In August of that same year, Mei sent word of Thompson's death, quiet and in his sleep. He had been ready. She buried him on the island where they had built their home and, after moving to Larksong, mourned a life well lived.

No one knew why Thompson's Gift finally failed without warning, but Mei told them that his last years were far and away their happiest together. That final night before he closed his eyes, he had turned to her and said, "It's been a good life, hasn't it, Mei?"

She had kissed him and replied, "Yes, my love. Good indeed."

To no one's surprise, Daniel proposed to Anwillik on Christmas Eve the same year they returned from Thompson's Island. In the spring, they were married at Stella Maris Mission and within five years, had three little ones running underfoot.

Alice Ann still remembered everything, but she chose to take each day as it arrived. Cade could better control his sensitivities, but there were still days when undue panic got the better of him. Every virtue had its vice. Every Gift had its weakness.

Were any of them more worthy to claim a Gift than anyone else? Who was to know? All they knew was that life was better for having received these talents. They would do their best to use them for whatever God called them to.

For years, Alice Ann and Cade sailed the fishing schooner along the coast with Julep and often Tleyuk at their sides. They sold fish and oysters, although they never became rich and never saw vast far-off places. Alice Ann never fought a pirate or a sea monster. As it turned out, she no longer minded.

There were still times, of course, when she imagined what could have been within those dreams that touched the sky. But, even in the midst of life's storms, the stars continued to glow brighter with every day—and every blessing—God bestowed upon them.

Blessings aptly named Julep, Simon, and Geraldine. The most beautiful stars she and Cade had ever fashioned. Brighter than any aurora, more breathtaking than a waterfall or a luminescent cavern. With each birth, she experienced some of the same darkness as when Julep had arrived, but this time, she had someone to walk her to the light. To tell her she wasn't damaged beyond repair. That some feelings were normal of motherhood, even when you loved your babies more than life itself.

And when that love eventually meant staying behind, she could peaceably watch Garrett take her place at sea while she remained beside her sisters and held her babies tight. It had taken time, but eventually Martha became one of her dearest friends. Sometimes jealousy for Julep's "other mother" still emerged, but Alice Ann knew there was room for both of them in her daughter's heart. Every night they prayed together for the missionary ship's safe return and that the gospel words they shared might bring hope to a hopeless people all along the Pacific coast.

"Because that is your true legacy, my darlings," she told her children as they waved goodbye to the *Gratia* from shore. Geraldine sat on her hip and Simon stood tall against her skirts. "Only that which the Lord has given you."

Simon tugged on her elbow. "But Mama, what if I don' getta Gift?"

She smiled at him, extracting one arm from Geraldine to ruffle her son's hair. He was only seven, but he already exhibited some of his father's insecurities. How she wanted to reassure him. "Then the Lord will use you in another way. Remember what Papa always says—"

"If God tells ya to lower the nets, don' be surprised when He fills 'em with fish."

She laughed. "Your father's interpretation seems to be veering a little off scripture, but yes. Trust in God and He will give you exactly what you need." She looked at her children, lovely faces she almost never had. Along with Julep, these were her true Gifts.

"Speaking of fish, how about we try to catch some for dinner tonight? Simon, you can be in charge of hooking the bait this time."

"Hurray!" he shouted and rushed for the ridge, racing to the fisherman's cottage at the top.

A lark floated past, and Alice Ann turned to listen as it sang. Offshore *Gratia*'s sails billowed in the breeze while Cade manned the helm, sixteen-year-old Julep and her new beau, Tleyuk working right alongside him.

Searching for their next passengers.

The next residents of Larksong.

The next set of prodigals, like her, longing to come home.

AUTHOR'S NOTE

Like the characters in *Stars in the Storm*, anxiety, post-partum depression, and marriage difficulties affect millions of people worldwide every day. If you, or someone you know, live with these conditions, you are not alone. Hope is only a call or click away.

Focus on the Family Christian Counselor Assistance
1-855-771-HELP (4357)
https://www.focusonthefamily.com/get-help/

Substance Abuse and Mental Health Services Administration
1-800-662-HELP (4357)
https://samhsa.gov/find-help/national-helpline

National Suicide Prevention Lifeline
1-800-273-8255 or Text "TALK" to 741741
https://suicidepreventionlifeline.org/

Post-Partum Support International (For both moms and dads)
1-800-944-4773
https://www.postpartum.net/

For Your Marriage.org Marriage Support
https://www.foryourmarriage.org/

Worldwide Marriage Encounter
https://wwme.org/

There are many additional resources available in addition to those listed. While some of the organizations listed above are United States based, similar organizations are available in other countries.

Have faith. Have hope. You have beautiful purpose.

HISTORICAL NOTES

C an you believe we've reached the end of Larksong Legacy? Although this was the shortest book in the series, it certainly didn't require any less research. In some ways, it needed more.

The Gifted:

Cade's Gift and related anxiety were inspired by something a therapist told me about my own anxiety: "Your greatest weakness can also be your greatest strength. Lightning harnessed is electricity, unharnessed is a thunderstorm. Harness your energy." I found this a fitting comparison to the physical ailments of anxiety, when sometimes you can't even describe why you feel a certain way. Like Cade, it can feel like a storm inside that you're struggling to escape. The scientific portion of his Gift is based on Barometric Pressure Sickness which occurs when a weather front is moving through, causing a variety of physical ailments. Throughout the story, he must find a way to harness these two afflictions together.

Alice Ann's Gift of hyperthymesia, also known as highly superior autobiographical memory, was one of the more interesting topics I've had to research, especially when paired with research on amnesia. In short, those with hyperthymesia can remember large portions of their lives in vivid detail from what they ate on an exact date to what someone was wearing to exact conversations. They also recall memories constantly while trying to form new ones. Understandably, this constant stream of information can become overwhelming, often causing anxiety and depression. There are currently fewer than 100 documented cases of hyperthymesia worldwide.

Linus Thompson's Gift is longevity. At the time of this writing, the oldest person according to the Guinness Book of World Records was Jeanne Louise Calment who died in 1997 at the age of 122 years and 164 days. There are also long life spans mentioned in the Bible, such as Methuselah at 969 years, Noah at 950 years, and Adam at 930 years. There is ongoing debate over the accuracy of these Biblical numbers, but who is to say that someone, through a mix of good health and environment, genetics, and God-given gifts, couldn't have an extremely long life?

Faith and Forgiveness:

While outlining *Stars in the Storm*, I knew that the sea and fishing were going to play a major role. So, when I searched for Bible verses about fishing and came across Luke 5:5, I immediately knew it needed to be included. In the Biblical story, Peter has been fishing all night and, having caught nothing, returns to shore. Jesus tells him to cast his nets out into deep water. Peter is, of course, skeptical, but still does as the Lord asks, saying, "Master, we have worked hard all night and have caught nothing, but at your command I will lower the nets." When he does this, the nets are so full, they begin to tear. Shocked, Peter says, "Depart from me, Lord, for I am a sinful man." Rather than send him away, however, Jesus says, "Do not be afraid; from now on you will be catching men." At that, Peter, his brother Andrew, and their friends James and John all left their boats and followed Christ. Likewise, Cade and Alice Ann must find trust in God to surrender their own lives and in the end, use their newfound faith to become missionaries of their own.

The other listed 5:5 verses are also taken directly from the Bible. It was another divinely inspired moment when I discovered that Matthew 5:5 about "Blessed are the meek" was the very one Alice Ann needed to hear.

Stars in the Storm is also inspired by The Prodigal Son parable, except in this case, Cade plays the role of both the father and the brother. He is torn between the emotions of joy at Alice Ann's return and hurt by all she's done. Only in Christ are both of them able to forgive and find forgiveness. In fact, Cade's ship's name *Gratia* is Latin for "grace."

The prayer that the Larks pray before leaving to find the source is taken from the prayer of St. Brendan the Navigator, the sixth century patron saint of travelers and sailors. He is one of my favorite saints and perfect for a story about the sea. You can find the original version of the prayer on the dedication page.

The sentiments Tobias mentions about the Song of Songs really are in the Bible. Would you like it if your husband compared your hair to a flock of goats? Apparently, it was considered a major compliment for Solomon!

Real-Life Research:

While many of the Pacific Northwest locations and events included are real, they are not always presented in their exact locations. It would have taken too long to travel between these places, so for the sake of the story's timeline, I took creative liberties and condensed their proximity.

- The **Copalis Ghost Forest** is a barren forest which was killed off by rapidly rising ocean water during the 1700 Cascadian Fault earthquake and tsunami. This is the same event that inspired the source of the Larks' Gifts and caused the mudslide that buried the *Oblique*. The excavation of the *Oblique* was inspired by an Ozette village that was buried under a mudslide resulting from the same earthquake and tsunami. Discovered in 1970, over 55,000 artifacts were excavated from the village over eleven years.

- **Astoria, Oregon** was founded in 1811; however, few photographs exist before the 1870s. The Oregon Historical Society was able to provide me with two photos from 1856 and 1866. Since *Stars in the Storm* takes place in 1859, I had to fill in the blanks of Cade and Alice Ann's visit as best I could.

- **Tintype Photography** was patented in the United States in 1856 by Hamilton Smith and was an inexpensive alternative to the daguerreotype. Tintypes were often created by street photographers and remained popular until the early 20th century. If you've read my novel, *Twisted River*, you may have recognized Henry Frye as the father of Hugo Frye, one of the novel's main characters.

- **Pacific Grey/Gray Whales** make the longest migration of any mammal, up to 5,000 miles from the Bering Sea to give birth in Baja California in the fall. The Larks could have potentially seen thousands of whales pass by during these migrations.

- While Thompson's Island is fictional, its location is the same as the real **Ben Ure Island** near **Deception Pass**. In the 1880s, Ben Ure and Lawrence "Pirate" Kelly used the island to illegally smuggle in Chinese migrants for slave labor throughout the Pacific Northwest. It is said that Ure's Native American wife would signal them from **Strawberry Island** when it was safe to transport the laborers and avoid the authorities. I chose to incorporate the reality of Chinese slavery through Mei's story while providing a better use for Ben Ure Island.

- The **Geomagnetic Solar Storm** Cade and Alice Ann witness is also known as a Carington Event, which took place over the night of September 1-2, 1859. A massive solar flare created auroras seen across North America and Europe, and its electromagnetic field caused many telegraph systems to literally explode. The lights were so bright that some people started work for the day, others believed neighboring towns were on fire, and a few wondered if the world was ending.

- The **constellations** of Cepheus, Cassiopeia, Pegasus, Pisces, and Cetus that Alice Ann sees prior to the solar storm are accurate for Ben Ure Island on September 1, 1859. Thanks to modern technology, you can view the full star chart here: https://skyandtelescope.org/interactive-sky-chart/

- The **Hoh Rainforest** is located on the western side of Washington's Olympic National Park and receives an average rainfall of 140 inches annually. Just like Cade and Alice Ann, visitors can experience its lush canopies, moss, ferns, and various other coniferous and deciduous species.

- The blue light that the Larks see in the cavern waters is **bioluminescence**, which is caused by single-celled algae and is most visible in Washington in late spring and early fall. There are many places to see this phenomenon, including on Whidby Island adjacent to Deception Pass.
- **Mount Ranier** is a volcano located in the Pacific Ring of Fire, about 59 miles southeast of Seattle, Washington. It experienced a significant amount of volcanic activity throughout the 1820s to 1850s and according to the Pacific Northwest Seismic Network, currently experiences seismic activity multiple times per month.
- Lava tubes run under many of Washington's volcanos with one of the most popular tourist spots being **Ape Cave** near Mount St. Helens. The ice cave from *Stars in the Storm* was inspired by **Natural Bridges Ice Cave** and **Guler Ice Cave**, both formed by lava tubes from Mount Adams.
- The cathedral-like cavern and sinkhole Cade and Alice Ann adventure through is based on **Vietnam's Sơn Đoòng Cave**, which contains the world's largest cave passage, its own weather system, a flourishing jungle, and a subterranean river with rumbling waterfalls. As far as I could find, something similar doesn't exist in Washington, but Sơn Đoòng Cave wasn't discovered until 1990, so anything's possible.

Acknowledgments

Thank you to my readers for staying with the series through four books and especially for giving Alice Ann a chance. I know she was a difficult character to forgive.

To my husband, Scott, and our children. As Alice Ann said, you are my true Gifts.

To my parents, Ken and Ruth, and my godmother, Mary, for always being there.

To my Grandpa George for Julep's "Thirteen Men in a Rowboat" story. I'll never forget how during my entire childhood, they all said, "George, tell us a story." He said, "Well, let me think...I know! There were thirteen men in a rowboat, and they all said, 'George, tell us a story...'"

To my fellow historical fiction author friends: Jennifer Q. Hunt, Susan Laspe, and Tanya E. Williams for helping me through many befuddled moments while writing this story, and especially to Rhonda Ortiz for your sailing advice and thoughtful criticism. *Gratia* would have capsized without you!

To authors, Allison Ramirez and Sarah Everest for your Pacific Northwest suggestions. To authors, Kortney Keisel and Diana Lesire Brandmeyer whose amnesia novels provided inspiration during the writing of this story.

To my beta readers: Ann, Jennifer, Mary, Rhonda, Sarah, Sharon, Susan, and Tanya. For your many comments, suggestions, and edits, thank you!

To my newsletter subscribers, the Catholic Writers Guild, my Walking With Purpose ladies, and everyone else who has provided reviews, posts, and well wishes.

To the many organizations who helped make my historical information accurate and believable, especially the Oregon Historical Society, Deception Pass Park Foundation, SkyandTelescope.org Interactive Sky Chart, Washington Trails Association, Pacific Northwest Seismic Network, University of Washington PNW Temperature, Precipitation, and SWE Trend Analysis Tool, Missouri Historical Society, St. Charles City-County Library, St. Louis County Library, The Library of Congress, The U.S. National Park Service, The Metropolitan Museum of Art, and all those whose historical stories were left behind. I hope you found the dreams you were searching for.

Most importantly, to my Lord and creator, Jesus Christ. Every good and perfect gift is from above. At your command, I will lower the nets. Without You, none of this could be.

ABOUT THE AUTHOR

Kelsey Gietl is the award-winning author of the early 1910s Over the Atlantic duology, the WWI War Across Waters duology, and the 1850s Larksong Legacy series. Combining Christian faith, family, and lessons from our past, her books provide inspirational stories with a dose of romance and a dash of intrigue.

She holds a Bachelor of Fine Arts in Theatre Design and Graphic Design and has made a career in fields from event planning and proposal writing to product management and communications.

She lives in Missouri with her husband, two children, and two dogs. She is a member of the Daughters of the American Revolution and the Catholic Writers Guild.

You can connect with her online at:
kelseygietl.com

www.ingramcontent.com/pod-product-compliance
Lightning Source LLC
Chambersburg PA
CBHW022038240626

47154CB00007B/2470